Blood
OR
Justice

Herbert E. Brown, Jr.

i

Some actual events have been taken out of their actual time sequence for the purposes of this novel. Any similarities of characters in this novel to any persons living or dead is purely coincidental. This novel is a work of fiction.

In *Step publishing*

P.O. Box 10235
Columbus, Ohio 43201

Genius can be denied,
but it can never be ignored.

Acknowledgement

First of all, I thank God in the highest and my two little girls who are too young to understand the madness of divorce and too innocent to stop loving either parent, for their unwavering love.

Next I want to thank my family for their love and support. My father, Herbert Elliott Brown, Sr.; my sisters, Loretta, Georgia and Betty; my brothers, Richard, David, Daniel and Carl; my brothers-in law, Tommy and George; sisters in law, Tina, Pat and Debbie. Furthermore I would like to thank my dear friends whose dedication and devotion made this book possible.

My reader who spent countless hours reading and re-reading, editing and re-editing this manuscript, Dick Termuhlen. I would like to also thank my typists, Pat Broadnax and Sonya Collier. Finally I would like to thank Miss Kathy Craig, Miss Shirley Little, Mr. Is Said and Mrs. Inaleigh Eisen for their support and encouragement throughout the writing of this novel.

Finally I dedicate this novel to my late mother, Maryetta Epps Brown and brother Larry Brown whom I sincerely hope to see again someday in that place where we shall never grow old.

Chapter 1

He sat on his front porch, staring pensively at the large, red ball sinking slowly on the western horizon. He blinked for a moment, then lowered his eyes to the woods just beyond the cornfield on the eastern side of the house. He marveled at how the scarlet glow of the dying sun fell over the vibrant green trees, giving them a yellow-gold sheen. "Wow!" he thought, "I sure wish I had the ability to capture that on canvas, just like that, with all its splendor and elegance and stump-down perfection, just like Mother Nature laid it out." His mind flashed back to the time when his seventh-grade class had taken a field trip to Washington, D. C., and they had visited an art museum. He had gaped in open-mouthed astonishment at the beautiful pictures he had seen there. He was especially enthralled with those paintings that featured outdoor scenes. He could hardly remember the names of any of the men who had done such wonderful work, for they all seemed so foreign and strange; but he knew one thing and that was that those men sure could paint. He had tried his hand at painting. He had always been quite good when it came to sketching, and he had won a number of school prizes for his work, but painting was new territory. When he had showed his art teacher his first effort on canvas, she had smiled brightly and said, in a voice that had stunned him, "Young man, you've really got some talent here. I haven't seen many college art students with this kind of ability." Jay-boy had beamed.

After that, his art teacher seemed to take more a special interest in him and had given him supplies and constant encouragement. However, when he had shown his work to his mother, she didn't seem all that carried away with it. His dad had just grunted and said, "Just something that's gonna cost money that we don't have and take up a lot of time." Jay-boy's heart sunk; his disappointment must have registered on his face, because immediately his dad had smiled and clapped him on the shoulder, saying encouragingly, "Hey, why don't you really concentrate on your ball playing? Now, that could definitely put some money in your pocket."

Although he felt somewhat put out because his folks hadn't shared his teacher's enthusiasm for his painting ability, he continued to paint. He found that the more he painted, the more he enjoyed it; he finally rationalized his folks' lack of interest by convincing himself that they just didn't have that cultivation of taste, that sophistication of the senses, to appreciate true art. So he persisted, blossoming under his teacher's careful instruction, using more and more of his free time to paint and sketch. He had decided that when he went to college, he would major in art and that, maybe someday, he would get a chance to go overseas, possibly France, and study the great masters. "Yeah," he thought to himself, "one of these days I'm going to come back here as a real professional artist and sit right down here and capture that-there sunset falling over those woods. It will be so beautiful that they'll ask me if I'll let them put it in one of those great art museums."

In the meantime, he was looking forward to his Wednesday art class. The last time he had shown his teacher one of his outdoor scenes, she had been so taken with it that she had asked if she could show it to one of her friends who was an art professor at Temple University. Jay-boy had beamed with pride and felt good clear through.

Presently, the sound of a car turning into the path brought him back to reality. He straightened, digging his toes into the soft, warm dirt, and stared hard through the glaring afterglow of the dying sunlight at a large, late-model car coming up the path toward the house. "They said they would try to be here before dark; I wonder if that's them?" His brow furrowed and his eyes narrowed as he peered intently at the oncoming car, trying to see if the license plate was an out-of-state one. His attention was riveted on the car as eager anticipation moved up his spine. How he wanted to see Bowknot! He had not seen him since they had moved away to Detroit four years ago. Bowknot was not only his cousin but had been his best friend; they had done everything together. They had even been in the same classes at school since the first grade.

The saddest day of Jay-boy's life had been when he found out that Bowknot's family was going to move away. One winter, Bowknot's father, Uncle George, had gone to visit his older brother Fred, who lived in Detroit and worked at the Ford Motor Company. Fred had convinced George to apply for a position with the Ford Company and had helped to get him hired. Jay-boy remembered how excited his Aunt Daisy had been when she had first come over to tell his mother the good news. He had been happy for them, but he hadn't had the slightest idea of how lonely and empty his life would be without his cousin and best friend. Right after they had left, he would often hear his mother talking to his dad about maybe moving away, too. His dad would always listen politely to her extolling the virtues of city living and, sometimes, Jay-boy's heartbeat would quicken at the prospect of living in Detroit and being reunited with his cousin. However, his dad would invariably wave his hand in a gesture—as if shooing gnats—and say, "No, no dice, baby. Right here is where I belong, farming my own land and being my own man. No, indeed, the city is all right to visit, but I certainly wouldn't want to live there; people too crowded together. Why, you can't even sneeze without spraying your next-door neighbor. I just couldn't live all crowded up like that." After Jimbo had come out of the army in 1944, he had worked a year on the railroad and saved his money. He had paid cash for the 200-acre farm early in 1946, just a few months before he had married Bessie. Jimbo had always been fiercely proud of his accomplishments, and Jay-boy could hear the pride in his voice and see the glow in his eyes whenever he talked about it. He would always wind up by saying, "Well, that just goes to show that if you really want something bad enough and put your all into trying to accomplish it, you can get it and the devil in hell can't stop you! Not if you're really bound and determined like I was." Often, he'd smile broadly and add, "Now, when I wake in the morning and go to work, I'm going to work for myself. Thank God that I don't have to beg anybody for a job or share-crop on anybody's land to feed my family. Mama may have, papa may have, but God bless the child that's got his own. Yeah," he would say, gesturing in a wide, all-encompassing motion, "Jimbo's got his own land and I know how to farm it, too!" Jay-boy would feel something stir inside of him when he observed his dad from time to time, talking animatedly to his wife or to one of his friends about his farm. He'd notice the light in his dad's eyes and the broad smile that would spread over his black face whenever he talked about farming. That it made him proud and gave him a real feeling of freedom and independence of spirit that very few colored folk in Greensville County knew.

Jay-boy could feel the nervous tension rising inside him. Finally, his grew wide with recognition: it was them. He whirled and hurried into the house. "Mama," he called, stepping quickly through the screen door. She was seated on the overstuffed couch, reading her Bible. Presently, she looked up, catching his excited gaze. "Mama, Aunt Daisy and them are here!"

"Say what!" she exclaimed, as if what he had said had not registered.

"Aunt Daisy and Uncle George are here. I recognized the Michigan license plates."

"Well, praise the Lord!" she said, heaving a deep sigh, "they finally made it here in one piece. Let me get out here and see them!" She laid her Bible on an end table next to the couch and rose abruptly from her seat. "Go tell your daddy; he's in there laying across the bed."

Jay-boy disappeared into the hallway. When he stepped into his father's bedroom, he saw him lying sprawled across the bed, his massive chest gently, rhythmically moving up and down in the long, luxuriant refrains of one in a deep, restful sleep. Jay-boy hesitated for a moment; he hated to have to wake him. Then, feeling the weight of the occasion pressing on him, he moved over to the bed and laid his hand on his dad's shoulder, shaking him gently. After a few seconds, Jimbo stirred and his eyes opened. "What is it, son?" he asked drowsily, blinking and rubbing his eyes with the back of his hand.

"Aunt Daisy and Uncle George are here!"

His father smiled warmly, then roused himself to a sitting position, cupping his head in his hands for a moment to try and free his wits from the dullness of sleep. He looked up at Jay-boy. "So, they finally made it, huh?"

"Yeah," Jay-boy replied, they finally got here."

"Well, tell them I'll be right on out." Jay-boy turned and quickly left the room. When he emerged onto the front porch, they had pulled up in the yard. The big, shiny, dark-blue Ford with white-wall tires was something to see.

Uncle George was the first one out of the car; Jay-boy and his mother bounded down the steps to meet him. "Lawdy, Lawdy, Miss Clawdy!" he grinned, straightening and stretching his giant frame to his full height. "Cut my legs off and call me Shorty! Great day in the morning, sis Bessie, if you ain't pretty as a picture!" He flung his large arms about her and kissed her on the cheek. He held her at arms' length and looked her up and down. "Lord, chile! How fine is you gonna get?"

"Oh, hush your mouth, George," she said, her face flushing as she struggled to hold back an embarrassed smile. Recovering, she said, "You don't look too bad yourself, Mr. Woods. All dressed up in your fine suit, looking just as handsome as ever. I bet Daisy has to carry a stick just to keep the women-folk away from you."

"No," Daisy broke in as she and Bowknot climbed from the

car. "I have to carry a stick to keep him straight." They all broke into laughter. Daisy and Bessie fell into each other's arms, raptured in fervent greetings.

"Well, look-a-here at you," Uncle George said, taking Jay-boy by the shoulder. If you ain't the spitting image of your daddy!"

Jay-boy smiled warmly and said, "I'm glad that you-all made it here all right. I know it was a long ride." Suddenly, Jay-boy felt a strong hand grip his arm and he looked around a tall, grim-faced young man with piercing dark eyes and a faint smile playing around the corners of his mouth. The young man was slightly taller than Jay-boy and bore a striking resemblance to Uncle George. Yet he lacked the jovial nature and easy humor that shone in George's eyes and the grimness of his countenance made his smile seem almost sardonic.

"What you say there, Jay-boy?" the young man greeted him. "Yeah, it's me!"

Jay-boy smiled congenially. "Bowknot," he gasped, his mind groping for some connection between this nearly grown man and the little runt he had known as Bowknot. "Man," he stammered, still stunned at how much his cousin had changed. "If I had seen you on the street, I would have never recognized you. You don't look nothing like that skinny little runt I had to take up for back when we were in school!"

"No, I guess not," the young man chuckled softly, his eyes moving over Jay-boy appraisingly. "You've changed a lot, too." He fell silent.

Jay-boy grinned. "I guess I have, at that, and anyway, four years is a long time."

"Yeah, you have grown a lot, too, Jay-boy," George broke in. "You and Jimbo can almost pass for twins."

Hearing the comment, Jimbo bounded off the porch, shaking with laughter, and grabbed George's hand, pumping his elbow excitedly. "Lord, I sure am glad to see you-all! And look-a-here at Miss Daisy! I declare, she looks like one of them-there movie stars," he quipped, as he gathered her up in his arms.

"Oh, go on," Daisy said, with an embarrassed giggle, falling into his embrace. She withdrew and looked up at him. "Dang, if you ain't been blessed in the good looks department yourself, and that boy of yours looks just like you! He's just like you for the world!"

"Well, you-all come on in the house and get you something to eat. I know you've got to be tired and hungry, too, after all that riding."

"Jay-boy," Jimbo said, "get their suitcases and bring them on in the house. Yeah," he continued, directing his remarks to the visitors, "you-all go on in and make yourselves at home. Me and Jay-boy will get your bags."

A short while later, they were all seated around the dinner table eating fried chicken, string beans, and potato salad and talking animatedly about the trip from Detroit. Jay-boy found that he was not very hungry; the anticipation of their coming and the excitement of their arrival had given him butterflies in his stomach. So he sat, quietly observant, his eyes moving from face to face and his ears cocked so as not to miss a thing. Finally, he joined in the conversation. "That sure is a nice automobile you got there, Uncle George. I bet she can really roll up some road."

"Yeah, son, she does all right," he said with a proud smile. "I bought it spanking brand new last fall. Since I work for Ford, I got an employee discount. Yeah, I got to say she's been good to me. I ain't had one minute's trouble out of her. She runs just like a top and rides just as smooth as she can be."

"Well," Jimbo broke in, "if the crops do all right this year, I reckon I just might get me a new car."

"Hey," George grinned, "if you get your mind set on a Ford, I'll see if I can't help you get a good deal on the price."

Jimbo laughed. "Well, now, I just might take you up on that."

"Hey, no problem!" George nodded, munching on a chicken leg. "Ford is the way and that's a fact. I know, because I'm right there helping build them."

"Daisy," Bessie broke in abruptly, "girl, how do you stay so trim and keep your skin so smooth and pretty? City living sure must agree with you."

"Oh, girl, I don't know," she laughed. "I guess I keep my weight down with all the running I do at the post office, because I sure haven't stopped eating."

They talked in lively spurts about one thing after another, long into the night. Finally, sleep began to steal over them one by one and they retired to their rooms. Jay-boy had noticed that, except for the few words Bowknot had uttered when they first arrived, he had remained conspicuously silent the whole evening.

Chapter 2

Everyone rose early the next morning. George and Bowknot accompanied Jimbo and Jay-boy on their feeding rounds while the women bustled about in the kitchen, preparing breakfast. As the four men started down the dirt path toward the barn in back of the house, the sun shone warm and bright and a symphony of animal sounds floating on the fresh morning air made George wax deeply nostalgic. "You know, Jimbo," he said, glancing out across the pea field flanking the east side of the house, "man, it seemed like it was only yesterday that I was getting up early in the morning, doing this very same thing. Man," he smiled, looking around at Jimbo, "I used to hate like hell to climb out of bed early in the morning to feed up, especially when it was cold and raining, too."

Jimbo said, "Yeah, I know what you mean. Sometimes you hate like the devil to even turn over, but them animals don't care nothing about it being cold or rainy or about you being tired." He chuckled. "All they know is, they're hungry and they want something to eat."

"Yeah," George laughed, shrugging his shoulders, "so you just got to get on up and get your butt in gear whether you feel like it or not. You know," he continued abstractedly, "what I wouldn't give sometimes to have the chance again to be able to get up in the morning and feed up. To wake up and walk outside and breathe this good, clean country air in my lungs, watch the sun come up, hear the chickens cackling and the hogs squealing. Now all I wake up to is the sound of cars running up and down the street."

Jimbo looked sympathetically at George, dropping his gaze when he saw the sadness in his eyes and heard the strains of regret creeping into his voice.

"You see, Jimbo," George continued soberly, "when a man is born and raised on a farm and one day up and leaves it, I believe he leaves a piece of his soul right there behind him. And no matter where he goes or what he does after, he knows that deep down in him there is something missing. Now, don't get me wrong" he said, slightly raising his voice for emphasis, "I'm not sorry that we moved away from here, because I'm doing better than I ever done in my life, as far as the money thing goes. I just don't have that inner peace, that sense of belonging and purpose that a man feels when he reaches down and picks up a handful of freshly turned earth at the beginning of planting season and gets that sweet smell of good earth in his nostrils. You know what I mean?" he queried, stopping a moment and staring hard at Jimbo.

"Yeah," Jimbo nodded in the affirmative, "I know exactly what you mean and that is why I ain't gonna leave this place until Gabriel blows his horn. I traveled all over Europe and all around most of these United States when I was in that man's army, and I couldn't wait to get back to the country. Man, out here is the only place that I have ever felt free, at peace and at home. Then again," he said, glancing at George, "I couldn't fault you for leaving here after the way old man Colfax was doing you. Hell, you wasn't gonna do a thing, fooling around with him, but work yourself to death for nothing."

"You got that right!" George quipped derisively. "I worked for that old bastard ten long years and came out owing him for every one of them except the last one. That's when I finally got enough sense to get the hell away from there." He paused a moment and stared reflectively out over the cornfield, then he continued. "I remember that morning I went by his house and told him I was going to leave. He reared back in his chair, rubbing his fat head like I had just broken his heart. 'Now, look-a-here, George, boy,' he said, 'what brought all this on? Ain't I been good to you all these years? Ain't I been dealing fair and square with you, boy? Why, it ain't been a time in the ten years you been working for me that you asked me for a favor and I didn't do it for you if I could!' 'No sir, Mr. Colfax, it sure ain't,' I said, trying not to make him feel that he hadn't been my lord and master and hadn't kept me in his divine care when, in fact, he had worked the hell out of me for nothing and had almost starved me and my wife to death. 'Why do you want to leave, George, boy?' 'Well, sir,' I said finally, 'it's my brother. You see, he lives in Detroit and works at Ford Motor Company and he wants me to come to Detroit because he is sure that he can get me on there, too.' I wasn't about to tell him that I had already got the job. Anyway, man, why did I have to even tell him that I wanted to go? Old man Colfax's face turned just as red as a beet and he jumped up and pointed his finger in my face and let me have it. 'So, that's it, huh? Some of them smart-ass northern darkies been filling your head with a lot of crap about big money and high living, huh? Well, I should have figured it was something like that. Let me tell you something, boy! Now, you can be a fool if you want to and let them fancy dandies swell your head with all that nonsense if you want to, but right here is where you belong. Now, let me tell you another thing, and you listen to me good. If you leave that farm, there ain't no way in hell I'm gonna let you set foot on my property again! Now, is that clear?' Man, that old white ape was so mad that his voice was trembling, and he probably would have hit me if I had said something back to him. He finally told me that he would give me until the next day to come to my senses and he would come by the house for my answer the first thing the next morning. Sure enough, he rolled up first thing the next day and I told him the same thing. He just stared hard at me for a moment and turned red all over again, then he blurted, 'Well, get the hell on, then!' He turned and stomped off, then he whirled around, shaking his old finger at me. 'I want you off my land this day,

boy, by sundown! Do I make myself clear?' 'Yes, sir, very clear.'
Then he whirled back around and stormed off."

"Yeah," Jimbo laughed softly, I bet he was sure enough mad
and mad clean through. He knew he wasn't gonna find nobody
else that was gonna work themselves to death for him for nothing. That's what he was so pissed off about. He knew that his
good thing had just played out. All right, Jay," Jimbo said, getting back to the matter at hand, "let me climb over and run
them back away from the trough and you hand me the bucket
of slop." The fifteen or so large hogs had crowded around the
feeding trough; Jimbo picked up a large stick and began to drive
them back. Then he quickly righted the overturned trough and
Jay-boy hurriedly handed him the bucket of slop. The hungry
hogs fell into the slop, squealing in wild ecstasy. Jay-boy handed
him a second bucket, which he poured in also.

"Son," Jimbo said to Jay-boy, "look in the corn crib and get a
bucket of feed and pour it in the dry trough over there and pour
a couple of buckets of water in this-here trough after they finish
the slop."

"Yes, sir," Jay-boy replied, walking back toward the crib.
Bowknot walked behind him. For the first time that morning,
Jay-boy had become actually conscious of his cousin and now
the observation had made him strangely uncomfortable. His
cousin was now almost a grown man, nothing like the puny
little kid who used to roam the woods with him. Why, sure, he
had the same large, brown eyes and the same sly smile as the
kid who had once been so close to him, but now he was about a
foot-and-a-half taller and his voice was a smooth, proper-sound-
ing baritone. Jay-boy's impulses were deadlocked and he really
didn't know what to think of his strange new cousin. "I really
hope that you'll like it here," he said over his shoulder in soft,
congenial tones.

"Yeah, I hope so, too," Bowknot replied drily.

When the two boys reached the corn crib, Bowknot paused at
the door while Jay-boy went in to get the feed. "Well, now,"

Jay-boy muttered, emptying half a bag of hog feed into a large bucket. "I reckon that ought to do it." He straightened, tossed the now-empty feed bag into a corner, picked up the bucket, and turned and stepped out of the corn crib.

As they headed back toward the hog pen, Jay-boy noticed that his dad and his uncle were now walking toward them and away from the pen where they had been admiring the large hogs. As the two men came abreast of them, Jimbo said, "All right, son, after you give them that feed and some water, you can feed the chickens and then you-all can go on back up the house and get ready for breakfast. I'll feed the mules."

"All right," Jay-boy nodded.

The two men strode wordlessly up to the barn and Jimbo went into the crib, coming out a few minutes later with a heaping bucket of corn. "Now," he mumbled thoughtfully, "I reckon this ought to quiet them down for a while." Stepping out of the crib, he closed the heavy door and the two of them walked around the barn to the corral where the mules were. The mules spotted them right away and trotted over to the edge of the corral and began to prance about, braying excitedly. Jimbo sat the bucket of corn down beside him and he and George started to shuck the ears, tossing them over into the corral. After a few minutes, the large, old bucket was empty. Jimbo stood eyeing his mules with great pride as the mules munched contentedly on the corn. "Now," Jimbo said, after a long moment, "let me fill their trough." He turned and walked over to the pump standing just outside the corral fence. George followed him.

"Man, them sure is some nice mules you got there," George said. "I bet they can plow up a storm!"

"Hey," Jimbo chuckled, smiling around at him. "I'll just say this much. I ain't scared to put them up against anybody's mules in the county. I can't complain a bit," he went on soberly. "You see, God's been pretty good to me the past few years. I've been doing nicely with my farm and, last year, I really had a fine crop. That's when I bought my new mules. I sold the other two I had. Now, they were good ones, too, but they were old and I had to get me some young ones. Yeah, George," he continued reflectively, "I've been doing all right. I'm gonna try and get that boy of mine a used car if the crops come pretty good this year. He's really done a good job helping me here on the farm, and he's also done a heck of a job in school. Why, he's almost a straight-A student," Jimbo beamed, "and a heck of a baseball-player, too. Shucks," he laughed, "his coach told me that he's already had a number of letters from colleges about Jay-boy, them wanting to offer him scholarships and things to come and play ball for them. He even told me that several of the pro team scouts had commented on how good he is. I'm sure gonna hate to see him leave this place, but I ain't gonna try and hold him back. I won't try to force him to be a farmer, if it ain't in him to be one. Anyway, after he finishes college or whatever, he might just want to get married and settle down right here. I've heard him mention it time and time again."

Jimbo picked up a jar full of water that he kept near the pump to be used for priming it and began to pour it slowly into the top of the cast-iron pumping mechanism, simultaneously pumping the long handle up and down jerkily until the cool, clear water began jetting from the spout. "All right, I got her some now," he grinned, refilling the jar and setting it back down on the round cement surface of the pump. Then he let the water jetting from the spout cascade down into a wooden, flume-like contraption that he had built, which stretched from the top of the pump through the corral fence, emptying into the mule trough about twenty-five feet away. This contraption enabled him to stand back at the pump and fill the trough without having to use a large bucket and make many trips. The sturdy brown mules walked jauntily over to the water trough and began to drink slowly and luxuriantly, their large, brown eyes sparkling and their ears pulled back. "Yeah, you-all enjoy yourselves, now, because day after tomorrow, you're gonna be back in the field," Jimbo said, smiling with boyish pride at his mules. He loved the farm and he knew that it was a part of him. It was as natural for him to be in that place as it was for the mules, the hogs, or the chickens, and the inner peace that washed over him with this realization made his spirit soar with infinite gladness. He lifted his face to the sky and drew in a big gulp of air, then released it slowly. He quietly thanked God. He knew that he was blessed, and he was beside himself whenever he stopped and realized just how blessed he really was.

After a while, he lowered his eyes and looked at George. Seeing the strange and deep sadness in George's eyes made Jimbo's glowing exhilaration melt like a late winter's snow in a warm, spring sun. For a while, their gaze held, but the pain and gloom in George's deep-set eyes made Jimbo look away. Presently, a hot feeling of shame flushed over him. How could he be so careless and cruel as to be bragging about his good fortune while poor George was standing here like he had the weight of the world on his shoulders? For a long moment, the two men stood in uncomfortable silence before Jimbo forced himself to speak.

"What is it, George?" he asked hesitantly. "What's the matter, man?"

"Well," George began somberly, "I don't want you to feel bad just because I'm having a few problems right now. Look here, man," he said, his voice brightening, "a man's got a right to be proud of what he has and the things he's accomplished. You've done all right for yourself and, really, I'm glad for you. I don't know how much Daisy's told you-all about the problems we're having with that boy of ours," he said, looking out over the corral. "But since you ain't brought it up, I don't reckon she's told you-all very much. Other than we wanted to know if you-all would let him spend the summer here on the farm, away from the city. We really appreciate you-all agreeing to let him stay."

"Oh, shucks," Jimbo broke in, "we're all family, ain't we? If you can't look out for your folks, what's the use of being kin in the first place?"

"Yeah," George said, looking around at him, his eyes full of gratitude, "but I still appreciate what you-all are doing for us. I tell you the truth," he continued, scratching his head wearily, "for the past two years, that boy's done almost worried me and Daisy to death. Playing hooky from school, in and out of trouble, hanging out in the streets all hours of the day and night. He done been arrested twice, once for gambling and once for joy-riding in some stolen car. He went mouthing off at the police trying to show off in front of his little buddies and got beat half to death. They charged him with resisting arrest, and I found when I looked into the thing that he was in the wrong. He had tried to lie and tell me they were just picking on him. Jimbo," George dropped his head, staring hard at the ground and shaking his head in bewilderment, "I done talked and talked and talked and now I just don't know what else to do. That boy's head is just as hard as a rock and he's done got just as mean as a snake."

Jimbo was visibly moved by George's anguished voice. He knew that George loved his son and he could see the deep hurt he felt at Bowknot's having gone astray. He knew that George had been a good father, and that he and Daisy had done all that they could to raise Bowknot up right, but somehow or another, Bowknot had been captivated by the allure of the good times and fast living of inner-city life.

"You know, Jimbo," George said, looking up and speaking in sober, far-away tones, "I wish to God that I had never moved to Detroit. Yeah, we got a lot of material things. We both got good jobs and all, but we've lost our son." His voice trembled as he struggled to stifle a sob in his throat.

Jimbo walked over and placed a sympathetic hand on George's shoulder. "Listen now," he said, "ain't no use in you going and blaming yourself. I know you wouldn't have gone to Detroit if you knew that this was going to happen, but hindsight is always twenty-twenty vision. Hey, you only done what you thought was best for your family, and ain't nobody can blame you for that. Look here," Jimbo said, trying to inject a note of hope into his voice, "all ain't lost yet. We still got a chance to turn Bowknot around. Maybe bringing him out here and letting him spend some time living and working on the farm might just be the best thing for him right now. It sure ain't that much for him to get into and I can find a lot of things for him to do that will keep his mind off a lot of devilment, too. Out here, where it's quiet and peaceful, he can have time to think and get a grip on himself. Another thing, too. Maybe Jay-boy will have a positive influence on him. Jay-boy is a pretty level-headed boy and, besides, they can get to know each other again. Listen, man," Jimbo said, staring hard at George. "I'll do everything I can to help Bowknot calm himself down and straighten out."

"I can't tell you how much I appreciate that," George repeated.

"Well," Jimbo argued, "if you can't help your kin, what good is being kin in the first place? And if one part of this family is in trouble, we're all in trouble. If someone in this family got a problem, we all got a problem. And we're gonna dig in our heels and fight this thing until we get it straight."

"Man," George smiled, his eyes brightening, "like I said, I sure thank you."

"Oh, don't mention it. It's no more than what I ought to do, anyhow. Now, come on; let's go in and get something to eat. My stomach's calling out loud, 'Feed me, man!'"

When Jimbo and George arrived at the house, they found everyone crowded into the kitchen, waiting for them. The house was filled with the delicious aroma of buttermilk biscuits and smoked ham. After a short while, they were all seated at the table, eating ham, eggs, fried potatoes, and Bessie's homemade buttermilk biscuits. Jimbo could tell by the troubled look on his wife's face that she and her sister had been talking about Bowknot. He stole a sidelong glance at George and quickly dropped his eyes into his plate when he again saw the deep sadness etched so vividly on George's face. The kitchen was silent except for the random clanking of metal eating utensils on china.

"Well," George said finally, trying to inject some humor into the uncomfortable silence and chase away the somber spirit that seemed to hang over them like a sagging rain cloud. "Lawd, have mercy, I ain't ate this good in years. You can't find this kind of good-eating ham meat in Detroit. Man, if somebody opened up a restaurant serving grub like this, folks would be battling to get a seat and I'd be right there with them." A volley of laughter went up from them as George reared back in his chair and began to rub his stomach with an exaggerated gesture. Eyeing him amusedly, Bessie broke into a lively giggle, "Lawd, George Broadnax, you ought to hush your fuss." Daisy looked over at her husband and crowed with laughter, as did the rest of them. George's antics seemed to have broken the somber mood and put to flight the dark melancholy that had permeated the room and weighed heavily on them, stifling their conversation, drying their throats, and making their food hard to swallow. Now they engaged freely in comical chatter, enjoying their meal until they all were satisfied. Finally, they got up and went to their rooms to get ready for church.

Chapter 3

An hour or so later, they all climbed into George's shiny new Ford and drove to the red brick church about seven miles away. When they arrived, many of the people were still milling around outside talking and exchanging local gossip, for the services had not yet begun. As George eased the car along the rocky church yard and nosed it into a parking space, heads turned and eyes grew wide with curiosity as people gawked at the new car with the out-of-state license plates. As they climbed from the car, folks started to gather around, recognizing Jimbo and Bessie and stepping forward to greet them. Suddenly, a man coming out of the crowd called incredulously, "George Broadnax?" George stared hard at the man for a moment, then bellowed, "Johnny Ross!" The two men ran to embrace each other, slapping each other's back excitedly. "Man, oh, man! Looka here, looka here! Man, how you been?" Deacon Ross exclaimed. "I ain't seen you since you left here."

"Well," George crowed, "I'm doing some of the things that folks say I'm doing, but I ain't doing all of them." The men broke up with laughter. "How you been doing, Deacon?" George asked.

"Oh, the Lord's been blessing!" He smiled delightedly, looking past George. "Is that Daisy? Well, now," he said, stepping forward and embracing her. "How you been doing, Miss Lady, with your fine self?"

Daisy laughed. "Oh, I've been all right."

"Well," the deacon said, his eyes sparkling, "it looks to me like the

Lord has been blessing you! How long you-all gonna be out here?"

"Oh, we're pulling out early in the morning because we got to be back at work Tuesday."The large crowd that had been staring curiously began to close in as the identity of the driver of the fine, out-of-state car became known. George and Daisy were besieged with affectionate greetings. There were endless hugs and slaps on the back amid loud exclamations of glee. Meanwhile, Jay-boy and Bowknot had slipped away from the crowd surrounding their parents and headed over to the picnic table near the woods behind the church where the young people congregated. Jay-boy's eyes swept the grounds, going over the young men and women dressed in their Sunday finery until he spotted Kathy. She was sitting on one of the wooden benches beside a picnic table with her best friend, Ruth, in the shade of a massive old oak.

"Who in the world is that good-looking boy, yonder?" Ruth whispered excitedly to Kathy.

"I don't know," Kathy said, following Ruth's gaze, "but they're coming over here."

As Jay-boy and Bowknot sashayed across the gravelly churchyard, Bowknot was conscious of the wide-eyed stares of the curious on-lookers. He threw back his head, donned a blissful smile, and broke into a rhythmic swagger, moving with the sophisticated suavity of an urbane gentleman.

"How you-all doing this morning?" Jay-boy greeted the two girls.

"How are you?" Kathy replied, a radiant smile lighting her brown eyes.

She was the most beautiful girl Jay-boy had ever seen, and it made him deliriously happy to realize that he was the one that she had chosen when she could have had any boy she wanted. He loved her with all the strength of his being, and his heart palpitated with sheer joy at the thought that she loved him just as much. Her best friend, Ruth, was pretty, too, and not a few boys were trying to win her affections.

"This is my first cousin, Bowknot," Jay-boy said, gesturing. "Remember him?"

Kathy's mouth dropped open in surprise. "This is Bowknot?" she repeated in disbelief. "The skinny kid that used to pull my ponytail when we were in the sixth grade?"

"Yeah, it's me," Bowknot confirmed, smiling slyly.

"Bowknot!" Kathy rose and slung her arms around him. She kissed him on the cheek and laughed uproariously, still finding it hard to believe it was really him. "Well, this is my best friend, Ruth," Kathy said.

Bowknot looked at Ruth and smiled, saying, "Pleased to meet you," as he extended his hand.

"Pleased to meet you, too," Ruth responded, giving him her hand. She noticed that he held on to it, beaming at her for what seemed like an unusually long time.

Soon a large crowd of young men and women had gathered around Bowknot, and the air was filled with the gaiety of old recollections and open-mouthed wonder at how he had changed. Those who had known him before gazed in absolute bafflement, finding it almost impossible to believe that the once-skinny little kid had metamorphosed into this tall, extraordinarily handsome young man. Bowknot enjoyed the fuss that they made over him. He especially reveled in the young women's adulation. He also felt a surge of pride in the way the young men gaped admiringly at his fancy clothes and his terse city accent.

After the hubbub died down and the crowd thinned out, Bowknot pulled a silk handkerchief from the breast pocket of his suit coat and mopped his forehead in mock exasperation. "Now, I don't believe that I got the name of this lovely young lady right." He motioned with his hand toward Ruth.

Kathy smiled. "This is my best friend, Ruth Redding. Her folks moved here about three years ago from North Carolina."

Ruth smiled shyly, her face flushing with incredulity as Bowknot eyed her admiringly.

"Well, Miss Lovely, Bowknot grinned, extending his hand,

"my name is really Leroy Broadnax, but everybody calls me Bowknot."

"Very pleased to meet you," Ruth said, her soft, feminine hand gliding into his.

"Well, ma'am," Bowknot chuckled softly, still holding her hand for what seemed more than necessary for a cursory meeting, "I hope we can become friends." He was staring straight into her dark eyes and she knew that he was no rookie when it came to the opposite sex and that there was no mistaking his intention in what seemed like an innocent request.

"Yeah," she smiled back at him, "I don't see why we can't become friends."

Bowknot shot a furtive, sidelong glance at his cousin and winked slyly, smiling to himself. Jay-boy smiled and chuckled in amusement, inwardly glad to see Bowknot so lively for a change. Most of the people who were milling around in the churchyard had disappeared into the building, for the morning service had begun. Those few who still remained, save for Jay-boy, Bowknot, Ruth, and Kathy, were hurrying toward the vestibule. Suddenly realizing that they were the only ones still in the picnic area, Jay-boy interjected, "I guess we'd better get a move on if we want to get a seat. You know that it's usually pretty crowded in here, especially on third Sunday."

They all headed across the yard around the side of the church toward the front door. Jay-boy and Kathy were walking side by side, and Bowknot and Ruth naturally fell in together. They had to wait for a while in the vestibule because service was already under way. In the crowded area just off the main sanctuary, they stood silent and solemn, waiting for one of the deacons to finish a long, fervent prayer.

"Lord, we know that you sit high and look low."

"Yes, Jesus," the refrain went up from the congregation with heartfelt solemnity.

"We come as humble as we know how, asking you to life up bowed-down heads and troubled hearts."

"Have mercy, Lord." "Yes, Jesus," voices called out in laconic refrain.

"Lord, we know that you're our strength and our refuge."

"Praise your name, Lord!"

"Father, we just want to thank you once more and again for letting us assemble here in the house of prayer."

"Yes, Lord!" "Thank you, Jesus!"

"Lord, we just want to thank you for our last night's sleep and our early rising this morning. Lord, we want to thank you for waking us up clothed in our right minds and able to start on another day's journey."

"Have mercy, Lord; please, Jesus!" "Thank you, Lord!"

"Father, we want to thank you for the food on our tables and the shelter over our heads."

"Yes, Lord, we thank you, Jesus."

"Lord, we thank you for the clothes on our backs. But most of all my Father, we want to thank you for your darling son, Jesus."

"Thank you, Lord!" "Praise your name, Lord!" "Have mercy, Lord," the refrain now floated forth fervent and spasmodic as the old deacon's voice rose with each supplication, passionate and quivering with emotion.

"Lord, we want to thank you for all that you have done, all that you're going to do, and all that you are doing right now, Lord."

"Yes, Jesus." "Thank you, Lord." "Please, Father!"

"Now, Father, when we've come to the end of our journey, we just want you to meet us somewhere down by the Jordan."

"Yes, Lord."

"Lord, we just want you to take our hand and lead us to that place where the wicked will cease from troubling and the weary shall be at rest. Where every day shall be like Sunday and the Sabbath will have no end."

"Yes, Lord." "Have mercy, Lord." "Please, Jesus." "Praise your name, Lord!"

"These things we ask in the name of the Father, the Son, and the precious Holy Spirit. Amen and amen."

The whole congregation joined in with a hearty "Amen." The usher opened the door and stepped aside smiling and Jay-boy, Kathy, Bowknot, Ruth, and the others who had been waiting in the vestibule filed quietly into the sanctuary and were directed by another usher to their seats. The four of them were seated together in the back. Jay-boy spotted his parents and his aunt and uncle sitting up front, near the "amen corner." As the choir took the stand and began singing a spirited version of "Come by Here, Lord," everyone except Bowknot seemed to have been swept into a frenzied torrent of emotion as they clapped loudly, stomping their feet in rhythmic cadence and singing along with the choir. Bowknot was peeping out of the corner of his eye at Ruth. She was quite lovely, and he especially liked the way the corners of her mouth turned up when she smiled. He also liked the lilt in her voice that made her words seem musical when she spoke. Presently, his peeping became an open stare, and the more he stared at her, the more distant the frenzy around him became. He was transfixed by the sheer wonder of her and his mind was totally captivated by her. He watched her lips as she sang, but the sound escaped his ears as his mind drifted farther and farther away from that place. He imagined him and her alone somewhere—anywhere, just alone. He imagined himself holding her soft, curvy body in his arms and staring deep into her sparkling brown eyes as he moved closer and closer until he finally touched her lips that he knew would drive him mad with passion. Suddenly, he came back to himself, realizing that Ruth was staring back in amazement as if to say, "What in the world are you thinking about?" Bowknot's face flushed with hot, burning shame and his eyes fell, staring miles deep into the plank floor, wishing that he could drop with the speed of light right down through those planks. He felt for certain that she had somehow read his thoughts and knew the desires of his heart; now he felt desperately ashamed.

Chapter 4

Jay-boy awoke to the sound of muffled voices coming from the kitchen and opened his eyes in the brackish dawn seeping through the thin curtains at his bedroom window. The delicious aroma of homemade sausage assailed his nostrils and made his stomach growl, reminding him that he was hungry. Yet, he lay still, engrossed in quiet reflections. He had enjoyed Uncle George and Aunt Daisy's visit, and it made him sad to think that they would be leaving in a few hours. They hadn't changed much; they had seemed just about like they had always been. Like he remembered them. Uncle George, always laughing and cutting up and Aunt Daisy, gentle and full of smiles. However, Bowknot had changed and changed a lot. He not only looked different, but sounded and acted different. Seeing him again had been almost like meeting a new person. Realizing that he no longer knew Bowknot made Jay-boy somewhat uneasy, uncertain what to expect. "Wow," he said to himself, shaking his head, "I didn't know that four years could make such a difference in someone. Well," he shrugged, "I guess I'm strange to him, too. Anyway," he chuckled, blinking his eyes in the morning light, "we got all summer to get to know each other."

Meanwhile, Bessie and Daisy were in the kitchen, busy preparing breakfast. "Well, sis," Bessie said soberly, "I sure enjoyed you-all. I just wish that you could have stayed a little longer."

"Yeah," Daisy agreed, "I wish so, too, but you know how it is, child, you got to get back to that old piece of a job."

"Yeah," Bessie said, straightening up from placing a pan of biscuits into the oven, "I know what you mean. You can't stay away too long because, before you know anything, they'll be giving your job to somebody else."

"Child, that they would," Daisy laughed.

"You know, Jimbo said if the crops do pretty good this year, he was gonna get him a new car and, if he does, I'm gonna see if I can get him to bring us out there for a visit around Christmas time."

"Oh," Daisy beamed animatedly, "honey, that sure would be nice. Oh, we would sure have ourselves a time. I'd take you around and introduce you to all my friends and we could just party from house to house. Child," Daisy flashed a wide smile at her sister, "you just be sure to write and let us know if you-all are definitely coming, because I want a chance to get everything just right." She chuckled delightedly. "Honey, we gonna pitch a wang-dang-doodle!"

Bessie laughed. "Now you know I'm a church-going woman." She winked at Daisy.

"Don't worry, baby sister," Daisy said, wagging her head. "I ain't gonna lead you too far astray and, besides, I'm sure the good Lord don't mind His children having a little fun now and then."

"Yeah," Bessie laughed, then a serious look came into her eyes. "You know, four years is a mighty long time between visits."

"Yeah, you got that right, and we ain't getting no younger, either."

Bessie nodded in agreement. "Yeah, and even though we write each other pretty often, a letter still ain't like seeing somebody in person."

Daisy continued, "Well, I'm sure going to be praying that you-all have a good crop and can make the trip. It would be the best thing I could possibly get for Christmas."

They fell silent for a few minutes, each engrossed in her own thoughts. Both of them were reflecting on how nice it had been to be together these past couple of days, and they now dreaded the sense of loss that always comes with parting. So, they busied themselves, bustling about around the large kitchen making breakfast and savoring every moment, knowing that these were the last moments of their visit. Bessie sat a large bowl of scrambled eggs on the table and sighed, "Let me go out here and get them."

"I'll get the plates," Daisy said, turning to the cupboard as her sister left the kitchen.

When Bessie stepped out onto the front porch, she saw George doing something under the hood of the car. Jimbo and the boys were standing around watching him. "You-all come on in and eat," she said.

George straightened up and looked around at her, smiling. "All right, I'll be right there."

Bessie returned to the kitchen and helped her sister finish setting the table. A short while later, they were all seated around the breakfast table.

"Honey, you gonna bless the table?" Bessie asked, nodding at Jimbo. He bowed his head and the others followed the gesture. "Lord, we thank you for this food which we are about to receive for the nourishment of our bodies. Amen."

"Well, now," George smiled, eyeing the table laden with delicious food, "a man could sit down here and eat himself right into bad health." The others laughed and George continued, "Now, if I could've afforded to eat like this at old man Colfax's place, I wouldn't never have left here." He paused a moment. No one else spoke, and he went on. "Shucks, them little few pennies he was paying me I couldn't hardly feed my chickens, much less a family." They all shook with laughter, knowing that what he had said was pathetically true.

Jimbo cleared his throat, and he passed the large bowl of eggs around the table. "Yeah, George," he said, "I heard about old man Colfax. His motto was 'work you like a mule and treat you like a fool.' And if you didn't like his way, he'd send you on your way." They all laughed loud and long at this, their hearty guffaws bounding off the walls and filling the room with gaiety.

Finally, Bessie said soberly, "I sure have enjoyed you-all. These two days have gone by so fast it made my head spin."

"Yeah," George replied, "we've enjoyed you-all, too. Maybe next time, we'll be able to stay longer. You know," he added, "four years is a mighty long time between visits." "Yeah," Daisy interjected, "me and Bessie was talking about the very same thing and we were thinking if the crops turn out good this year, you-all could put that new car on the road and come on out to visit us in Detroit."

Jay-boy's eyes brightened and his dad smiled as George said excitedly, "Yeah, that would be nice. Man, we could really show you-all a time, brother-in-law!"

Jimbo laughed amusedly. "Well, we'll see how the crops do. We're about due for a nice, long vacation.

As the fading twilight melted into dusk, Jay-boy sat on the edge of the porch, half-listening to his mother and Mrs. Ruth, a neighbor lady from just down the road, swap local gossip. He rose and stirred their smoke back to life for them. It was a pile of old rags set ablaze, then slowly smothered so as to give off a lot of smoke. This was to keep the mosquitoes away so that they could enjoy the fresh, cool night air without being run inside by the pesky creatures. So, on those balmy summer nights when it was just too hot to stay indoors, they would make a smoke and sit outside, carefully angling the direction of the smoke away from them to avoid irritation of eyes and nose but close enough to keep the mosquitoes at bay. Jay-boy straightened, glanced down appraisingly at his handiwork. A thick, billowy stream of blue-gray smoke rose steadily from the pile of rags. He sighed softly, feeling pleased with himself, then turned and walked back over and took his seat on the edge of the porch.

Jay-boy sat, smelling the acrid scent of the smoke in his nostrils and feeling the soft caress of the night air on his face. He wiggled his toes in the warm dirt and stared past the large oak tree in the yard, out over the peanut field toward the road. He could see lightning bugs dancing in the distance and, now and again, an occasional automobile passed by, pushing an avenue of yellow light before it, droning along the paved road. It had been almost a week now since Uncle George and Aunt Daisy had gone back to Detroit, and things had settled back to normal. Or had they? Jay-boy glanced quickly over his shoulder at Bowknot, who was sitting in a chair further back on the porch. He had angled his body so that the front legs of the straight-backed chair were tilted up as the back rested against the outer wall of the house. He had a somber look about him, a quiet, brooding that made Jay-boy feel that he almost resented having to stay with them. Most of the time, Bowknot's manner seemed so cold and downright hostile that it discouraged any attempt at casual conversation. Bowknot was definitely no longer the wide-eyed, happy-go-lucky kid that he had grown up with. That Bowknot was gone and this one was a stranger. What had happened to him? The last time he had seen Bowknot, although it was four years ago, he had been nothing at all like this. He was then still the same old Bowknot that he had grown up with and had grown to love like a brother although they were cousins. He remembered how empty and sad he had felt the day he learned that Bowknot's family was going to move to Detroit. He had moped around for weeks, maybe even months, after they left, thinking, remembering, and crying a little now and then, trying to adjust to life without his best friend. Now the boy who he had grown to love like a brother seemed like a total stranger to him although they were now only sitting a few feet apart on the porch. Jay-boy knew that they were miles apart in reality. This fact pained and perplexed him and he shook his head and narrowed his eyes as if peering into an invisible microscope trying to see some tiny organism, some germ that lay at the root of his perplexity. What really happened to Bowknot in Detroit that had turned him into this stranger, this narcissistic, spiteful, sardonic young man who made him feel awkward and uncomfortable?

"Well, I reckon I'll get on to the house," Mrs. Ruth was saying, lifting her arms and yawning lazily.

"I'll walk with you a ways," Jay-boy's mother said, rising slowly from her chair. The two women rose and started walking away from the house toward a small footpath that ran across the pea field to the gravel road. Mrs. Ruth lived in a large, old, weather-beaten house that sat just beyond the road. It was in plain sight of the Johnson house, diagonally across the pea field in a straight line with the ancient footpath that busy feet kept packed hard and firm despite the fact that it was plowed asunder every spring. Neighbors used the path as a shortcut on the way to the Johnson house, opting not to take the longer route around by way of the hard-surface road to their gate. People had used this path ever since Jay-boy could remember, and it seemed that it had always been there. It seemed strange those few days or so in the spring when it wasn't there, but the goings and comings of their neighbors quickly fixed that. Jay-boy watched the two women as they made their way along the narrow path across the field toward the road. He rose, walked over and picked up the two chairs in which they had been sitting, and brought them back and placed them on the porch. Then he went over to the smoldering fire and put out the last of the dying coals and gathered up the left-over rags. He tossed them into a metal bucket, which he replaced between the large roots of the giant oak standing in front of the house. He straightened for a moment, glancing out across the pea field in the direction that his mother had gone. He could barely see her slight form, now moving back toward their house. He started off to meet her, for it was full dark now and the overcast sky covered with a blanket of clouds had denied the moon its radiance.

"Who's that? You, Jay-boy?" his mother called out as he came near, her soft voice floating on the warm night air.

"Yes, ma'am," he replied. "I just came to walk back with you. It's gotten so dark out here now."

When he came up to her, he turned and she slipped her arm

through his, laughing softly. She beamed at him in pride and said, "Looks like I've raised me a fine son here. You're quite some gentleman, you know that?"

Jay-boy chuckled softly, but said nothing. Mrs. Johnson was very proud of her son. He worked hard on the farm, he was smart in school, and he had never given them a moment's trouble. He was a good boy, she thought, and I thank God for it, too.

"Well," Jay-boy said after a long silence, "I just wanted to make sure that the wolf don't get you.

She laughed and patted his cheek playfully. "You think you're a man now, huh?"

Jay-boy said nothing, just laughed to himself. Neither spoke for a long while, enjoying the companionable silence as they walked. Finally, Jay-boy said, "Ma?"

"Yes?" she answered.

He hesitated, and before he could speak, his mother broke in. "It's Bowknot, isn't it?"

"Yeah, Ma," he frowned, sighing in exasperation. "I don't know what's the matter with him. He hardly ever says anything, and when I try to talk to him, he just acts all surly and junk like he ain't got nothing to say."

"Well, son," she said sympathetically, "I know that it's hard, but just try to bear with him. He'll come around after a while. He's had a lot of problems. He just got mixed up with the wrong crowd and got himself in some trouble. Your dad told you, didn't he?"

"Yeah, Ma, he told me that Bowknot was arrested with some boys in a stolen car. He said that Bowknot started to mouth off at the police and they beat him up and charged him with resisting arrest. Still, that ain't no reason for him to walk around with a chip on his doggone shoulder, mad with the world," Jay-boy blurted disgustedly.

"No, I reckon not, son, but people deal with their problems in different ways. You see, when Bowknot was arrested with them boys for stealing that car and Daisy and them got the call that he was locked up, they were mad as they could be when they got down to the jail and found Bowknot all beat up. Daisy said he looked like he needed to be in the hospital and they did take him straight to the doctor. The first thing next morning, she and George went down to the police station to find out why Bowknot was the only one of the boys that had been beat. They were told that Bowknot had smart-mouthed the two arresting officers and told them that he wasn't going no damn where with them, because he didn't know that the car had been stolen. The guys just came by and asked him if he wanted to ride. While they were arguing, two other police showed up and they tried to arrest Bowknot. He started fighting with one of them and all four of them jumped on him and beat him pretty bad. And then they charged him with resisting arrest. They don't know why he just didn't let them go on and arrest him like the other three boys. Maybe he was trying to show off, but whenever Daisy and George tried to ask Bowknot what had happened, he just said that the police started it, that they were picking on him, but that he would die before they'd ever put handcuffs on him again. A few days after Bowknot had told them that," she paused and sighed heavily, "Daisy said that she found a thirty-eight in Bowknot's room and they knew that it was time to get him out of the city and away from that crowd he was running with, before something serious happened."

Chapter 5

The sun was hot and the air was heavy and still. Jay-boy paused and leaned heavily on his hoe, staring down the long row. A dust devil danced about in the tobacco plants as Jay-boy spat and pulled a handkerchief from his back pocket, wiping his brow. He looked around at Bowknot, a few yards behind him?

"Tired?" he asked.

"I was tired when I started," Bowknot replied sourly.

"Well, I guess it's about time to knock off for dinner, anyway. I've got twelve straight up."

Jay-boy stood erect and started toward the house, leaving his hoe right where it was to sort of mark his place. Bowknot followed.

"It sure is a scorcher out here today," Jay-boy said, venturing an attempt at conversation. The two of them had worked side by side chopping tobacco all morning, and had not said twenty-five words to each other.

Bowknot was silent. He walked on, head tilted down, arms swinging loosely at his side.

"You know," Jay-boy said thoughtfully, "I bet you it's ninety degrees out here, and that's in the shade!" He laughed drily. Still, Bowknot was silent; he merely grunted, half-acknowledging the comment.

As they neared the back of the house, Jay-boy saw his dad pulling up to the barn with the mule team.

"How's it going, fellows?" his dad called to them.

"All right," Jay-boy replied.

"He ain't working you too hard, is he?" Mr. Johnson directed this question at Bowknot.

"No, sir," came Bowknot's laconic reply.

Having reached the house, the two young men climbed the steps, crossed the back porch, opened the screen door, and entered the kitchen. Jay-boy's mother was bending over, taking something from the oven. She straightened as they entered.

"I've been expecting you-all. Go on and get washed up and I'll set the table. Is your daddy out there yet?"

"Yes, Ma," Jay-boy said, "he just pulled up. I reckon he'll be on in here in a minute." He dipped water into a large tin and picked up a piece of soap from a small table beside the door. He carried the tin of water to the back porch and placed it on a stout wooden table beneath the kitchen window. He washed the dirt from his hands and arms and, after he had finished, Bowknot took the tin and did the same.

While Bowknot was washing, Jay-boy returned to the kitchen and took a seat at the table. His mother brought in a large plate of pork chops, a bowl of collard greens, and a pan of hot biscuits. "Well," she said, "you can help yourself." Jay-boy did. Then he closed his eyes and whispered his blessing.

"It sure it hot out there," he said.

"Yeah," his mother responded, "the weatherman said it was going to be ninety-three today, but we're supposed to get some rain tonight or early tomorrow morning."

Bowknot came back in, letting the screen door slam softly behind him.

"Come on, sit down here and help yourself, son," said Mrs. Johnson. "There's plenty here, and I don't want to see nothing go to waste."

"You heard from Mom and Dad yet?" Bowknot asked quizzically.

"No, not yet," she said, "but I haven't checked the mailbox yet today."

Bowknot helped himself to the food before him and said nothing else.

The screen door opened. "Well, now," Jimbo laughed, "I see it was so good that you-all just couldn't wait for me, huh?"

"Don't worry," Bessie laughed softly, "we got enough to go around."

A few moments later, Jimbo had washed up and was seated at the table enjoying the meal.

"Huh," he grunted with satisfaction, "you sure know how t cook for a working man. This is the kind of food that will stick to your ribs and help you hang in there and stay with it." He glanced at his son. "You think you-all gonna finish that tobacco today?"

"I don't see why not; we're just about half-way right now, and we haven't really been pushing real hard because of the heat."

"Yeah," Jimbo said thoughtfully, "this heat is something else. I've had to keep a close eye on my mules. Well," he said, changing the subject, "if it don't rain tomorrow, I want you-all to plow the peanuts back over yonder in the bottom. If you can get started early, you can probably finish up tomorrow evening."

Jay-boy nodded. Glancing at his cousin, he saw him frown. Bowknot cleared his throat and got up from the table abruptly; he pushed his chair back under the table with a sharp shove and strode out of the kitchen.

"He didn't hardly eat a thing," Bessie said, looking at his plate.

"Guess he's not hungry."

"Well, I guess he's just got a lot on his mind," she sighed, rising to clear his plate from the table. "Jimbo?" She paused, turning her gaze on him, a serious, somber look coming into her eyes. "Jimbo, you don't think we're working the child too hard, do you?"

He hesitated before he answered, glanced at Jay-boy, then lifted his eyes to hers. "No, no harder than we're working our own son. Now, baby," he went on reflectively, "George brought the boy down here to work on the farm. He asked me to keep him busy." He stopped to take a piece of pork chop on his fork, and chewed and swallowed it before he continued. "Now, I have a farm to run and plenty of work for him to do."

"Yeah," she said, "but I don't want us to overwhelm him. Let him get adjusted; he can't keep up with Jay-boy. Jay-boy is used to the farm and all."

Jay-boy could feel the tension mounting, and he knew that an argument was brewing. He kept his eyes buried in his plate and hurried his pace, now starting to gulp his food, looking for the earliest opportunity to make an exit.

His dad sighed in exasperation. "Bessie, baby, I didn't say that I was going to kill the boy. I know he can't keep up with Jay-boy and I don't expect him to, but I do expect him to pull his weight." His voice was beginning to take on a quality of sternness that was rare—he only used that tone when he meant to have things his way and was utterly convinced that his was the right way.

"Now, Jimbo, Bowknot has been through a lot, and he is going to need time to get himself together and a lot of patience from us, too." She was insistent now.

Jay-boy had finished his meal, so he quickly rose and made a quiet retreat. He glanced back over his shoulder as his dad laid down the fork and sighed heavily.

"Now, honey, I'm not a what-do-you-call-it, a psychologist. I'm just a man trying to work his land and take care of his family the best way I know how. George asked me to take the boy and let him work here on the farm, and that's what I'm going to do. Now, I ain't got time to baby no half-grown man—I don't baby Jay-boy and I ain't gonna baby him. The only problems I see that he has is being hard-headed and sassy."

"Shhhh," she said, holding her index finger to her lips, "he might be listening."

"No," he said, even more loudly, I'm not gonna shhhh! This

is my house and, furthermore, I know that I'm right. Now being hard-headed and sassy will get you in trouble every time and I'll tell him so to his face!" He pounded the table to emphasize his point. "I'm not going to stand for it! I've already told him so, too, and I also told his daddy!"

The sweltering heat was almost intolerable when they returned to the field. The glaring sun had reached its apex and was now descending ever so slowly toward the western horizon. The sun's heat was trapped beneath a blanket of haze and the high humidity made the atmosphere heavy, steamy, and oppressive. The mingled fragrances of cedar, pine, and honeysuckle permeated the air. Somewhere a bird sang lazily, and now and again a busy little bee buzzed among the young tobacco plants.

The two young men worked steadily, methodically, and silently up and down the long rows, each engrossed in his own thoughts. Now and then, Jay-boy would throw a quick glance back over his shoulder. There he was, not more than ten yards behind him. His eyes riveted on his work, his mouth drawn into a tight line that curled into a sneer at the corners. Bowknot's face seemed to be frozen into a perpetual frown. He had no cause to act like this, no matter what had happened in Detroit. After all, he and his folks hadn't done anything to Bowknot but try to make him feel welcome. He had his nerve, walking around mad with the world because he had gotten his behind beaten for smart-mouthing a cop. Shucks, he could just drop this hoe, turn around, look him right straight in the eye, and tell him about his damn self right now. Suddenly, Jay-boy's stomach muscles flexed taut and rage bloomed behind his eyes. It was all he could do to restrain himself. He shook his head abruptly, fighting for control. He couldn't do this—what would his mother say? How would she feel? What would his dad say? Probably nothing much, but there was his mother's reaction to really consider, and he knew that she would be hurt. She had almost pleaded with him already to bear with his cousin and try to understand. Yeah, he would try to understand; he would try to be patient. Yeah, but why is it that people who have a problem themselves always seem to want others to be patient and try to understand them while they carry on being a total pain in the ass, not having the slightest regard for anybody else's feelings?

Jay-boy blinked his eyes, trying to force these thoughts from his mind. Finally, the memories of earlier times flickered across his consciousness. He remembered the time he had pulled Bowknot from a pond and probably saved his life. He, Bowknot, and Old Man Burnside's grandson had gone fishing at the Burnside's pond. After they had all caught long strings full of fish and were making ready to leave, Johnny Burnside decided to dive into the pond and take a swim. "You guys come on in and let's swim a while before we go."

Jay-boy shook his head and said wistfully, "We can't swim."

Johnny's face broke into a wide grin, and he said tauntingly, "You guys are thirteen years old and can't swim? Well, ain't that just a doggone shame, now!" He whirled around and dived under the murky brown water. In a couple of moments, he surfaced and smiled condescendingly. "I could give you-all some swimming lessons, but then again, I don't know if I want to be responsible if you happen to drown before you learn. Now I just couldn't stand that on my conscience."

By this time, Bowknot's face was livid with rage. "Speak for yourself, Jay-boy! I know how to swim!" He was determined not to be mocked. Yeah, he was going to show this uppity white boy—who he really didn't like anyway and only bothered with him because he worked from time to time for his old granddaddy and by fooling with him, they could come on the place and fish often. Before Jay-boy could frame a response, Bowknot had pulled off his clothes and dived into the pond. He sank immediately; he sank like a rock. Suddenly, he came up, face flushed and eyes wide with horror. He was flailing the water, thrashing about wildly, and immediately sank again. Jay-boy was terrified: his eyes watered, his throat went dry, and his heart hammered against his ribs. He had to do something. Again Bowknot came up. "Help, Johnny! Please help!" Now he was heaving gulps of water and his voice had risen toward hysteria.

"Oh," Johnny laughed, "I thought you said you could swim." Then he exploded with prolonged laughter and there was a glint of cruel amusement as his face flushed red with glee. Meanwhile, Jay-boy's eyes canvassed the banks for a long stick, a sturdy reed, a deadfall—anything that he could reach out and let Bowknot catch hold of. There was nothing, and watching Bowknot thrashing about in the water filled him with a sickening dread. Finally, an idea flashed like lightning into his mind. He shucked his shirt and pants and hurriedly tied the arm of his shirt to one of the legs of his pants and did the same with Bowknot's clothes. There. He had made a rope of sorts, long enough to reach his cousin. He quickly tied a chunk of wood to the end of the makeshift rope and slung it with all his strength out to Bowknot. "Here," he shouted, "catch hold of this!"

By now, Bowknot was almost listless with horror and there was a hopeless look of resignation in his eyes. Quickly, Jay-boy picked up another chunk of wood and threw it hard, striking Bowknot on the arm with it. The blow seemed to jar Bowknot back to his wits. "Grab hold of the rope!" Jay-boy shouted at the top of his lungs, not asking him, but demanding that he do so. Bowknot obeyed and Jay-boy started pulling with all his might, towing his frightened cousin to shore. When Bowknot reached the edge, Jay-boy scrambled down and helped him up onto the bank. Bowknot was trembling with fear, and clung to Jay-boy like a frightened child, crying uncontrollably. After a long while, he managed to quiet his cousin. "There, that's all right, Bowknot."

"Don't tell Mama," he begged. "Please don't tell Daddy either, they'll kill me. Please don't tell," he pleaded pitifully.

"I won't tell," Jay-boy promised. "I promise I won't tell a soul."

All this time, Johnny was sitting at the edge of the water on the opposite side of the pond, looking on. When Jay-boy looked up and noticed him there, his eyes were cold and his lip curled into a hateful sneer. "I'm going to beat you for this!"

"Why?" Johnny howled. "It wasn't my fault he jumped in the water!"

"Yeah," Jay-boy hissed, "but you egged him on and you wouldn't do nothing to try to help him, but sat there and laughed like a jackass."

"What could I do?" Johnny protested. "My folks always told me never go near a person who's panicking in the water because they could drown you."

"Well, then," Jay-boy spouted, "they should have told you to keep your big mouth shut and not to make fun of people just because they don't know how to swim and you do. Now, you may as well come on over and get it now, because I'm gonna beat your behind and I don't care who you tell."

Jay-boy and Bowknot dried themselves and donned their clothes as Johnny sat watching, looking scared and forlorn, wishing that they would go and leave him alone. After they had dressed, the two of them stood and watched Johnny sitting there at the edge of the pond, red and frightened, wanting to come over and get his clothes but afraid of what Jay-boy would do to him.

"You may as well come on over and get your beating now," Jay-boy said, his eyes glaring, his tone determined and merciless, "because if I have to run you down, it's gonna to be twice as bad."

"I ain't done nothing to you-all," Johnny whimpered. "I can't help he jumped in the water."

"Shut up!" Jay-boy blazed. "Now, you come on over here right now or I'm coming around this pond and get you."

Johnny looked behind him and then on both sides, everywhere seeing thick vines, dense saplings, and briar-laced underbrush that would slice his naked skin like a knife if he tried to make a run for it. What if he was caught? They would probably beat him unmercifully then. Finally, realizing the utter hopelessness of his plight, Johnny lowered his head, slunk back into the water, and started swimming slowly back toward the two boys. When he reached the bank and started to climb up, his eyes were red with tears.

"I'm sorry," he said, "I didn't mean to make fun of you-all, honest, I didn't."

He was a pitiful sight, and to look at him now suddenly filled Jay-boy with disgust. Jay-boy strode over to him, snatching him up violently by the arm and sticking his face in Johnny's. "You make me sick, you know that?" Jay-boy spat out.

Johnny said nothing, his eyes frightened, his body trembling with dread.

"Listen, you ain't worth the energy it takes to beat your ass, but I am gonna take your pole and your fish, and I dare you to tell anybody."

"I won't tell, I won't!" Johnny pleaded pitifully.

"Get out of my sight!" Jay-boy viciously shoved the boy, almost pushing him to the ground. "Come on, Bowknot, let's get the hell away from here."

Bowknot had never seen Jay-boy so angry before, and it almost frightened him to think of what he might do to Johnny. They gathered up their gear along with Johnny's pole and fish and left.

That had been the last time they had gone fishing with him, though they still worked now and again for his granddad. The next time they had seen Johnny, he had grinned sheepishly and acted like the whole thing had never happened, but he kept his distance from then on.

Chapter 6

Then Jay-boy remembered the time about a month before Bowknot and his folks moved away. Spring had fallen over the landscape. She had dressed the woods up in vibrant greens. She had dappled the wildflowers with bright reds, yellows, blues, pinks, and violets and arrayed them in a mosaic of picturesque splendor. The morning was warm and the sun was bright. The air was filled with the music of the children's laughter.

Jay-boy had been playing marbles with five other boys on the hard-packed dirt behind the school. He was kneeling, getting ready to take his shot, when little Leon Petterson came running up to him.

"Hey, Jay-boy!" Jay-boy looked up into the boy's excited face. "They messin' with Bowknot around there!"

"Who's messin' with him?" Jay-boy asked, his voice low and his eyes hard and serious.

"One of them high-school boys. He . . . he done took Bowknot's lunch money and when Bowknot tried to get it back, the boy knocked him down and got his clothes all dirty!"

Jay-boy stood up. "Hey, Roy!" He gestured to a boy who was watching the marble game but who had not been a player. "You can take my turn." Then Jay-boy turned sharply around and said to Leon, "Come on, show me who this boy is."

The two of them started around the corner of the old weather-beaten school building to the area where the high-school students had congregated to wait for their buses. Bowknot had tried to leave to tell a teacher what was going on, but the boy had kept pushing him back and had told Bowknot he would whip him good if he did tell.

As Leon and Jay-boy approached, Jay-boy was silent, but his eyes were hard and his face was set in a frown. "There he is, Jay-boy." Leon's finger shot out like a pistol as he pointed to a heavy-set boy leaning against the side of the building.

Jay-boy looked at Leon. "Where is Bowknot?" he snapped, his eyes flashing, his voice trembling with anger.

"There he is!" Leon shouted, pointing to Bowknot, who was sitting with his head bowed, idly scratching in the dirt. Jay-boy strode over to his cousin and as he came closer, he could see patches of dirt in Bowknot's hair.

"Bowknot!" he called. When the boy looked up, Jay-boy could see that his eyes were red from crying. Suddenly his heart started to hammer against his ribs and his blood began to boil like lava. "Bowknot," he said sharply, pointing to the boy Leon had shown him, "did that boy take your money?"

"Yes," Bowknot said sadly, "and he told me that if I told, he would beat me."

"Well, I guess we'll just have to see about that," Jay-boy hissed. "Come on, Bowknot," he said, taking his cousin by the arm, "let's go and get your money."

They strode up to the boy. By now, a crowd had started to gather as the word had flashed around the schoolyard about what was about to happen. Jay-boy moved in front of the boy and stuck his face right into the boy's face. His eyes were flashing with anger, but his voice was level and cold. Taking Bowknot's hand, he thrust it forward and said, "Give him back his money."

The older boy smiled, then looked around amusedly, winking at several of the other boys standing around, and laughed. "Now, just who is going to make me?" The other boys laughed.

Jay-boy spoke again, his tone still level and his eyes still hard. "I said give him his money back."

The boy was taller and heavier than Jay-boy and now he

bristled, moving forward a little. "I'd just like to see you try and make me!"

As soon as the last word slid from his lips, Jay-boy's fist smashed him full in the mouth. The boy went down. Eyes were wide and mouths hung agape at the speed and power of the smaller boy's blow. The high school boy looked up, shocked and furious as he spat blood. His lip was cut, but his face went black with rage. He leaped up and lunged at Jay-boy. Jay-boy stepped quickly aside and tripped the boy, putting out his leg and then connecting with another right hand, smashing the boy in the temple. His heavy body hit the ground with a thud.

When he turned over and started to rise, Jay-boy was standing over him, his fist tight and his face contorted with rage. "Now you give him his money before I beat you senseless, and I'm not going to tell you again."

The boy grabbed at Jay-boy's leg. As Jay-boy shifted, the boy missed but with the same movement, rolled to his knees and lunged to his feet. "Now," the high school boy said, his lip twisted in a sullen sneer, "I'm going to beat your ass, just like I done his."

"Come on, then," taunted Jay-boy, "I'm waitin'."

The boy came at Jay-boy, swinging savagely. Jay-boy met him, throwing up his left arm, blocking the boy's right and connecting hard just below the boy's left eye. The boy screamed and grasped at his face, then Jay-boy swung again with all his might, smashing the larger boy in the stomach. The bully sank slowly to his knees, then to the ground, and lay still.

"Get up, you big bully!" Jay-boy shouted derisively. "Get up!" He kicked the boy, not savagely but hard, in the ribs. The boy's eyes rolled back and he sprawled in the dirt. Jay-boy bent down over him, rolled him over, and removed his wallet roughly. He snatched it open and snapped his head around to Bowknot, who had been watching. "How much money did he take from you?"

"Three dollars," Bowknot said softly.

Jay-boy snatched three dollars from the boy's wallet and threw it down on him as he lay groaning in the dirt. "Now, you get this," he said, kicking the boy again, hard, in the thigh, "don't you ever, as long as you breathe oxygen, mess with my cousin again, or next time, I won't just bust your lip, it will be your ass!"

Jay-boy looked around at all the wide eyes, spat, then turned sharply and said, "Come on, Bowknot, let's get away from around here."

Suddenly, the school bell rang. Somewhere, someone shouted excitedly, "Here comes the teacher!" A sense of fear seemed to flash through the crowd and everyone began to scatter, not wanting to be involved or connected with the fight. After all, it could mean suspension. So, as the buses pulled up and began loading, the crowd quickly dissipated. Jay-boy remembered that his teacher had confronted him about the fight later and that Leon and a number of the other kids had stood up and said that the high school boy had started the whole thing. The last Jay-boy had heard was that the boy had indeed been suspended for starting trouble on the school grounds. After that, the kids had dubbed Jay-boy "Joe Louis," and he had had no more trouble at school.

Chapter 7

Bowknot was jubilantly bobbing his head and popping his fingers to Marvin Gaye's "How Sweet it is to be Loved by You" when Jay-boy eased the car off the hard-surfaced road and nosed it along the dirt path up to Kathy's house. The headlights threw their hard, yellow glare on the weather-beaten boards of the two-story frame house. It had a tin roof and a porch that ran lengthwise across the front of the structure. There was a swing at one end of the porch and two old metal porch chairs on either side of the front door. There was a large old oak tree standing at one corner of the house and it towered above the house like some gothic statue, looming huge and ghostly in the harsh yellow light.

"Well, here we are," Jay-boy smiled as he pulled up in front of the house. Suddenly the porch light came on and, looking up, Jay-boy saw the curtains move at the large window beside the door. He smiled to himself, "That was Mrs. Walker, no doubt, peeping to see who's out here." After turning off the engine and lights, Jay-boy glanced over at his cousin and said, "Let's go, my man."

The two of them climbed out of the car and strode up the front steps onto the porch and across to the front door. Jay-boy knocked. "Who is it?" a voice came from inside. It was Kathy's mom.

"It's me, Jay-boy, and my cousin, Bowknot, Mrs. Walker," he called. The door opened and there was Mrs. Walker, standing smiling.

"Well, you-all come on in." They opened the screen door and

entered, letting it close softly behind them. Mrs. Walker was a short, stout, woman, neat and soft-spoken with a pleasant, folksy nature. She loved to talk and was a superb cook. She had a way of putting one at ease immediately and a rare insight into the passions and problems of adolescence. Her good cooking and her hearty but gentle manner made her a friend and confidant to many of the young people of the neighborhood. This also made her house a popular gathering place because Kathy had inherited all of her mother's traits, which made her as beautiful internally as she was externally and made Jay-boy the envy of many a would-be young suitor.

"Let me go upstairs and get Kathy," she said, leaving them in the front room. "Oh, you-all have a seat." The room was modestly furnished and reflected the homely elegance of the family. A large, black-and-white television perched on its mahogany stand, flanked by a large, old record-player sitting smugly on a table along one wall. A well-worn couch stretched along another wall, attended by an end table holding a ceramic lamp wearing a pleated cloth shade. Along the other wall were two large pillowed chairs; the end table between them was adorned with a beautiful ceramic vase festooned with an interesting bunch of artificial flowers. The fourth wall held the fireplace, on either side of which were artificial floor plants; several wooden chairs were placed throughout the room. The two boys seated themselves: Jay-boy on the couch and Bowknot in one of the pillowed chairs.

A few moments later, Mrs. Walker returned, smiling. "Would you boys like something to eat? I have some neck bones and cabbbage in there. You know you're welcome."

"No, ma'am," Jay-boy nodded, "we just finished supper. But thank you just the same." Bowknot nodded in agreement and muttered softly, "No, thanks."

Jay-boy noticed that his cousin seemed nervous under Mrs. Walker's gaze. He constantly shifted his weight in the chair, drummed his fingers on its arms, and kept his eyes averted, staring miles deep into the linoleum floor.

"Well, you know that you-all are welcome to it." She sighed, lifting her arms and running her fingers through her soft, mixed gray hair. "You, son," she said, staring hard at Bowknot. "You are the spitting image of your daddy. I mean you are just like him, cute as you can be and shy as you can be. Now, that daddy of yours was a mess! Could dance and always as sharp as a tack. I tell you he was the life of the party after he had had gotten him a couple of drinks. Laughing and joking. I mean you couldn't shut him up. But he was always nice and friendly to everybody. Seem like a drink or two would just melt that shyness right away. Now, Jay-boy, your daddy was a live-wire, too. He didn't need nothing to drink to get him started. He was always cutting the fool. He had a string of girls after him, too. It was a sad, sad day around here when he and your mother announced that they were getting married." She laughed heartily, slapping her thigh. The two boys laughed, too. "Yeah," she continued, "we had our day and we didn't miss much either. On Friday nights like this here, we would have that old Victrola jumping and, child, we would be stomping the dust out of the floor!" She chuckled reflectively. "Yes, child, we had ourselves a time!"

"Oh, yeah!" Kathy laughed, peeking over her mother's shoulder at them. "I bet you were a frisky little something when you were young," she said, patting her mother playfully on the cheek. She had glided down the stairs so quietly that they had been oblivious to her presence until she spoke. Then they all turned and stared in wonder, and her mother laughed, half-embarrassed and half amused at the young men's obvious interest in her story.

"Well," she laughed, shaking her hips and popping her fingers rhythmically, "I ain't always been old and I still ain't forgot how to shake a leg." The young people laughed uproariously.

"You'd better cool it, Mom," Kathy laughed, "you'll be walking around here crying about Arthur and Rumer tomorrow!"

"Oh, I ain't worried about them righteous brothers," she chuckled. "We understand each other—I don't bother them and they don't bother me. That's why I'm gonna leave all this dancing to you young folks. I just want to let you-all know that I might be old, but I ain't cold and I still got some soul and know how to let the good times roll!" She broke up with hearty laughter and so did the rest of them. Their laughter bounced off the walls and the ceiling and filled the room, making them glad to be around Mrs. Walker, basking in the glow of her warmth and humor. Even Bowknot, Jay-boy noted, had relaxed. His eyes were flashing bright with laughter and a wide smile creased his face.

"Well, Mom," Kathy said finally, "we're gonna get going."

"All right," Mrs. Walker said, "you-all be particular now, you hear!"

"We will," they all answered as they walked out.

Bowknot climbed into the back seat and Kathy and Jay-boy rode in the front. Jay-boy had opened the door for Kathy and helped her into the car. His heart had quickened when his hand held hers and his head had reeled from the effects of her hypnotizing beauty and the divine fragrance of her perfume. She was without a doubt the most beautiful girl that he had ever seen. Each time their eyes met, they would hold and the unspoken tenderness in her large brown eyes pronounced her love for him louder, stronger, and deeper than any words could ever express.

Kathy was an angel of a girl—sweet, intelligent, and vibrant. She was full of life, full of hope, and laughter always seemed to lurk just behind her soft, brown eyes. She had wanted to be a teacher ever since she could remember, and she could hardly wait to finish her last year of high school. She wanted to attend Fisk University and, after graduating, she wanted to return home and teach. Her father had been killed in the Korean war and her mother had never remarried. Her mother had bought a house with his insurance settlement, and with a widow's pension and domestic work for a prominent white family in town, she had managed to make a reasonably good living. Mrs. Walker was a strong believer in education and she had always insisted that Kathy do her best. Kathy had not disappointed her mother; she had been a straight-A student since grade school. Why, she seemed to have it all: intellect, elegance, and the sweetest personality in the world. She could have had any boy she wanted, but she had chosen Jay-boy.

Jay-boy started the engine and turned on the lights and the radio. He slid the car in gear and eased it back out toward the hard-surfaced road.

"Where are we going?" Kathy asked.

"To Ruth's house, I thought," Jay-boy said, puzzled. "Then I was going to the shack and we gonna pitch a wang-dang-doodle all night long!" He laughed. Kathy chuckled, too.

As Sam Cooke crooned "You Send Me" on the radio, the three of them sat quietly. The only other sound was the steady drone of the engine and the whining of the rubber tires on the road. After a while they were pulling up in front of Ruth's house, a small frame house that sat about thirty yards back from the road in a hard-packed clearing. An old rust-covered truck was parked in the yard, and about fifteen yards from the house was a well. Jay-boy pulled up beside the old truck and blew the car's horn. A light came on over the stoop and the door opened.

"Light and come on in, light and come on in!" a deep, husky voice called congenially. It was Ruth's dad, a large, barrel-chested man with a pot belly and huge, calloused hands. He was a sharecropper, and the family had come to Virginia from North Carolina in search of a better life and a better piece of land to farm. Ruth was the oldest of five children, so she was sister and mother to her three younger brothers and small sister. This often meant that she would have to spend long hours running the house while her mother was away helping her father in the fields or doing domestic work in town. She often missed days from school and would struggle to keep up with her class. Kathy would often help her with her homework and, as a result, they had become best friends.

Ruth was not so sure of what she wanted to do with her life after school, which was probably due to the fact that her life had never seemed like her own in the first place. She had always been told what to do and when to do it. It seemed that her mother always had some task waiting, and one thing after another filled her days and left her tired at nightfall. However, Friday night was different. It was the only time that she could call her own, and she really looked forward to it. So when the three climbed out of the car and entered the house, Ruth was ready to go. She was standing in the middle of the floor, smiling excitedly. "I had thought you-all wasn't coming, there for a while," she said. "I thought you had forgot me."

"How could we forget you, Ruth?" Jay-boy laughed. "Bowknot wouldn't have stood for that." He smiled, teasingly nudging his cousin in the ribs with his elbow. Bowknot just smiled and said nothing.

"Dad," Ruth said, smiling at Bowknot, "this is Jay-boy's cousin, Bowknot."

"How do you do, son?" the older man said, extending his large, calloused hand. "Nice to know you."

"Nice to know you, too, sir," Bowknot replied softly.

"Oh, and Mom . . ." Ruth went on and introduced Bowknot to her mother and the host of siblings milling about the room. After a short while, the two couples left, with Ruth's dad admonishing, "Don't you-all stay out here too late. And be careful; you know there's a lot of wine-heads out here trying to drive tonight!"

"Well, here we are," Jay-boy sighed as he nosed the car carefully into a space between an old Chevy and a late-model Dodge.

"It sure is packed here tonight," Kathy observed, her eyes canvassing the lot full of cars of every make and description. The hard dirt yard in front of the place was full of people laughing, talking, slapping hands, dancing, and gesticulating in every manner. The large, one-story, weather-beaten house that everyone called "The Shack" seemed to vibrate with the thudding of the electric bass. It swayed and creaked in rhythmic cadence to the beat of "Baby, Baby, Where did our love go?" blaring from the oversized jukebox. The old house seemed to be a living thing, animated and electric in the harsh yellow glare of the spotlights mounted on three light posts around the building.

"Well, now," Bowknot said, trying to mask his excitement, "are we going in or not?"

"You two go on in, we'll be on," Jay-boy replied.

Bowknot opened his door and stepped out and went around to open the door for Ruth. She slid out and the two of them started to weave their way through parked cars toward the place.

"Don't be too long, now," Bowknot threw back over his shoulder with a hint of amusement in his voice.

Kathy laughed drily, a little embarrassed at his insinuation. "We'll be on soon," she said reassuringly.

After the other two were out of sight, Kathy glanced at Jay-boy. "Ruth is falling for Bowknot, you know. That's all she's been talking about all week. She was so scared that you-all weren't coming by tonight and she wasn't gonna get to see him."

"I thought her and Pigfoot Parker was supposed to be going together."

"Oh, she really don't like him that way. I mean, he's a nice guy, but he just isn't her type."

"Well, why does she keep hanging around with him, then?" Jay-boy said sharply.

"Jay," Kathy said, leveling a reproving stare at him, "she said that he is a nice guy and fun to go out with, but she is just not in love with him. Can't people just be friends?"

"Yeah, I reckon so, but that guy thinks she's his woman. I've heard him bragging about that at school. Now, if that really ain't the case, then somebody better tell him."

"Listen," she said quickly. "Ruth is a big girl, and I'm sure she can handle her own affairs. Now," she said, taking his hand in hers and sliding close to him, "let's talk about us."

Jay-boy looked deep into her eyes and became as oblivious to the world as a man sleepwalking under a hypnotic spell.

"I love you, Jay-boy," she whispered. The words were soft, and they seemed to caress his mind like beautiful music and made him giddy with delight. Then she was in his arms, soft, gentle, like a flower. To him, she was the very personification of love. She was the essence of ethereal elegance. As he drank the sweet nectar from her voluptuous lips and caressed the silky softness of her arms and shoulders, he found himself suspended somewhere between dream and reality. After a while of smelling her, tasting her, feeling the soft contours of her body molded against his, his heart hammered against his ribs and his blood sang through his veins with throbbing desire. He tore himself from her embrace. Yes, he wanted her, but in the right way. He knew that she wanted him, too, but also in the right way. Therefore, they would have to wait. It seemed like it would be forever, but he knew that he could wait because she would wait for him. There had never been anyone else for either of them. He held her hand and stared deep into her eyes. She leaned against him and planted feather-like kisses on his lips. "I can't wait until we're married. I couldn't love you any more if you were already my husband," she whispered, closing his mouth with a kiss before he could reply.

When she pulled away from his lips, he whispered, "I love you so much, Kathy. I just can't explain it. All I know is that I just couldn't live without you." He sighed heavily and continued. "When I think about you, my mind just seems to reel like I'm in a dream or something." He straightened and stared hard at her, lifting her chin slightly with his fingers so that he could look full into her eyes. "Kathy, you are the only girl I've ever loved, and I feel like the luckiest man in the world to have a sweet woman like you. Every night, I pray to God that you never change or stop loving me."

"Oh, Jay," she said reassuringly, "you don't have to worry

about that. I know that you are the only man for me. You don't know how I miss you when you're not around, how I still dream about you at night; sometimes I want to see you so bad that my heart just aches and I get physically sick!"

"Baby," Jay-boy interrupted, "if it was up to me, I would come to see you every night, but I knew that when school was in you had your schoolwork and things you had to do around the house. Plus, your mother would think I was taking you away from your studies. And then, too, I just don't want you to get tired of seeing me!"

She laughed, reaching up and patting him on the cheek. "I never get tired of seeing you, Jay-boy, you know that."

Jay-boy was quiet for a long time, and finally Kathy reached up again, taking his face in both her hands and kissing him full on the lips. She drew back slowly, and stroking his earlobe with her index finger, she asked, "Now what's wrong?"

He sighed heavily and cleared his throat. "When we gonna get engaged?"

"First you got to ask me to marry you, silly!"

"Okay." He smiled, then turned and opened the car door and made his way around to her side and opened her door. She stepped out and he immediately dropped to one knee. Looking up at her with all the seriousness he could muster, he said, "Kathy Marie Walker, will you marry this here poor old farm boy?"

She smiled down at him, her eyes alight with pride. "Yes, yes, and yes, I will marry this poor old farm boy," she said. "Now get up and get that dirt off your pants."

"You know what, baby?" he said excitedly, brushing the dirt from the knee of his trousers and straightening up, "I'm gonna give you an engagement ring on your graduation day. I'm gonna start saving up for it right away."

"Oh, that is so sweet!" She came close, leaning her head on his shoulder. He slipped one arm around her and she nestled close to him.

"Kathy," he said, looking down at her, "baby, you're the greatest." "Well," he said thoughtfully, "I reckon we'd better get on inside before Bowknot comes back out here looking for us." They picked their way among the cars toward the building.

Chapter 8

As they drew near The Shack, their senses were over-whelmed with a symphony of sights and sounds. The air was filled with vitality and gaiety abounded as folks preened and pranced about in the bug-filled glare of the outdoor lights. They wanted to be seen and heard, to impress and be impressed. The young men strutted around like peacocks. Young ladies strut-ted, too—especially those who were alone—like mincing, co-quettish peahens. Cotton, polyester, and gingham dresses clung to metronomic hips and hugged protruding behinds as yam-, cinnamon-, and nutmeg-colored arms and legs shuffled, shim-mied, and shook to the bump-and-grind rhythms of the synco-pated beats. Driving drums overlaid with horns were background to melancholy, elated, or sassy voices talking about love lost, love found, or love in transition. They were bathing in an ocean of sound and letting themselves be whisked away on waves of emotion. Smiling and laughing with the highs, faces dropping in sadness with the lows, but all in all, it was party time and everyone had come to live the experience to the fullest.

"Jay-boy!" a voice called out loudly from the front of the crowd as he and Kathy approached, hand in hand. Jay-boy's eyes searched for the source of the voice and his eyes lighted on Billy-boy Banks coming toward them. "What's happening, home?" Banks said, extending his hand to Jay-boy.

"Ain't nothing much," Jay-boy replied, grasping the young man's hand.

"How you doing, pretty lady?" he said, smiling at Kathy.

"Oh, fine," she smiled back.

"I can see that, Miss Kathy," he laughed wistfully. "You-all just get here?" he asked, turning back to Jay-boy.

"Yeah," Jay-boy said, " and it looks like everybody and his brother is here tonight.

"I know, man," Billy-boy laughed. "I guess everybody came out tonight because this is the first full week since school closed and they know that it won't be long before they're gonna have to grab them hoes and hit them fields. And you know," he added, "looks like this here is shaping up to be a sure-enough hot summer."

Billy-boy was a thin, wiry boy, shorter than average but deceptively strong and quick for his size. He was the short-stop on the varsity baseball team. He was an extremely good all-around player, and with his superb hitting, running, and fielding, had drawn the interest of several professional baseball scouts. He had been elected team captain for the past three years not only because he was the best player on the team but also because his bubbling personality made him the hands-down favorite. Jay-boy was a pretty good player, too; he had been chosen co-captain for the past two years and had also drawn attention from a couple of professional scouts. The Wyatt High Panthers had won the state championship for the last three years running. Their coach had already assured them that they would be offered scholarships from a number of colleges and urged them to take advantage of this source of basically free education.

"Well," Jay-boy said, looking around at the steady stream of clean dudes and fine ladies pouring into the place, "I guess we'd better get on in here before we miss something." The three of them shouldered their way through the crowd milling about in the doorway and on into the place. The atmosphere inside was hot and steamy, like a sweltering summer day after a brief rain. The air was heavy and oppressive, permeated with the mingled odors of cigarette smoke, fried chicken, beer, and accented here and there with the screaming fragrances of cheap perfumes and colognes. However, no one seemed to mind in the least.

The Shack had been converted from a large, four-room frame house into a dance hall. Dallas Green, the owner, had knocked out the dividing walls between the two front rooms and made the rooms into one very large room, which served as the dance area. The jukebox was in one corner of the large room and in the corner diagonally across from the jukebox, he had cut a square window in the wall. From this window, he could serve food and beverages from one of the two small back rooms. A door a few feet to the left of the serving window opened onto a narrow hallway that led to the back door of the house. About half-way down the hall the doors to the two small rooms faced each other. The room that wasn't used for serving held a small bed and a pot-bellied stove; Dallas often spent the night there after The Shack closed. He also kept much of his stock in this room, so this door and the door to the hallway were usually locked. Green would often laugh and say, "Ain't nobody got no business back there unless I invite them."

The dance room was lit by two low-wattage bulbs at either end. The hard stream of light that flowed from the serving room and the yellow glare from the jukebox provided the only other light, leaving the room bathed in shadow. Wooden benches were positioned along the walls and, in addition to the front door, there was another door at the side near the serving window. These two doors were always open for ventilation and, especially during the warmer months, made the place bearable.

"Hey, there, home!" a voice called as a hand slapped Jay-boy on the shoulder. Jay-boy looked around, into the face of Red Williamson, a tall, slender boy with copper-colored skin and short red hair that had earned him his nickname.

"Hey, what's the word?" exclaimed Jay-boy, reaching out and clasping the boy's hand.

"Thunderbird!" Red boomed gleefully. "How is the lady?" he continued, nodding politely at Kathy.

"Fine," Kathy replied.

"So, you-all finally made it in, huh?" Bowknot broke in, smiling sheepishly and winking at Jay-boy.

Jay-boy laughed and said, "Well, let's party, you-all!"

As a Marvin Gaye song boomed from the jukebox, they merged into the crowd and started dancing. Then before anyone could recover, Rufus Thomas was asking "Can Your Monkey do the Dog?", and they all made the building rock and sway under the shuffle of their feet and the rhythmic lurching and twisting of their bodies. Beads of sweat formed on Jay-boy's forehead, and he could see the same on Kathy's, but neither of them seemed to care. As soon as the Rufus Thomas tune faded and people started to sit, the Isley Brothers beckoned them to "Twist and Shout" and the dance floor was immediately crowded again as arms gestured, behinds shook, and feet shuffled to the cadence of the music. Sweaty and almost spent, Kathy brightened when she heard the strains of Otis Redding's "That's How Strong My Love Is." She melted in Jay-boy's arms and laid her head gently on his shoulder. He looked down at her and felt glad to be alive and in this place. He inhaled the fragrance of her hair against his cheek and his fingers caressed the contour of her back as they glided serenely on a calm sea of sound. Feeling her soft body nestled against his, he felt intoxicated by the magnetism that emanated from the very essence of her being. Otis Redding sang out; words that he seemed to tear from the very depths of his soul: "If I were the sun way up there, I'd go with love most everywhere. I'd be the moon when the sun goes down, just to let you know that I'm still around." Redding seemed to say the very things that Jay-boy was feeling, but hadn't the poetry in his soul to put into words. The singer seemed to be reading his thoughts and projecting his passion as if he had invaded the innermost sanctum of Jay-boy's being. He held Kathy a little tighter, caressed her more soothingly, and bending down whispered to her, "Listen, baby, that is exactly the way I feel about you."

Kathy swooned in his arms and, looking up, her large brown

eyes caught his. She tilted her face up to him, planted a soft kiss on his lips, and whispered, "And this is the way I feel about you, too." Then she laid her head back softly on his shoulder.

At that moment, Jay-boy knew that he must be the happiest man alive. He was not only in love, but was possessed by love. Each time he was with the woman he loved, the experience lifted him to a higher height of euphoria and his blood bubbled with bliss and sang through his veins like water cascading through a meadow brook.

Suddenly, Bowknot was tugging at his elbow. "Hey, Jay, the record is over."

Jay-boy looked up in astonishment and gasped with embarrassment. Kathy looked up, her face flushed. Then they released each other and clapped their hands over their mouths and broke up with laughter. All those who had been watching in amusement for the past two or three minutes exploded with loud and prolonged laughter. "That young man is sure enough in love," a husky voice called.

"Yeah," another voice called from the shadows, "whatever he's got, he's really got it bad!" Again the room erupted with laughter.

"That's all right, sister," a woman called out, "ain't nothing wrong with being in love, honey!"

The two of them, having partially recovered, moved slowly with sheepish grins to the side of the room.

"Hey, young man!" a voice called. Jay-boy looked around into the face of a pot-bellied, middle-aged man moving toward the jukebox. "You just hold on to what you got, because what you got sure looks good!" There was another volley of laughter. "Now, I'm gonna play this record just for you and your lady." The man punched the buttons on the jukebox and the voice of Joe Tex exhorted "You Had Better Hold on to What You've Got." Again, couples moved onto the dance floor, as did the still slightly embarrassed Jay-boy and Kathy. After a few moments, everyone seemed to be caught up in their own reflections.

Kathy glanced over at Ruth and Bowknot; Ruth caught her glance and smiled broadly.

Kathy wondered to herself, just how strong were Ruth's feelings for Bowknot and, moreover, how far would things go between them? This gave her an uneasy feeling, a sense of foreboding that worried her. She didn't want to see her friend hurt, but maybe she was just over-reacting. After all, Ruth was a strong-willed girl who could surely take care of herself. Nevertheless, the uneasiness that washed over her like a cold rain when she looked at them together made her shiver with a nameless dread. She thought about confiding her fears to Jayboy, then thought better of it. She really could be over-reacting and, anyway, if Ruth wanted to date him and he wanted to date her, how could anyone stop them? She glanced again quickly at Ruth gliding around and around the floor in his embrace. Ruth's white teeth would flash and her bright eyes would sparkle whenever she saw Kathy looking. Once Bowknot caught her gaze and smiled wryly.

When the record ended, Ruth came over to Kathy, beaming with delight. "I'm so glad that you-all came by to get me tonight," she said. "Girl, it's really happening; you hear me?" Suddenly the collar of her blouse shivered with the boom of the electric bass as the Supremes asked, "Baby, Baby, Where Did Our Love Go?" Ruth looked around for Bowknot and, just as her eyes found him, she saw a slender hand reaching to grab his and lead him back onto the dance floor. Ruth frowned and grunted with disgust.

Kathy drew her off to the side and, placing an arm around her shoulder, she said consolingly, "Don't let it get to you, girl, that don't mean nothing."

"Yeah," Ruth retorted, "but that Josephine Johnson just couldn't wait until I turned my back for a second before she came jumping on him like some alley cat!"

"Calm down, girl," Kathy interrupted, "they're just dancing, that's all."

Jay-boy stood silently beside the two girls, leaning against the wall and watching the dancers. He tried not to listen to Kathy and Ruth talking excitedly beside him. As his eyes canvassed the room full of young men and women twisting, shuffling, and gyrating to the beat of the music, he had to admit that Bowknot was quite a dancer. Yes, he could really cut the rug, and he moved like he knew it, too. Jay-boy noticed that quite a few heads had turned and eyes were fixed on his cousin as he moved in and out of dance routines that were thoroughly unfamiliar to the rest of them. Many of the curious onlookers had closed in around him, and girl after girl would cut into the circle, saying "Show me that step, Bowknot!" or "What do you call that, Bow?" or "You people from Detroit can really shake 'em down!"

Jay-boy glanced over at Ruth. Her mouth was drawn in a tight line and he could see that she was obviously annoyed. For the next several records, Bowknot seemed to be the center of attention—at least among the girls—and an obvious object of envy among most of the boys. "Your cousin sure can dance," Kathy leaned over and said in Jay-boy's ear.

"Yeah, he sure can," Jay-boy said, "but I don't think his date is too thrilled with him getting all of that attention." Bowknot was indeed a superb dancer. His deft, catlike movements, splendid timing, and graceful execution made him the focus of attention. The young ladies watched, transfixed in open-mouthed admiration as the young men, for the most part, gaped in green-eyed jealousy. The floor had cleared around him as he shimmied, shuffled, and twisted his way in and out of all the local dance steps and introduced new ones. The girls lined up and clamored for a chance to dance with him.

"This guy can really shake 'em down," a short, coffee-brown girl said to her date, who gave her an irritated frown and stood in silence.

Another girl, overhearing the comment, turned and replied, "Oh, can't he though!"

Another girl broke in, "Who is he, anyway?"

"I really don't know," the short, coffee-brown girl said. "I heard somebody say he was some kin to Jay-boy Johnson."

Bowknot held them suspended in awe. Like a great performer plying his craft, he seized them by their collective collars and dared them to blink lest they miss something. The young people stood gaping, their feet nailed to the floor, their eyes riveted on Bowknot, the succession of girls moving up offered their gyrating salutations and faded back into the crowd in gratitude and wonder.

Kathy glanced over at Ruth and was visibly moved by the lines of irritation etched on her face. She touched her friend's shoulder and said, "It's pretty hot in here. Would you like to go outside with me for a while?" She desperately wanted to spare Ruth from the hurt that showed in her now-downcast eyes.

"We weren't, like, going together," Ruth said nonchalantly, trying to feign composure.

"Listen," Jay-boy said, trying to bring a note of cheer to the situation, "let me bring you-all something to eat and drink."

"We'll be out by the car," Kathy said as the two girls turned and made their way toward the front door. Jay-boy looked over at his cousin still dancing like a demon and sucking up all that attention like he was on stage, and a sense of irritation moved over him. It was all right to dance with other girls, but he didn't have to just totally abandon the girl he brought to the dance. He would talk to Bowknot about that; that wasn't cool at all. Ruth was a nice girl, nicer than most, and he had been the one dying to go pick her up. Now here he's gonna get here, dance with her a few times, and just ditch her like some broken-down car while he showboats around like he came by himself. These thoughts agitated him the more he thought about the whole situation and he had an urge to go over and straighten him out right now. He found himself shouldering his way through the crowd toward the semicircle where Bowknot was dancing. He stepped full in front of his cousin and glared in reproachful silence. As soon as Bowknot caught his eyes, he stared miles deep into the floor and his face flushed with guilt, for Jay-boy had said it all in his cold, accusing stare.

Jay-boy turned and walked off, making his way back through the mass of bodies over to the serving window. He glanced briefly back over his shoulder and noticed that Bowknot had melted back into the crowd and the floor had now filled with other dancers. The building creaked and rocked and the jukebox boomed as a sassy and somewhat husky female voice cried, "We're gonna pitch a wang-dang-doodle!" Electric guitars screamed, drums pounded the message home, and the electric bass stomped out the beat with its deep reverberations.

"Jay-boy!" Dallas Green called out congenially, glancing up from a piece of paper that he was writing on. "What's the word, son, what's shaking?"

Jay-boy smiled. "Oh, ain't nothing shaking but the leaves on the trees, and they wouldn't be shaking if it wasn't for the breeze."

Green laughed heartily at their banter, then reached out to shake Jay-boy's hand. "How is Jimbo?"

"Oh, he was at the house laying down when I left. He been busy plowing all week."

"Yeah," Green said thoughtfully, "I've been out there trying to finish up my little plowing, too, before we get a sure-enough good rain and the weeds take over."

Dallas Green was a giant of a man, standing about six feet, four inches tall and weighing well over two hundred pounds. He had a hearty laugh and a jolly disposition. No one was a stranger to him. He was congenial and easy-going with a sharp sense of humor; he was thoroughly at home among the young people who frequented his place, though he himself had children their ages. He was well liked and fun to be around, but most folks knew he had another side that was seldom seen. When it was seen, it definitely left a lasting impression. He was the kind of man who would give you the shirt off his back, but he didn't stand for no foolishness, namely, fighting and carrying on in his place. He would say, "Anybody is welcome here as long as they know how to behave. Now if they come in here with any mess, they gonna have to mess with Dallas Green."

He had been known to grab many an unruly customer by the nape of the neck and send him sprawling out the front or side door to the hard-packed earth. He had also been known to scatter a few violent ideas with his huge fist, on occasion leaving some unfortunate rabble-rousers who had ignored his warnings to wake up wondering where they were and what had hit them. It was also known that he carried a gun and wouldn't hesitate to use it if some fool pushed him. He was, for the most part, respected as a man not to be trifled with.

"What can I get you, son?" he asked Jay-boy.

"I'd like four pieces of that there fried chicken, a pig foot, and three sodas."

Green turned and started preparing the order. Glancing up, he said, "You still gonna help me in tobacco this year, ain't you?"

"Yes, sir, I'll be right there if nothing happens," answered Jay-boy, glancing sidelong at the door as a slender, gray-haired man entered.

"What you say there, Jay-boy?" the man said, slapping him on the arm. It was Bumsey, an old codger with thinning gray hair and a grizzled gray beard who hung around The Shack and helped Green for a few dollars and free drinks.

"How you been doing, Bumsey?" Jay-boy asked, smiling, expecting Bumsey to launch into one of his poetic salutations.

"Well, son," he said, his flat eyes showing a sparkle of light. "I feel like a lemon ain't never been squeezed, like a wagon wheel that's just been greased. You see," he gestured elaborately with his hands toward a pretty young lady who had come up behind Jay-boy to buy something, "I'm the man that hobbles the lightning and thunder, just for you to see that doggone wonder. I walked a barb-wire fence forty feet long, with two elephants under each arm. The mule may kick me and bruise my hide, the rattlesnake bit me, then crawled off and died. I been shot five times with a forty-five and left for dead, but still ain't died." Then he slapped his thigh and laughed uproariously. Jay-boy and Green, who had overheard, also broke up with laughter. When Jay-boy turned slightly and looked out of the corner of his eye, he saw the cinnamon-colored young lady who had been standing behind him, her shoulders shaking with laughter, too. When Bumsey recovered, he beamed with pride and smiled broadly, satisfied that his earthy wit was sharply effective. "Well, that's all old Bumsey gonna tell you for now," and he moved off and disappeared in the crowd.

A hand touched Jay-boy lightly on the shoulder; he turned around and found himself looking into the face of the girl who had been standing behind him.

"Hi, there," she said shyly. "My name is Linda," she went on, extending her hand.

He shook it politely and said, "My name is Jay-boy Johnson."

"I know," she said. "I've seen you around school. You go with Kathy Walker, don't you?"

"Yes."

"I heard that the tall, slim boy who was dancin' so good was some kin to you," she said coyly.

"Yeah," Jay-boy said, "he's my first cousin."

"What's his name?"

"His name is Kevin, but we just call him Bowknot."

"Well, he sure can dance. Is he from around here?"

"No, he's from Detroit, but he's spending the summer out here with me."

She paused for a moment, smiled broadly, and said, "Would you give him a message for me?"

"Sure," Jay-boy answered. "What do you want me to tell him?"

"Tell him I think he is a fantastic dancer and quite good looking and that I would like to meet him sometime."

"All right, I sure will," Jay-boy said, "but he is still around here somewhere and if I can find him, I'll tell him tonight."

"Look." She pointed out the side door. "You see that big tree over there? We parked just on the other side of it in a gray Corvair. Ask him to stop by if he can."

"All right."

"Thank you," she said.

"Okay, here Jay, I fixed you right up here, buddy," Green said as he placed the food and beverages on the counter. "That will be a dollar and thirty-five cents." Jay-boy paid him. "Now, don't forget me," Green said.

"I won't. You know I got my cousin out here with me this summer from Detroit. He'll probably want to work, too."

"Do he know how to pull tobacco?"

"Yeah, he grew up out here. I'm sure he hadn't forgot in four years."

"Well, you know how folks is when they get a taste of that city living, they ain't got much truck for getting their hands dirty on the farm no more."

Jay-boy glanced at Green as he picked up his change. "I'm sure that he'll want to help. He'd like the chance to make some spending money, too."

"Well, you let me know now, you hear?"

"I will." Jay-boy turned and shouldered his way back through the crowd, heading toward the front door and scanning the room for a glimpse of Bowknot.

Chapter 9

"All right, youngblood, you gonna roll the dice or just sit there and hold them all night?" a man said gruffly over a small paper cup he lowered slowly from his full lips.

Bowknot said nothing, nor did he look up from where he was stooping on a large piece of plywood beside an old Chevy in the bug-filled glare of the post light. Ignoring the big man, he shook the dice thoroughly in his right hand and, glancing up at the other three men standing in the circle, he flashed a broad smile and said, "Mama got the blues and baby sure needs a new pair of shoes." Then he threw the dice. "Seven!" he shouted, "there it is!" He pointed to the dice, then reached down and snatched up the five one-dollar bills. He stuffed them into his hip pocket and threw the dice again. "Eleven!" he boomed, reaching out to snatch up the money again.

"All right, put your money down, let's go another round." Their money had barely hit the ground before Bowknot shouted "Seven!" again and was reaching for it. He glanced up at them, beaming with confidence, his eyes bright with pride as they moved around the circle of faces. However, the four young men had no offerings of friendship in their eyes for Bowknot. Instead, their faces were hard and expressionless, except for the largest one. He was Big Tiny Oliver. His face shone with open contempt and his dark eyes registered a cold hostility. Tiny was a large, thick-set man with powerful shoulders and large, calloused hands. His blunt features seemed to thrust forward, and he always stood with his legs apart and had a habit of leaning slightly forward when he talked, which made him appear menacing.

"All right now, you-all put your money in and let me roll these bones again because I just can't seem to lose with the stuff I use." The four young men dropped their money sullenly. Here was this city slicker trying to show off on them. First he gets up and profiles in front of their women with all his fancy dancing and now he sits here and wins their money. And has the nerve to make fun of them while he's doing it, too!

"Are you gonna rattle your teeth all night, man, or roll the damn dice?" Big Tiny queried, sounding disgusted.

Bowknot never looked up. He just grinned and shook the dice in his hand, then he tossed them down. "Seven or eleven, come on home! I'm tired of looking at these dollars roam!"

"Eleven!" he shouted, then reached down and again snatched up the money.

"Man, that guy is lucky!" a slender, copper-faced boy said in exasperation as he reached into his pocket to retrieve another dollar.

"All right," Bowknot said, "put your money in and let's try it again." He shook the dice and threw them. "Four," he said.

One of the boys smiled with satisfaction. He felt sure now that Bowknot would "crap out." Glancing up at them quickly, Bowknot caught the boy's smirk and retorted boastfully, "If I don't make this four, Virginia ham ain't lean and poke salad ain't green!" Then he threw the dice. "Four!" he shouted with glee. "I told you-all I'd make it!" He snatched up their money and laughed, gloating with self-satisfaction.

A short, stocky, coffee-brown boy shook his head and muttered to the boy beside him, "Man, I ain't never seen nobody this lucky before!"

Bowknot paused a moment. "You-all still game?" His eyes moved over their faces.

"Ain't nobody said they wasn't, did they?" Big Tiny spat out.

One by one, the young men dropped their money in the pot. The short, stocky boy knew that something was about to happen as his eyes moved back and forth between Big Tiny and

Bowknot. He knew that Big Tiny hated to lose and he also knew that the corn liquor he had been sipping from the small paper cup had by now lit a fire in him and it wouldn't take much to make him start something. Tiny had a long-standing reputation for being a rough customer, especially when he was drinking. Bowknot was apparently new to the area and couldn't have known about Big Tiny's reputation, so he had no idea who he was antagonizing. None of them was about to tell him, either. Perhaps a good butt-kicking was just what he needed to cool him off a bit.

"Seven!" Bowknot called out loudly and reached down quickly and grabbed up the money. Stuffing it into his now-bulging back pocket, he began to shake the dice and made as if to roll them again when Big Tiny spoke.

"Hold it! Don't you go another fu'ther!"

The words seemed to strike Bowknot like a blow; his arm froze in mid-motion. Recovering after a moment, he glanced up quizzically at Big Tiny. Tiny's big hand shot out toward him. "Here," he demanded angrily, "you take these dice here. It ain't natural for somebody to be that lucky nohow."

Bowknot frowned, glancing around the circle at the other boys. They all stood mute, including two other boys who had come up to watch the game. They all stood silent and stone-faced. They knew what was coming and wanted no part of it.

Bowknot straightened up slowly, never taking his eyes from Big Tiny's face. "You didn't ask nobody else to change dice," he protested, his voice still conversational.

"I'm not asking you, I'm telling you, city boy. I'm telling you now, either you play with these here dice or you get out of the game."

"Is that so, now?" Bowknot asked, smiling. "And I suppose you gonna put me out, too, right?" he added with cold disdain.

The big man glared balefully, his face set with hostility and his full lips curled into a sneer.

"Now, looka here, man," Bowknot said. The atmosphere

vibrated with tension and the other boys stepped back a few paces, clearing the way for what they were glad was coming and, to a man, hoping that Bowknot would get the worst end of the affair. "You just looka here, you been flapping your gums all night at me, and for what? You just pissed off because I was winning your money. Now if you can't stand to lose," he continued, his voice rising slightly as he stared hard into Big Tiny's dull, flat eyes, "you just keep your damn money in your pocket."

As soon as the words had fallen from Bowknot's lips, the huge man lunged at him like a grizzly. With catlike quickness, Bowknot shifted his feet and drove a hard right hand at his oncoming foe, smashing him just under the left eye. The blow stunned him momentarily, but the big man shook it off and came again, barreling in with both fists swinging. Bowknot threw up his forearm and blocked the man's thudding right. Then leveraging himself from his toes, he drove his right fist with all the strength in his body straight into the man's mouth, feeling teeth give under his knuckles. Blood spurted from Big Tiny's mouth as he staggered backward for a moment, then let out a savage yell and came again.

Bowknot ducked and dodged, pounding blows home until his fist ached and Big Tiny's face was covered with blood, and still the big man came. He seemed almost invincible, exuding the strength of a gorilla and the savage determination of a grizzly. Finally, Bowknot looked around, almost pleadingly, at the onlookers but not a soul stepped forward to help or to try to break it up.

Pain now shot through his hands and arms like needles as he heaved with exhaustion, but he dared not stop moving, ducking, and smashing blows to the blunt-featured face and rock-hard head of his relentless pursuer.

Suddenly out of breath, arms and shoulders aching with fatigue, Bowknot dropped his fists and stood still to recover. That was all it took. Big Tiny's large, calloused hands went straight to his throat and his fingers locked around Bowknot's neck like steel claws. Slamming Bowknot hard against the old Chevy a few feet away from where they had been fighting, Big Tiny began to squeeze and Bowknot gasped, feeling the air rush from his lungs. He brought his knee up sharply and with all his might into the big man's groin. Big Tiny let out a yell and released Bowknot for a surprised instant, but that was all the time Bowknot needed, too. When Big Tiny leaped again, all he saw was the brief flash of the steel blade in the hard yellow light.

Bowknot met him, driving the hawkbill blade deep into the man's left shoulder, then slashing him across the right cheek. Blood streamed down over his neck and shirt. The onlookers gasped in horror and someone cried, "He's stabbing him! He's cutting him to death!"

Another voice cried, "Somebody go get Mr. Green!", and feet scurried away as the others looked on in panic.

Shifting the knife to his left hand, Bowknot slammed his right fist squarely into the man's left temple. For a moment Big Tiny tottered like a giant old tree, then went crashing to the ground with a thud. As soon as he hit the ground, Bowknot jumped astride him and, placing the steel blade of his knife firmly against the man's throat, he hissed coldly, "If you ever cross my path again, I'll kill you!"

Big Tiny lay bleeding profusely, his flat dark eyes now pleading as his full lips trembled with terror.

"You see this?" Bowknot held the knife a few inches away from the man's eyes. "Now, I don't want your blood on my knife, so you lick it off." The onlookers held their breath, gaping in fascinated horror. "Lick this blood off my knife, sucker, or I'm going to open you up like a hog."

Bowknot's voice was trembling with hate, and there was no doubt in Big Tiny's mind that he wasn't bluffing. So, with tears streaming, the big man stuck out his tongue and began to lick the steel blade of the knife.

Suddenly, Bowknot felt someone pulling at his shoulder. "Let him go, Bow." It was Jay-boy; someone had gone and gotten him. "Let him go, Bow. He's had enough." Bowknot looked around at his cousin, and slowly recognition came into his eyes. He raised up, releasing the sprawled man, and allowed Jay-boy to lead him through the crowd and away.

Chapter 10

The mid-morning sky was a leaden gray. The air was heavy and humid and there was a brief let-up in the torrential rain that had drummed steadily on the tin roof of the house and soaked the earth since the early morning hours. There was still, however, a light drizzle and a lingering mist that hung over the trees that made the landscape look dull and gloomy. The car sat idling, its frame shaking slightly with the vibration of the droning engine. Jimbo sat silently behind the steering wheel, his eyes staring abstractedly out over the fields. Jay-boy sat sprawled in the back seat, staring at the front door of the house, wondering when his mother would appear and hoping that his parents would not question him too much about Bowknot's insistence on staying home.

Suddenly, the front door swung open and his mother appeared with a large purse in one hand and an umbrella in the other. Pausing a moment on the porch to let up the umbrella, she walked gracefully down the steps and around to her side of the car. Jimbo leaned over and pushed the door open for her; she let down the umbrella and slid into the front seat beside him.

"Huh," she said wistfully, "I sure hope this-here rain quits soon because I sure don't feel like walking around in the rain all day."

"Yeah, I did want to finish plowing that cotton back over yonder in the corner today, but the good Lord changed all that. I just hope it does quit soon, too, and maybe we can get enough sun to dry things out enough to get back in the field on Monday before the grass takes over." Jimbo slipped the car into gear and nosed it around the large oak tree.

"Jay-boy," his mother said, haltingly, "what's the matter with Bowknot? Seems like he's been chomping at the bit to get out all week and now he's laying in there across the bed like he ain't even thinking about going nowhere."

Jay-boy's stomach muscles tightened and his throat felt suddenly dry, but before he could speak, his father broke in. "I reckon the boy is just tired, baby," his father said softly. "He ain't used to all this-here hard work like us and I reckon he's just plain beat and wants to get himself some rest."

Jay-boy relaxed, glad that he had been spared having to give an explanation and also that his father did not share his mother's suspicion of his cousin's motives for staying home. For a while, they rode without talking; the only sounds were the drone of the motor and the rhythmic swish of the windshield wipers. Jay-boy sat watching the lush, green countryside careening by, wondering not if, but *when*, his folks would find out what had happened the night before at The Shack. Bowknot had begged him not to tell and, though he had agreed not to, he had insisted that they would find out and that would only make things worse for both of them. Now he was really in a fix and he knew it. Maybe he should just go ahead and tell them and get it over with, but they would hold him responsible. The agony of his indecision made his temples pound, and his heart hammered against his chest as his stomach churned sickeningly, leaving him feeling weak.

"I got to get me a hair trim," Jimbo said to his wife. "I hope they ain't too crowded in there this morning. I'm gonna leave the car in Mitchell's parking lot and the keys with you so when you finish making grocery, you can come on out and put it in the car."

"All right," said Jay-boy's mother, "it shouldn't take me but an hour or so to get my little mess. I'll walk on up to the barber shop and wait on you if I get done before you do."

"All right," he responded. "I got to stop at the feed mill, too, and the hardware store to pick up me some nails."

"You know, Jimbo, I just feel kind of uneasy somehow about that boy wanting to stay out there by himself like that."

"Baby, you worry too much and there ain't nothing to worry about. If the boy wants to stay home and rest or whatever, that's all right. He's been doing all right so far; he's a good hand, he keeps his room clean, and he get his chores done. I really think him being out here working on the farm is gonna help him get himself together, but like you told me, we just got patient with him and give him a little time. Stop questioning every move he makes and looking for something that ain't there. Baby, you know how the old saying goes: 'If you set out looking for trouble, you'll surely find it.'"

"Yeah, I guess you're right." She sighed heavily. "Maybe the boy *is* just tired and wants to rest. He'll probably want to go out tonight anyway."

Jay-boy had been sitting still during their exchange, staring abstractedly out the window, his brain barely comprehending the snatches of their conversation that were filtering through to him. His head had begun to ache in earnest as he deliberated about whether or not he should tell his folks what had happened at The Shack.

"All right, here we are," his father said, pulling the car into a parking space in front of a large, red brick building bearing a white sign with blue lettering that read "Mitchell's Grocery." His door swung open and he stepped out. Then he went around the car and helped his wife out. Noticing that Jay-boy had not so much as changed his position on the seat, Jimbo ducked his head back inside the car and asked, "Son, you gettin' out?"

Jay-boy snapped out of his daze, his face flushed with embarrassment, and smiled, trying to shrug off the fact that he had sat oblivious to what was going on around him.

"Son," his father stared hard at him, "is everything all right?" He spoke softly, with a note of concern in his voice.

"Oh, I'm all right." Jay-boy smiled, looking quickly around, avoiding his father's searching gaze. "I was just sitting back here nodding; I guess I'm a little tired, too. Maybe I should have stayed home and caught up on a little rest, myself."

"Well, we won't be down here too long," his father said, as he straightened up and closed the door. Jay-boy stepped out on the other side and, leaning over the top of the car, he said, "I'm going around to the pool room for a while. I'll be back and if I don't see you, Mom, I'll just wait here by the car."

"Okay, then," his mother said. They all turned to go their separate ways.

"Well," he said, raising his arms and stretching lazily as if he had really been asleep, "I'll see you-all in a little bit." As he turned and started to walk away, he could feel their eyes on him and it made his scalp tingle and his temples pound and he wanted to shrink from their sight. Finally, when he faded around the corner of a building, disappearing from their view, his muscles relaxed and his heart slowed. He tried to push the whole situation from his mind.

"I'm going around here and shoot me some pool and shoot the breeze with the fellows," he thought. "They can't hold me responsible for everything Bowknot does, anyway. And anyway, that damn mean-ass Big Tiny Oliver had it coming, always messing with people, throwing his weight around, bullying people. They all knew how he was. He had cut up a few people himself and now it was his turn, that's all. Bowknot hadn't started the fight, he was just protecting himself. And he sure had a right to do that, didn't he?"

"Jay-boy," a voice broke in on his thoughts as he approached the pool room. He looked up to see "Blue" Hicks, a tall, cocoa-brown, loose-limbed boy, flashing a wide smile at him. "What's happening, home?" the boy boomed, extending his hand.

Jay-boy grabbed his hand and shook it excitedly, saying, "You got the business, man; I'm just the customer." They both laughed heartily.

Clearing his throat, Blue said, "You think you want to drop a few dollars at the table, man?"

"Yeah, man," Jay-boy said, "you know you got to bring some to get some, right?"

Blue laughed briefly, then smiled, thinking about the last time they had played pool and how he had won. "I'm game," he said.

The two of them sauntered into the pool room. "Mornin', youngbloods!" a big, bass voice called out to them as they entered.

"Mornin'," they answered. The voice belonged to Big Buck Saunders, a large, hulking man, the owner and manager of the pool room. He had a broad, flat nose, a receding hairline, a large pot belly, and huge hands. His looks could strike fear into a man's heart, however, he had a jovial disposition and could make anyone laugh. Jay-boy's eyes canvassed the room. All eight tables were occupied, and excited conversation was punctuated with a volley of loud laughter now and again.

"Well," Blue said regretfully, "looks like we're gonna have to wait a spell." "Yeah," Jay-boy replied.

"Can I get you boys something?" Big Buck asked.

"Yeah, I reckon I'll have a soda." This from Jay-boy.

Blue laughed. "Now, don't spend all your money before I can get a chance to win some of it."

Jay-boy was silent as he walked to the counter to wait for his order. He turned slowly toward Blue and said, "I'll call you as soon as a table is ready."

"Make sure you don't forget about me, now," Blue said, smiling.

Jay-boy answered, "I won't. I'm just waiting for the chance to wipe that smile off your face. After you pay me, you gonna reach in your pocket and come out empty-handed."

"Sure, sure, my friend. I'm so worried my teeth are rattling and my hair's turning white," Blue retorted.

"Here you are, young man," Big Buck said, calling Jay-boy's

attention back to the counter. Jay-boy paid Big Buck for the bottle of soda. Taking the money, Big Buck smiled congenially and said to Jay-boy, "So, what's shaking, youngblood?"

"Ain't nothing shaking but the leaves on the trees."

"Now they ain't even shakin' cause there ain't no breeze," a voice boomed over Jay-boy's shoulder. Jay-boy turned around and saw Skeet Taylor, a ginger-colored man in his late twenties who had just come in. "What's happenin', home?" he chuckled wryly, grabbing Jay-boy's hand and pumping his elbow."

"Like you just said, not a thing," Jay-boy smiled.

"So, what's the word, Big Buck?" he said, releasing Jay-boy's hand and glancing at Buck.

"Thunderbird!" Buck bellowed heartily. The three of them laughed together.

"Yeah, a nice, cold bottle of that-there Thunderbird would make a body feel right nice, wouldn't it?" Skeet said in a wistful tone.

Skeet was a thin, wiry man of average build whose sunken eyes and drooping lids gave him the appearance of being always half-drunk. The creased corners of his mouth and his lined face made him look much older than he actually was. He was a permanent fixture around the pool room, always cutting the fool and shooting the breeze, and always trying to hustle someone out of a dollar or two to keep him in cheap wine. He would run errands and do odd jobs for Big Buck, who rewarded him with a few dollars now an again. However, on occasion, he would get a regular job and work until he drew a couple of paychecks. Then he would invariably concoct some story of illness in order to take off a few days, never to return.

"Hey, Buck!" Skeet called, "give me a cigarette, will you?"

The big man sighed and stared at him for a moment. "You know something, Skeet?" he began. "You're just like them-there B-52s—when you ain't hummin', you bummin."

Skeet laughed drily. Jay-boy smiled as Buck reached into his shirt pocket and brought out a package of cigarettes. Holding the pack out for Skeet to take one, Buck said plaintively, "Here, just go ahead and take the lighter now, too, cause I know you gonna be asking for a light next." Skeeter smiled sheepishly and took the cigarette and the lighter.

Jay-boy, taking leave of the patrons at the counter, said, "I'll be talking to you-all." He picked up his bottle of soda and walked over toward the nearest table, where two boys were engrossed in a game of pool. He leaned against the wall, sipping his soda and watching the game. From the serious looks on the boys' faces and their total absorption in the game, Jay-boy surmised that they were playing for money. They moved carefully, staring at the soft, green surface of the table, their foreheads wrinkled in concentration as they meticulously plotted their shots.

Jay-boy took a long gulp of soda from the bottle, feeling the carbonated liquid gurgle slowly down his throat. It burned slightly and made him belch; he leaned forward, cupping a hand to his mouth. He straightened again, and leaned back against the hard plaster wall, letting his eyes move over the room and take in the whole scene. He saw faces ranging in color from high yellow to cinnamon red to cocoa brown and ebony black, registering a multitude of expressions depending on the disposition of their fortunes. The owners of the faces stared nervously, shifted and fidgeted uneasily as opponents knelt carefully and aimed with precision, slamming the cue ball into its target. Some faces beamed with delight and others dropped in consternation as the targeted ball would go bounding into a pocket. Jay-boy spotted Blue standing down at the other end of the room, intently watching a game. Letting his eyes shift back to the two boys near him, he saw that the one now holding the cue stick was smiling broadly and the other stood, his face expressionless, his eyes somber and riveted to the green surface of the table.

Suddenly, the door swung open and a short, fat, copper-colored man walked in, carrying a handful of keys dangling from a large ring. Jay-boy turned his head slightly and their eyes met. "How's your hammer hangin' there, young man?" he greeted Jay-boy.

"I'm all right; how you doin'?"

The man smiled affably and strode over to the counter where Skeet and Big Buck were. He had on a white, ill-fitting orderly's uniform. His coat looked a size too small, and his shirt was tucked carelessly into his pants which hung dangerously low beneath his huge belly and fell down atop his rocked-over shoes. He thrust out his hand to Skeet as he approached: "Give me some skin, there, Skeeter Rabbit!"

Skeet immediately reached out and grasped the man's hand, shaking it excitedly. "What's happening, home!" he said, smiling broadly.

"Man, ain't nothin' cookin' but the peas in the pot, and they wouldn't be cookin' if the water wasn't hot!"

The men laughed heartily at his witticism as Fat Daddy drew his hand back and shoved it toward Big Buck, saying loudly, "Give it up, man!" Big Buck shook his hand, still laughing.

Big Buck gave him a quizzical look. "Man, what you doin' down here this time of day? You still workin'?"

"Oh," Fat Daddy replied, "I'm on my lunch break. I just thought I'd get out of that place and catch me a little fresh air, so I decided to mosey on down here and see what was goin' on. I see you got you a full house," he continued, glancing around.

"Yeah," Big Buck nodded.

"These boys are anxious to get down here and drop their little paychecks," Skeet broke in.

Fat Daddy laughed drily. "Yeah, I kinda thought that. I might take time to shoot me a couple of games and relieve somebody of a few dollars if it's burning their pockets that bad."

Big Buck laughed, then said thoughtfully, "I doubt if most of them would even play you, man. They know it would just be like giving away their money."

Fat Daddy's face with animated with pride and self-satisfaction.

He could soak up praise like a sponge, and the fact that most of the people around town considered him the best pool-player made him gloat often. Every once in a while, one of them would get up enough nerve to challenge him, but they would never play him for more than fifty cents a game. Nor would they play too long, fearing the prospect of leaving the table with empty pockets and the inevitable pitying eyes of onlookers saying "I told you so" with their silent stares. The losers would always try to disguise their shame, slapping Fat Daddy on the arm and saying resignedly, "Fats, you still the best!"

"Hey, you-all know that somebody cut up Big Tiny Oliver last night," Fat Daddy said, matter-of-factly.

"Say what?" Big Buck exclaimed, moving closer and leaning over the counter and cupping his chin in his hand.

Skeet stared in disbelief at Fat Daddy. "Hush your fuss! Nobody's bad enough to mess with Big Tiny!"

Jay-boy's flashed to attention, straining to hear every word yet trying to appear nonchalant.

"Yeah," Fat Daddy continued, "they say that Wallace McNair brought him in about one-thirty last night, bleeding like a hog." Buck and Skeets listened in amazement, with their eyes glued to Fat Daddy. "They say that he was unconscious and that if he hadn't got to the hospital when he did, he would have been watching pine roots grow by next week."

"Who did they say done it?" asked Big Buck, still stunned.

"Well, I saw Minnie, his momma, this morning, and she said they told her that three boys jumped on him and just cut him up pretty bad."

Jay-boy leaned his head slightly nearer, his eyes moving back and forth between the three men talking and the two boys playing pool in front of him, still trying not to appear that he was listening to the conversation. The effort made his head ache. When he heard Fat Daddy's remark that three boys had jumped Tiny, his mouth flew open in surprise and he lowered his head to conceal his expression.

"Yeah," Fat Daddy went on, "she said Wallace told her they had got to fighting over a crap game. Said somethin' about one of the boys was cheating and that Tiny tried to make him get out of the game and then they all jumped on him."

Skeet listened intently, then straightened up and began to finger his mustache thoughtfully. "You know," he said slowly, "something about that sounds fishy to me. Now if he caught one man cheating and asked him to get out of the game, why would the others side with the man who was cheating? He was cheating them, too. You know, a couple of weeks ago, I was down at the shack and me and Tiny and two other boys from over the state line was shooting craps. Everything was going along all right until Tiny started losing, and then he just stood there drinking that corn liquor and mouthing at everybody, trying to start something. After a while, I quit and he cussed me out to a dog, but I just walked on away. Then after a while I went back around to where they had been playing and the other two boys had gone and Tiny was just standing there beside his car by hisself. When he saw me, he put his hand in his pocket and started walking toward me. 'I ought to cut your damn balls off,' he said, and he wasn't grinnin' a bit. I didn't say nothin' to him, I just turned around and walked off. Later on that same night, he jumped on some young boy because the boy didn't want Tiny pullin' on his girlfriend; he beat that boy to a pulp." Skeet leaned back and, gesturing with his hand, he said, "Dallas Green had to come out and pull Tiny off the boy. Then he still kept walking around there pickin' at people. He didn't leave till, finally, Dallas threatened to whip him."

Big Buck broke in, "You know that Tiny Oliver is a mean somethin'. He done been in here starting trouble. About a month ago, he jumped on a boy in here because the boy had beat him out of his money. I had to pull my pistol, and I told him that I'd blow his head clean off if he hit that boy again. He heard me cock the hammer, so he knew I meant business, and he went on out of here cussing under his breath. He's been back in here since then tryin' to start some mess, but I told him that he'd better take it on out of here. Man, I tell you the truth! I hate to see him coming, especially when he done had a little bit to drink."

"You know," Fat Daddy said soberly, "he goes for bad but I ain't never had no truck with him and no use for him."

"Well," Skeet said, "it's bad that he got cut up like that but, then again, he had it coming. He just met somebody that was a little badder than he was, that's all." Skeet continued excitedly, "He just got a taste of his own medicine. Man, he's been bullyin' people around for years, now somebody done peeped his hole card. Whoever," he laughed derisively, "whoever them boys was, I'd like to shake their hands. I'm glad they didn't kill him, but he needed a good ass-whippin'. Maybe now that'll make him think before he come messin' with people and maybe it'll keep him from gettin' killed."

"Anybody know who the boys was?" Big Buck asked, looking at Fat Daddy.

"No, Minnie said that Wallace told her that somebody told him they were from across the state line. Maybe so; you know them North Carolina boys believe in bladin' you. They'll blade you in a minute."

Three boys had jumped on him, Jay-boy thought in amazement. So this is the story they're putting out. He knew that at least five boys had seen exactly what had happened. Did they concoct this lie out of fear that when—or if—Big Tiny got well, he would come looking for them? The whole thing was preposterous; there wasn't no three boys, just Bowknot alone who had done the damage. And not only had no one raised a hand to help him, now they were lying to make that bully look good. He felt a strange impulse to leap over in front of them and shout to the top of his lungs, "There wasn't no three boys! Just Bowknot, my cousin, Bowknot! He did it all by himself and I'm glad that he fixed that bully. Now they're trying to explain their way out of the fact that he got his ass kicked thoroughly, and not by three men but only one man—Bowknot!" Jay-boy's blood coursed through his veins like lava shooting from a volcano, and he shook his head rapidly to control himself and restrain his wild impulse.

Chapter 11

When Jay-boy stepped into Long's barber shop, his eyes took in the surroundings at a glance. He noticed that the place was not as crowded as it usually was on Saturday afternoon. He recognized Lightning Wilson, a fortyish man with arms that seemed too long for his body and large, lumberjack hands that looked like catcher's mitts. A stout, middle-aged woman he did not know was sitting near the window with two small boys who fidgeted nervously in their seats, watching her slyly out of the corners of their eyes. Bobo Hicks was also there, sprawled in a chair, legs crossed, leaning back with his head resting on the wall, puffing lazily on a cigarette. Everyone looked up and spoke as Jay-boy entered.

Shorty Long took his eyes away from Jimbo's hair long enough to say laughingly to Jay-boy, "I'm almost finished with him. I know you came to get him."

Jay-boy nodded and smiled, then said, "My mom's not quite done yet, anyway. I left her standing in the store talking to Mrs. Banks."

"Lordy, Lordy," his father replied with a chuckle. "If she's talking to Mrs. Banks, then there ain't no telling what time she'll be ready."

Jay-boy strode over and took a seat beside Bobo. "So what's the word, there, Jay-boy?" He grinned broadly, bringing the front legs of his chair down softly on the floor.

"Oh, man, ain't nothin' shakin' but the leaves on the trees, and they wouldn't be shakin' if it wasn't for the breeze."

Hicks laughed. "You got that right. Say, they tell me somebody cut up Big Tiny Oliver pretty bad last night at The Shack."

Jay-boy looked up, trying to act surprised. "You say what?" he asked, raising his eyebrows slightly. He glanced quickly at his father and saw that his eyes were lit with curiosity. Even Shorty had paused momentarily, staring, with his mouth slightly agape.

"What's that you say, there, Bobo?" Shorty prompted.

Bobo cleared his throat and straightened up in his seat; a faint smile played around his lips as he realized that he was suddenly the center of attention. "I heard that somebody cut Tiny Oliver up pretty bad last night. You see, I reckon it was a little after twelve by the time I got down there. Just as I turned the curve up there by the gin, somebody passed me like a bat out of hell, with both blinkers on." He paused and took a long draw from his stub of a cigarette and glanced around the room to make sure that everyone was listening. Then he continued. "Soon as I pulled up at The Shack and got out of the car, I saw Pigfoot Parker. He told me that somebody had just cut Tiny and that Wallace McNair had took him to the hospital. They tell me Tiny was bleeding so bad they was wondering if he was gonna be getting his mail from the groundhog from now on. At first, they was saying that three boys from over the state line had jumped on him."

Jay-boy could feel a tightness in his chest creeping up into his throat and restricting his breathing. Every now and then, he stole a glance up at his father and watched his father's eyes move back and forth between Bobo and him.

"Well, how did it happen?" Shorty nudged again.

"Well," Bobo said, heaving a long sigh and wagging his head slightly, "I don't exactly know, but the way I heard it was that they were shooting dice around in the back and Tiny accused one of the boys of cheating and told him to get out of the game." He took a last long draw from the dying cigarette and smashed the butt into the ashtray near his chair. "They say that Tiny tried to make the boy get out of the game and the boy wouldn't. So Tiny jumped on him and the other two took it up."

Lightning Wilson had been sitting quietly, listening intently from the beginning of Bobo's monologue. He spoke up. "You know," he said, clearing his throat and glancing over at Bobo, "that-there Big Tiny Oliver is a mean son of a gun. Them boys was probably winning his money and he just got pissed off about it and picked a fight."

"I reckon he did it count of the others taking it up, though," Shorty interjected. "Them boys from over the state line don't take a lot of foolishness."

"That's right," Bobo responded. "Man, them guys will blade you in a minute. I reckon it was about two months ago me and ol' Bookertee Powell was over there at a club in Gageburg, just sitting down listening to the music and eating some barbecue. Man, two great big, corn-fed-lookin' dudes walked over to our table and just stood there looking down at us. Finally, one of them said, 'You-all ain't from around here, is you?' Me and Bookertee just looked at each other. 'Aw, shit,' I said to myself, 'these pugwood guys want to start something.' Then the other one spoke up: 'I believe the man just asked you-all a question.' Both of 'em stepped closer to the table and I could smell the corn liquor so strong I almost got drunk off the fumes. Bookertee looked up and said, 'No, we ain't from around here, we from across the line.' The first man cut him short and said, 'Well, ain't they got clubs over there?' and almost before Bookertee could say 'no,' the man said, 'Why in the hell you feel you got to bring your ass over here, then?'

"I looked around and I didn't see but one way out of that place. I kicked ol' Bookertee under the table and leaned over like I was reaching for my beer. I told him, quiet-like, 'Man, don't you start nothing. Look; there's about five more guys standing over there by the door, just looking over here.' Then all of a sudden, one of 'em bent over and spit right in Bookertee's plate and laughed and said, 'Now, what you gonna do about that, Virginia Boy?' Man, I was about to kick ol' Booker's leg off.

I knew that my gun was in the car and I didn't even have a fingernail file in my pocket, much less a knife! Man, we was sitting there sweating bullets and finally ol' Booker broke out laughing and said, 'Man, I ain't gonna do nothin' about it. That ol' barbecue didn't taste that good nohow. Come on over to the bar and let me buy you boys a drink.' Man, they both broke out laughing and slapped ol' Booker on the back and said, 'You Virginia boys ain't all bad.'

"We got up and bought them drinks and, just as I thought, about four more who had been standing watching came over and we bought them drinks, too. Man, we sure dodged a major ass-whipping that night! We even wound up having a pretty nice time. One of the guys finally told us that a carload of boys from across the line had come over and cut up two boys the weekend before, and one of them was his cousin. So that's why they had us picked out to get our butts kicked."

The room was quiet for a moment, then Lightning said reflectively, "Yeah, them North Carolina boys don't play."

Jay-boy's temples were pounding and sweat had collected under his arms and was running around and down into the small of his back. He kept his face averted, but still he could feel his dad's eyes on him, accusing eyes, probing into his thoughts.

"You know," Bobo said, rearing back on his chair again, "I don't know how true this is, but later on I run into Bobby Lee Adams and he told me there wasn't no three boys that jumped on Big Tiny."

Jay-boy's stomach muscles were tying themselves into knots, and he could feel beads of perspiration popping out like pimples on his forehead. Nevertheless, he tried to appear calm, still keeping his face averted and his eyes from his father's eyes.

"Bobby Lee said," Bobo continued, glancing around at the faces of his audience whose mouths were open, waiting to devour each word that fell from his lips. He noted that all eyes except for Jay-boy's were riveted on him, and Jay-boy's seeming nonchalance goaded him somewhat. So he directed his words and attention to Jay-boy. "Yeah," he started again slowly, "Bobby Lee said that he saw the whole thing. He was sitting out in his car with his girl, watching them shoot craps. He said it was about four of them, and a tall, well-dressed boy that he heard had come from New York or somewhere like that was winning the money. Well, he said it seemed like that anyway cause the boy held onto the dice a real long time and kept picking up the money. He said he couldn't really hear what they was saying, but they didn't seem to be arguing at first and anyway he wasn't paying much attention. Then, all of a sudden he heard some loud cussing and the boy stood up and Tiny jumped on him. He said that he didn't try to get up close because he was with his girl. Plus he didn't want to be involved in it cause he didn't know who had what and he wasn't about to get shot or cut for nobody else."

Each time Jay-boy would sneak a look at his father, he would see two accusing eyes staring right back at him, through him. His father's gaze stabbed at him like a sword, making him twitch and squirm in pain and reproach.

Bobo paused for a moment, and smiled with self-satisfaction at his ability to hold them spellbound. "Yeah, he said that young boy fought like a prize fighter, bobbing and weaving, ducking and dancing, putting fist all in Tiny's face! Man, Bobby Lee said that boy was hitting ol' Tiny so hard and so fast that he didn't know way to turn. He just kept on charging in like a big ol' bull, swinging like a windmill and beating up the air cause that boy was too fast for him. He said," Bobo continued, taking a match stem from his shirt pocket and placing it between his front teeth, "that he was hoping somebody would break it up, cause he knew that if Tiny got his hands on that boy, he would hurt him awful bad."

Suddenly, the door swung and Dallas Green stepped in. His dark brown eyes took in the situation at a glance and the uncomfortable expression that registered on his face was a tell-tale sign that he knew he had interrupted something. The sudden hush that had fallen over the room at his entrance made it all the more evident that whatever they had been talking about somehow involved him.

"Gentlemen, gentlemen, gentlemen," he said, walking over to sit beside Lightning Wilson. They all spoke politely, then stared at him, their eyes lit with curiosity, waiting for him to speak. Green's eyes moved slowly over their faces and he smiled amusedly. He surmised that they had been talking about what had happened last night at his place, but had dropped the discussion when he had come in. Now their closed mouths and open stares seemed to indict him for what had happened. He could feel the blood rush to his temples and his jaws tighten. The room was still silent except for the steady whine of the clippers that Shorty dexterously manipulated as he neatly trimmed Jimbo's hairline. Green looked over at Jimbo and was glad to see that he was not staring—though it was partly because of the way his head was tilted while Shorty was trimming a patch of hair behind his ear.

Green cupped his hands on his knees and asked, "Anybody seen Bumsy around here?"

"No, not today," Shorty answered.

"He told me he would be through here around twelve or one o'clock, and it's about one-thirty now."

"No," said Shorty again, "he ain't been in here."

Bobo, realizing that he was not longer the center of attention, laughed sarcastically and said, "Oh, Bumsy's probably somewhere trying to find him a bottle of wine."

A ripple of laughter went around the room. Green chuckled softly, knowing that Bobo's speculation about Bumsy's activities was most likely correct.

"Hey, Dallas," Bobo continued, "what about that fight at your place last night?"

Green looked up, staring into each person's eyes by turn. He had known that this was coming. "What about it?" he asked, matter-of-factly.

"They tell me somebody cut up Tiny Oliver pretty bad."

"Yeah," Green nodded.

"Do you know who done it?" Bobo asked.

Green paused a long time and finally said, "I think so." Green looked around the room at the eager faces of the people waiting for juicy details. He sighed heavily, glancing over at Jay-boy, who he noticed did not exhibit the same feverish anticipation as the rest of them. Neither did Jimbo, he noted, after a quick glance over at him. This realization made him temper his response. He sighed again heavily and cleared his throat as his mind struggled to frame a response that would not offend—or incriminate—anyone.

"Son, I didn't say that I knew who cut Tiny, I said I think I know." He paused a moment and stared hard at Bobo, not a threatening stare but more a concerned, fatherly stare of the kind that often preceded an admonition. "Now," he continued," I said that I thought I knew. Now if I am wrong, I'd just be adding to the rumor mill like a lot of folks are doing right now." His words seemed to smite Bobo like a blow, and the way his eyes dropped, Jay-boy could tell that the words stung him.

"Son," Green continued softly, "Tiny was cut up pretty bad. I helped Wallace put him into the car. I told Wallace to put his blinkers on and put the pedal to the floor, because we didn't know if Tiny was going to make it. Now if you wasn't there and didn't actually see what happened, I advise you to watch what you say or you might find yourself explaining it all to the police." Bobo was silent, his mouth drawn into a tight line.

"Well, I'll be seeing you-all," Green said, standing up and walking slowly over to the door. "I got to find that-there Bumsy. He's supposed to help me put a radiator in my truck today."

When the door slammed behind Green, silence rushed in to fill the vacuum he had left. The silence was heavy and oppressive, weighing on their shoulders, stifling their speech, and sealing the echo of Green's words tight inside their skulls.

Chapter 12

Jay-boy's stomach muscles had tied themselves into knots; his temples had pounded until they made his head ache. When he reached out to pull back a chair and sit down at the dinner table, eating was the furthest thing from his mind. Finally, his mother took her seat after placing a large bowl of mashed potatoes on the table. They bowed their heads of one accord and his father began, "Lord, make us thankful for what we are about to receive for the nourishment of our bodies. Amen."

Jay-boy, sitting across from Bowknot, kept his eyes averted, being careful not to even look in his dad's direction. As the food was passed around, he put some on his plate simply to have something to do, anything that would delay just a little longer what he was inevitable. He noticed that Bowknot kept his eyes fixed on his plate as he ate, chewing his food slowly and mechanically, as if he were eating only to be polite or accommodating, not out of any sense of hunger or want. For a long while there was only the sound of silverware clanking on china and ice cubes rattling in glasses. These otherwise insignificant sounds would have gone unnoticed had it been just an ordinary Saturday evening, but now they were stentorian. The sounds were juxtaposed to the piercing silence that filled the room like a pungent odor.

Finally, Jimbo broke the almost painful silence, which allowed them to begin breathing normally for the first time since they had sat down to dinner. "Bowknot, you want to tell me what happened at The Shack last night?" Bowknot's head snapped up, and he threw a hard stare at Jay-boy; Jay-boy caught it as he raised his eyes. It was an accusing stare, and it brought Jay-boy's blood to a slow boil. His words eliciting no immediate response, Jimbo spoke again. "Bowknot, I said do you want to tell me what happened at The Shack last night?" This time his words had a harder edge and his gaze was piercing, almost threatening.

Bowknot lifted his eyes to meet Jimbo's briefly, then dropped his gaze to his plate again. "I was shooting craps," he began slowly, "with these guys back behind the place." He paused for a moment to take a sip of Kool-aid from his glass, then continued haltingly. "Well, everything seemed to be going all right until I really started winning the money."

Jay-boy glanced up quickly at his father. He noticed that Jimbo was chewing his food slowly, listening attentively, and it seemed that his eyes had softened a bit. He looked surreptitiously at his mother, and saw that she sat barely eating, sipping her Kool-aid now and then, with a troubled look in her soft, brown eyes as she listened.

"Well, when I started winning the money, this one big guy started getting mad."

"Did you know who this man was?" Jimbo interrupted.

"No, sir. Like I said, when I started really winning the money, this big guy started getting mad. He started mouthing at me, but I just ignored him and kept rolling the dice." He paused and let his eyes move around the table, trying to ascertain whether his story was being believed. He took another sip of his Kool-aid and continued. "Finally, he shoved another pair of dice at me and told me to use them. I asked him why; everybody else had used the same dice, why should I change? He told me to use the dice that he was handing me or get out of the game. I asked him says who, and he said him. I asked him was he gonna try and put me out, then I stood up and he jumped on me."

"Didn't nobody try to break it up?" Jimbo queried.

"No, sir."

"Didn't nobody go and get Dallas?"

"No, sir. They just stood there and watched."

"Well, what's this about the knife?"

"Well, see, at first we were fist-fighting and I was getting the best of him, but I wasn't really hurting him that bad."

"What do you mean?"

"Well, I was hitting him and everything, but he just kept coming. I couldn't keep him off of me. Then I got so tired that I dropped my hands for a minute and he grabbed me."

"What did he do then?"

"He picked me up and slammed me against a car, and then he started choking me. I thought he was trying to kill me! None of the other boys standing around lifted a finger, no sir! Nobody went to get Dallas, no sir!"

"So what did you do then?"

"Well," Bowknot paused for a moment and sighed heavily. "I finally kneed him in the groin and he turned me loose for just a moment. He came right back at me, but by then I had grabbed my knife and I just started cutting him. When the others saw what was going on, somebody ran to get Jay-boy and Mr. Green."

"Was you trying to kill him?"

For the first time, Bowknot raised his voice slightly. "He was trying to kill me and they was just standing there watching and nobody, not a soul, lifted a finger to try to stop him!"

Suddenly, Mrs. Johnson wheeled in her seat. "So you were trying to kill him?" Her words came in a gasp and her eyes were wide and flashing with amazed disgust. "Listen here," she said, straightening up and leaning forward, "we are responsible for you." She raised her hand and was now shaking her finger at him. "Your folks left you here in our care. Do you hear me, boy?"

"Yes, ma'am," Bowknot muttered softly, his eyes fixed on his plate.

"Look at me when I'm talking to you, boy!" she blazed. Her voice was now trembling with anger. Bowknot raised his head, flinching as her words lashed him like a whip. "If you go out here and get in trouble, Jimbo and I are going to be the ones who'll have to get you out. In the first place, you had no business down there gambling anyway, and in the second place, you have just quietly walked away from that mess." She paused for a moment as if to catch her breath or to let what she had just said sink in. "Son," she sighed, her voice softening a bit, "you ain't in Detroit no more. This is a small town and people talk. You ain't been here three weeks, and look at what's happened! "I'm going to write your folks and tell them what has happened here and I'm going to tell you right now I'm not going to have that kind of mess out of you. Do you hear me?" Her voice rose again to emphasize the point. "We don't put up with that from Jay-boy and we ain't going to put up with it from you, fighting and cutting and raising hell like some alley cat!"

"Jay-boy," she turned on him, "I'd like to know why you couldn't tell us what had happened." Jay-boy glanced up quickly at his mother, then he just as quickly dropped his eyes again. He was silent as he felt the blood to his face and his scalp tingle with shame under her reproachful stare. "I'm listening," she said, the words bouncing off his skull like blows.

He finally murmured in a low voice, "I don't know, Mom."

"Did you-all think we wouldn't find out?" she snapped.

The silence in the room became deafening after his mother's tirade, and seemed to stifle not only Jay-boy's speech but his very thought processes. His brain felt shut down. He knew he should have told them. He'd had every opportunity, but had elected not to do it. Why hadn't he told them? He didn't tell Bowknot to go around there gambling with Tiny Oliver and them, did he? "I'm sorry for not telling you-all," Jay-boy said softly. "I . . . " he started to say more, but thought better of it.

His dad spoke. "Son, I'm disappointed, not so much in Bowknot as I am in you." His father had not raised his voice, he had spoken softly and stared straight at Jay-boy. The deep sense of hurt in his voice made the words burn themselves on his brain like a hot branding iron. The words filled him with self-recrimination, and scalding tears boiled up in his throat as he fought valiantly to keep them down. "I'm disappointed," his father went on, "because you didn't feel that you could come to me and tell me, son. You know that if you are in trouble, no matter what it is, you can come to me. You know that I'll stand behind you no matter what the situation might be. Haven't your mother and I always been there for you, son?"

Jay-boy answered, "Yes, sir." His words were choked slightly above a whisper.

"So, son," his father sighed exasperatedly, "I just hated to hear about the thing in the barber shop when you could have told us. You had all the time in the world," he said, disgust creeping back into his voice.

"That's right," his mother spoke again, "you had all the time in the world to tell us."

They both were staring straight at him and the weight of their stares settled on his shoulders like lead weights and pressed down, down, grinding him to dust. Finally, Bowknot stood up. His voice was hesitant and weak, but still he spoke: "Jay-boy promised me that he wouldn't tell."

"What?" Mrs. Johnson's eyes swept to Bowknot's face.

"I begged him not to tell you-all! He didn't want to keep it away from you-all, but I begged him!"

"Why?" Jimbo broke in. "Didn't you-all know we was going to find out?"

"I don't know, sir, I was just scared, just scared, that's all."

"Son, this ain't nothing like a schoolyard ruckus or something. A man was almost killed! You almost cut that man to death."

For a long time, no one ventured to speak as the hard, cold facts of what Jimbo had said settled around them like fine dust. Finally, Jimbo said, "Jay-boy should never have promised something like that and you should never have asked him to, either. Now you-all need to think about what has happened and how both of you-all have behaved. You guys are almost grown men.

Now I know that that-there Tiny Oliver is as mean as a snake. All of them Olivers are mean. They been cutting and shooting folks for years. Tiny's older brother, George, killed that boy up at the fairgrounds a couple years ago. His sister, Brenda, stabbed a girl in the cafe two, three years ago, didn't she, baby?" He nodded to his wife.

"She sure did," Mrs. Johnson said, adding, "Tiny is the worst one. He's been raising hell around here for years. Every time you turn around, he done cut or shot somebody. He ain't been that long got out of jail for cutting that boy from across the state line over at the barbecue place."

"Now maybe we were just a little too hard on you-all, because I know that Tiny goes for bad and maybe you couldn't walk away. But son," Jimbo said, a deep note of urgency in his voice, "you've got to learn to stay away from them kind of people. You've got to be smart enough to see trouble coming and man enough to walk away from it before it gets there or you're gonna find yourself in it deeper than anybody can get you out."The sound of a car horn interrupted them. "Who in the world is that?" Jimbo said, as he rose from the table and headed for the door. He pushed the front door open and saw Dallas Green sitting in front of the house in his old, blue Chevy, chipped paint peeling off it. "Light and come in, light and come in!" he greeted.

Green climbed out and started toward the house. "I been rippin' and runnin' all day," Green said, as he stepped onto the porch. He pulled up one of the wooden chairs and sat down heavily. Jimbo took a seat. Green reached into his shirt pocket and drew out a package of cigarettes. "Here, have one," he offered. Jimbo took a cigarette out of the pack and passed it back to Green. Green lit his own cigarette and handed Jimbo the box of wooden matches.

"Well," Dallas Green said, after inhaling long and blowing a large cloud of smoke. "I came by here to talk to you about what happened at the place last night. When that boy of Lula Adams' came and told me that somebody had cut up Tiny Oliver and I ran around there where they was, I saw Big Tiny layin' in the dirt, bloody as a hog, with Wallace McNair standing over him with a towel or somethin'. There was about twenty or thirty people standing around looking and I helped Wallace get him into the car and told him to get to the hospital as fast as he could. Tiny was unconscious and limp as a dishrag." Green paused a moment and took another long draw from his cigarette; he exhaled slowly, the smoke curling around his head like a halo.

"After Wallace was gone, I started asking people what had happened and Tiny's sister—you know the one who cut that girl in the cafe that time—told me that three guys from over the state line had jumped on Tiny. She said that they had been gambling and Tiny caught one of them cheating and the other ones took it up and jumped on him, saying that he was trying to start trouble. Everybody else I asked said that they didn't see nothing or gave me the same story that his sister had. So I went on back in the place. I asked a few more people who I knew played dice in back of the place regularly and they said that they hadn't seen a thing."

"Then," he said, dragging deeply on his cigarette and releasing the smoke, "just as I was about to close up, that Adams boy came up to me and told me the whole story. He told me how tiny had jumped on the boy and the others just stood there and watched and wouldn't help him or try to break it up or come and get me. Then when he started cutting Tiny, they ran to get me, but by then I was already out there because Bobby Lee had already came and got me."

"So Tiny jumped on Bowknot, huh?" Jimbo said thoughtfully.

"Yeah," Green said, "you know that Tiny is a mean something, He's always coming around there starting something, always picking at people. Well," he paused, leaned over, and spat a stream of saliva into the dirt, "maybe that Tiny has finally got a dose of his own medicine."

"Yeah," Jimbo replied, exhaling a spiral of cigarette smoke, "somebody was bound to get that Tiny Oliver sooner or later. I just hate that my boys have to be mixed up in this mess. You know," he said, looking over at Green, his eyes serious and his voice sober, "all them Olivers go for bad and I don't want to have to kill nobody."

"Oh," Green laughed, "I don't think nothing is going to come of this and anyway you and I have been friends too long for me to let anybody bother them boys."

"I know that, Dallas, and I appreciate it, but you can't be everywhere. Like you said, when they came and got you, everything was all over."

"Yeah," Green nodded, looking out over the field. Then, as much to himself as to Jimbo, he said soberly, "You know, maybe this-here thing was a blessing in disguise. Maybe now tiny won't be so quick to go picking with people. I ain't had nothing but trouble out of him for years and I frankly wouldn't mind a bit if he didn't show his face around my place anymore. I told his mother so, too." He cleared his throat and continued, "She screwed her face all up like she didn't like it, but I don't care. As soon as I can, I'm going to get up there to that hospital and have a talk with him personally. Just as soon as they let me see him, I'm going to get his ass told. I'm going to tell him something that might keep him from losing sight on the world."

Jimbo glanced up and saw the kind of glint in Green's eyes that signified that the man really meant what he was about to say.

"I'm going to tell him that he got one more time to bring his ass around my place starting trouble, then I'm going to take it up and see how bad he really is. If I don't tell him, I hope I drop dead!" he exclaimed, lips quivering in disgust.

The door opened as Mrs. Johnson stepped out onto the porch. "Oh, hey, Dallas! I didn't know you were out here. How have you been?"

"Oh, I've been all right. I just stopped by here to let you-all know what really happened last night. I didn't want to say nothing in the barbershop about it. Like I told Jimbo here, Tiny Oliver is a mean bastard, and I ain't had nothing but trouble out of him for years. One thing after another, almost every weekend." Green straightened up and looked around at Mrs. Johnson, who was still standing. "He had it coming. If it wasn't that boy, it would have been somebody else and, like I told Jimbo, maybe it was all for the best. Now he'll have some time to think while he's laying there in that hospital. When he gets out, maybe he'll have sense enough to stop picking with people now that he knows how it feels to be cut up and laid up in the hospital." He leaned back in his chair and heaved a long sigh. "So, don't you-all be too hard on the boy, because I know Tiny started the whole thing and the boy probably had to cut him or get cut up himself. You know that Tiny is known for blading people and now he just got a taste of his own medicine, that's all. And I just hope he learns some sense from it."

Jimbo and his wife nodded in agreement, then they were all silent for a while. Finally, Green leaned forward, slapping his knee with a palm and saying, "Well, I guess I'd better be getting on then. I just wanted to stop by and talk to you all a minute and set things straight. Listen now, that boy is welcome at my place anytime he wants to come and you tell him ain't nobody gonna bother him, either, and I'll guarantee that."

"All right, Dallas," Jimbo said, "we appreciate that and I'm glad you came by, too."

"All right," he said, rising from his chair and tossing the dead cigarette butt to the ground. "I just didn't want to say anything about this in the barbershop. You know I don't believe in gossip and, anyway, it was none of their business. If they want to believe these lies floating around, let them. Tiny's sister started that lie about three boys from over the state line jumping on him because she just don't want nobody to know that Tiny got his ass whipped by just one boy, that's all. You see, if that really got out, that would ruin his reputation because he always bragged that no one man was bad enough to whip him. Well, one did and now they made up that lie because they can't stand for people to know the truth. Well, let them keep on lying and let people believe what they want. With that he stepped off the porch and strode across the yard to his car. "You-all take care," he said, and opened the door and slid in.

They waved their good-byes as he started the engine and drove off. Mrs. Johnson came and sat down in a chair near her husband, staring hard at him.

He looked up. "What is it, baby?"

"You know," she said, "I hope we weren't too hard on the boys."

"Yeah," he sighed. "That Tiny Oliver is mean as the devil and the boy was only standing up for hisself. That is what we've always tried to teach them."

"Yeah," she nodded thoughtfully. Then she stared out across the field, watching Green's car disappear around the curve at the edge of the woods. "I just don't want Bowknot out here getting in trouble. They left him in our care and we are responsible, and that's why I want him to know that he has to learn to be more responsible. He should have seen that coming."

"Yeah," Jimbo responded, "but you know how these young folks are. He may not have wanted to fight Tiny, but he didn't want to look like a coward in front of the other boys. You know how that sort of thing goes."

"Yeah," she said reflectively, "but he has to learn how to use his head more."

They both turned toward the screen door as Jay-boy came outside. His eyes fell under their direct stares. "I was just coming out to see how wet it was. I was gonna walk out to the road and catch a ride down to Kathy's house."

"Jay-boy," his father spoke up, "son, we didn't mean to be so hard on you-all. We can't hold you responsible for everything Bowknot does, and maybe he didn't have no choice in what he did."

"Yeah, son," his mother nodded in agreement, "we just wish you had told us, that's all."

"Yes, ma'am," Jay-boy said in a barely audible voice.

"Son, you can use the car," his dad said. "You don't have to catch a ride no where. Take Bowknot with you if he wants to go. What's been done is done; let's forget and go on. There ain't no need to keep talking about it, but from now on, don't you ever promise nobody that you'll keep nothing from us. Now, do I have your word on that?"

"Yes, sir," Jay-boy smiled broadly. His parents smiled back at him and his heart melted and a tremendous burden lifted from his sagging shoulders. Now he was reinvigorated; like a wilting flower after a warm summer rain, he bloomed and blossomed again.

Chapter 13

The next two weeks drifted by uneventfully. The hot, dry days and the shimmering heat that folded over the land made the corn, cotton, tobacco, and peanuts droop sickly. Jay-boy watched his father's strongly boned face grow more and more haggard with worry as he lurked around the radio, ears cocked for some word of rain. There wasn't very much to do around the farm now save for taking care of the livestock and doing a little hoeing now and then; the hot weather was stunting the growth of weeds as well as that of the crops.

The few times Jay-boy and Bowknot accompanied Mr. Johnson into town for hog feed or to have some farm implement repaired, they noticed that wherever the older men gathered, their conversation was dominated by talk about the weather. "I sure hope we get some rain soon." "Man, it sure is hot, and dry as a bone." "The weatherman says that this is the hottest July we had in the last five years."

Jay-boy knew that his father had borrowed money and had bought twenty more acres of land. Yes, he had invested heavily in his farm and now everything was in jeopardy. Each morning as they got up early to feed the livestock, he secretly watched his dad walking out across the field. Jimbo's eyes were quiet and troubled, and a look of helpless dejection was stamped on his face that no amount of feigned optimism could hide. Jay-boy looked out across the fields at the once-lush green pea vines and the once-vibrant corn with firm green bayonets held skyward now drooping and turning a sickly yellow. This made him sad, for he knew that his father was an inextricable part of his farm and what was happening to it was happening to him. He noticed that there was little laughter in the house. The conversation, what little remained, was polite but lifeless, as though the blistering heat had sapped life from them as thoroughly as it had done the crops.

"Would you like some more Kool-aid?" Kathy offered.

"Yeah, I don't mind if I do," Jay-boy replied.

Kathy smiled, took his glass, and turned and disappeared through the screen door. A fly droned now and then, bouncing off the wire screen and sailing away. Jay-boy watched the red afterglow of the dying sun and sighed heavily, trying to recall how it felt to be cool. The heat was stifling and the hot breath of the sun lingered long after the blazing sphere had fallen below the horizon. Presently, Kathy returned with another cold glass of Kool-aid. She sat down beside him on the porch swing. He looked at her and saw tiny beads of sweat collecting on her forehead and lifted the glass to his lips.

"I know you're worried about your dad's farm," she said softly.

He nodded and lowered the glass.

"Don't worry," she said. "I know it's going to rain; I been praying every day."

Jay-boy smiled as an inexplicable sense of peace moved over him. She placed a hand on his and smiled into his eyes, then leaned over and kissed him lightly on the lips. Straightening up, she leaned back against the swing. He slid his hand from beneath hers and, raising his arm, placed it around her shoulders. He inhaled deeply, then emptied his lungs with a long, heaving sigh. "You know," he said quietly, "if we don't get some rain soon, folks' crops are gonna burn right up in the fields." As he spoke, he looked out over the dust-covered fields with their wilting, yellow-brown vegetation. The heat stifled, stunted, oppressed everything. Even their conversation had grown steadily more lifeless, listless, and shallow, making the effort of speaking itself a laborious task. They talked less and less and, then, because the process of thinking was becoming an exercise in tedium, they stopped thinking. So they sat speechless, suffering in the sweltering heat and suffocating humidity. Jay-boy and Kathy sat for a long time, watching the evening deepen into dusk as the velvet cover of night crept slowly and steadily across the sky. Occasionally, they gazed lovingly into each other's eyes, but they remained silent in their own reflections.

The area had gone for three weeks now without a drop of rain. Jay-boy's father had invested everything he had into the farm. It just had to rain soon, it just had to. Jay-boy found his lips moving and heard the words inside his head. "Oh, God, please let it rain. Please, please, God, let it rain." Presently, he came to himself and, glancing at Kathy, thought he saw her lips moving, too. Her face was placid and her eyes stared back at him, but there was no indication that she was aware of his presence. He moved his hand slightly, caressing her shoulder; she moaned slightly, awareness coming into her eyes.

"Praying?" he asked softly.

"Yes," she said, "for rain. You praying?"

"Yes, I think we're gonna get some rain soon, you watch." Jay-boy set his glass down on the porch and took her hand. "Kathy Walker, you are the sweetest woman in the whole wide world! You know that?"

"Yes," she laughed teasingly, "but it's still nice to hear sometimes."

Now it was completely dark and the stars hung like lanterns and the moon rose over the trees, bathing the night in silvery iridescence. The moon was so bright that its brilliance carved vivid shadows as it sifted down through the limbs of the large, old oak next to the house. Jay-boy stared hard at Kathy and was almost overwhelmed at how beautiful she appeared in the moonlight. He involuntarily pulled her closer to him and the stunning sight and sweet smell of her made the burden that had sat heavily on his shoulders and clung to him like an evil thing relinquish its tenacious hold and slide into oblivion. He leaned over and kissed her full on the lips and felt her arms go up around his neck. His mind and soul were lifted on waves of gladness.

She drew back slowly and looked into his eyes. "Jay-boy," she said softly, then pausing to clear her throat, "I love you."

The words quickened him, made his blood sing through his veins and his heart dance with delight. He smiled widely and replied, "Baby, I love you, too; you just don't know how much I love you. Why, if it wasn't for you, I don't know what I would do."

"I feel the same way," she said, running her hand along the molding of his jaw, then gently drawing him down to her waiting lips.

It seemed like the smothering heat was finally subsiding, and the cool night air dried their perspiration, leaving their faces dry and salty. Kathy wriggled up into Jay-boy's lap and nestled against his chest, laying her cheek against his. They gloried in each other's presence, melted in each other's embrace as each seemed to feel beyond the fire of passion and beneath the weight of words that each had, indeed, found a soul mate in the other.

"You sure don't talk much about yourself," Ruth said.

"There ain't really nothing to tell," Bowknot replied matter-of-factly, staring at the headlights coming down the road.

"I mean," Ruth paused a moment, following his gaze, "you don't really talk much about anything."

"Well," he said, now watching the red taillights disappear in the distance, "I'm just not a big talker."

Now there was silence again. Ruth had forgiven him for the way he had carried on with the girls that Friday night at The Shack, and had even allowed him to start seeing her regularly. She really liked him. There was a certain something about him—even beyond his tall, slender handsomeness—but she couldn't put her finger on exactly what it was and it troubled her. She would often find herself lying awake at night thinking about him. She enjoyed being with him, despite the fact that she generally had to pull conversation out of him. Sometimes when he took her in his arms, it felt so good that it was frightening. She had never gone all the way with anyone before and she had set her mind that she was not going to, either, until she was married. However, when she was locked in his embrace, her heart pounding, her breasts tingling, and her midriff throbbing with desire, she had to tear herself away. It was as if he had the power to release something inside of her, something that titillated as well as frightened her. The pressure of his full lips on hers and the sensation of his hands caressing her body, steadily and gently, seemed to awaken something that had lain dormant in her, something that made her body ache and throb with passion and tremble with a need so intense that she felt she would explode unless he entered her and released her from her quivering agony. No other boy had made her feel like this before. This was totally new to her and she didn't have the slightest idea of how to deal with it. She didn't love Bowknot, and doubted that he loved her, but she did like being with him.

"Do you really like it out here?" Ruth asked, glancing up at him.

"Oh, it's all right," he answered.

"What do you think about these country girls?"

"They're all right. I'm especially fond of one." He leaned over and winked at her. "Come here," he said, pulling her to him.

At first she resisted, looking up into his eyes. "What if I fell in love with you and then here you go on back to Detroit?" She paused a moment, staring at him. "Now, where would that leave me, huh?"

He was silent for a moment, then he said, "Suppose I fell in love with you and had to leave. Don't you think it would be hard on me, too? Come on," he said softly, drawing her to him. Again she stiffened for a moment, then relented and melted into his arms. He kissed her hard and long, with tongue and teeth predatory. She felt her body yielding under him, her passions aflame, her emotions boiling as she panted in his arms.

Suddenly, he drew back and stood up, taking her by the hand. "Come on," he said, leading her down off the porch and out to her dad's truck. He opened the door and half-lifted her inside, then closed the door behind her and went around to the other side and climbed in. He gathered her up in his arms and kissed her, caressed her, fanned the flames of her desire until she was weak and her body was pliable and yielding. She felt her blouse open and the elastic base of her bra being pushed up. Then she felt his hand full of her breast. Her hands went up to push him away, but desire sapped her physical strength and her strength of will. Her passion made her long for more as she moaned and panted, her mind reeling between delight and disaster. Finally, she felt his hand, his fingers, exploring the fleecy black hair between her thighs. Then he was pulling at her panties and needles of fear shot through her, sending her bolt upright on the seat as she snapped her legs shut, snatching his hand away.

"I've never been all the way with a boy before," she said quietly, her head bent slightly forward.

"There's nothing to it," he said, "just relax. I'll take it easy with you." He pushed her back gently onto the seat and his hand moved up her thigh, but she kept her dress down and legs pressed tightly together. Trembling, she wanted to let him have his way, but her mind could not find a good enough reason on which to hang the decision to lose her virginity.

"Bow, we are not in love yet," she said weakly.

"Oh, baby, it will come! And anyway, you don't always have to be in love to do it," he said, his hands still caressing her thighs and trying to reach the zone between her legs.

Suddenly, she drew back and slapped him hard across his mouth. He reeled backward against the seat and gaped at her in shock.

"Is that all you think of me, just somebody you can lay with?"

His mouth hung open, but nothing came out.

"I like you and I care a lot about you, but I'm not going to be a whore for you!"

"Well, just what the hell do you want from me, then?" he asked disdainfully. "Ain't nothing wrong with doing it. I know that you want to and you know that you want to, so who do you think you're fooling, huh? One minute you want to be a woman and the next, you want to be a child. You've got to make up your damn mind!" With that he turned, opened the door, and stepped out of the truck. He walked slowly over and sat down on the edge of the porch. After a long while, Ruth got out of the truck and walked to the porch, where she sat down at its corner.

There was a tense silence between them, an invisible curtain that separated them as completely from each other as if they were physically miles apart. They each sat brooding, engrossed in their own thoughts, as the tree frogs and cicadas lifted their shrill voices in a throbbing symphony, pulsating rhythmically in the warm night air.

Bowknot watched with longing eyes the intermittent procession of westbound headlights moving along the highway. His heart ached with anticipation each time he saw a pair of headlights break over the hill. He watched the hard yellow beams intently, waiting to see if the car was slowing down to turn into Ruth's driveway. It seemed an eternity before a pair of headlights illumined the driveway as the long-awaited car turned in. He suddenly became aware again of the girl sitting a few feet from him on the other side of the small porch. The fact of her presence made him nervous, and he fidgeted about in his place on the porch's edge. He drummed his fingers on the rough boards, feigning composure and nonchalance.

When Jay-boy pulled up into the yard and stepped out of the car, Bowknot rose to meet him. Jay-boy started to speak, then looked from one to the other and thought better of it. He stopped in his tracks and asked quietly, "You ready to go, Bow?

Bowknot replied in a soft monotone, "Yes, I'm ready." Bowknot turned and threw over his shoulder as he made his way toward the idling car, "I'll be seeing you."

Ruth did not respond; she got up and walked toward the door, opened it, and stepped inside without a word. As the door slammed behind her, Jay-boy looked at his cousin and asked, "Is something wrong?"

"Aw, no, nothing's wrong."

The two of them climbed into the car. Jay-boy slipped the car into gear, turned it around, and eased it back out over the hard-surface road.

"Jay," Bowknot said, glancing over at him, "can I . . ." his voice trailed off and his eyes dropped.

"What is it, Bow?"

"Oh, never mind. That's all right."

"What's on your mind, man?" Jay-boy prompted.

"It wasn't nothing."

"Come on, what is it?"

Bowknot sighed deeply and cleared his throat, then started haltingly. "I was just wondering if you would let me drive a little bit."

Jay-boy didn't answer immediately, then he asked, "Do you have a license?"

"I've had it for a year," he said, shifting his weight on the seat so he could pull his wallet out of his back pocket. He opened the wallet and showed the license to his cousin.

"I didn't know you had your license!" Jay-boy exclaimed. "Why didn't you tell me?"

"You never asked," Bowknot replied, as he returned the wallet to his pocket.

Jay-boy slowed and eased the car over to the side of the road. He came to a stop and, leaving the engine running, stepped out and walked around to the passenger side. He motioned for Bowknot to slide under the wheel and climbed in. As Bowknot was pulling back onto the road, Jay-boy noticed that he handled the car with the ease and poise of one who was no stranger to the art of driving an automobile. As the engine droned and the tires whined, the yellow headlights cut an avenue of light through the heavy darkness.

Jay-boy leaned his head back and rested; his muscles relaxed as though he had just fallen into a soft, comfortable bed, and his mind settled into the peace that induces sleep. Nevertheless, he forced himself to resist sleep's beckoning invitation, feeling that Bowknot wanted to talk. He glanced over at Bowknot, then shifted in his seat and said, "So, Bow, what's the story with you and Ruth?"

Before Bowknot could answer, Jay-boy continued, "You know that she's mighty sweet on you, don't you?"

Bowknot waited a long time before he answered. "Well, all I know is that she wants to get real serious, and I ain't ready to get serious with nobody right now. I told her that, too. I told her that I just want to play things real loose. I don't wanna be tied down to one girl right now; I want to play the field and just have some fun."

"Did you make that clear to her?"

"Yeah, but I don't know if she wants to accept things that way. That's what we were talking about before you drove up. She wants to get real serious. I mean, fall in love and junk like that and, man, I just ain't ready. I told her so, too, but she just got real salty with me."

"Well," Jay-boy sighed heavily, "you can't let nobody force you into anything you're not ready for. I can't blame you for that and, besides, she should be able to understand how you feel."

"Man," Bowknot interrupted sharply, "these girls out here now just want to control a guy and make him into what they want him to be. Then if you ain't willing to dance to their music, they really get the ass with you and try to make like you've done something wrong to them."

Jay-boy raised his head and stared out for a long moment

into the darkness. "If you ain't ready to go steady, don't let nobody force you into it. Now, Ruth is a nice girl, don't get me wrong, but she ain't the only available girl in the country."

Bowknot lowered the window and spat into the wind. "I told her that we could still be good friends if she wanted to, but I was definitely not ready to settle down with no one girl right now and nobody was going to push me or make me feel bad for wanting to just play it loose and enjoy myself."

Bowknot was slowing the car as the glare of the headlights fell over the mailbox standing opposite the path to their house. He nosed the car off the road onto the hard-packed dirt path, moving it along with meticulous care over the uneven ground toward the house.

"By the way," he said, almost as an afterthought. "I'm sorry for frowning up at you like I did at the dinner table. At first I thought that you had told Uncle Jimbo about the fight at The Shack. I just want to say that I'm sorry, that's all."

Jay-boy just nodded his head. "No problem; don't mention it."

Jay-boy was rather awed at Bowknot's openness, his willingness to talk freely about things that were private and personal. A warm sensation moved over him and the tense, uneasy feeling that had tugged at him when he found himself in Bowknot's presence fled. He realized that a closeness was growing between them, and he was glad. He loved his cousin, and he liked the Bowknot that was finally coming out. He had known that the real Bowknot would emerge if he remained patient, but his selfless waiting had drawn his nerves taut as a bow string; many were the times he had almost let the arrows of disgust and impatience fly with ripping passion. He was overjoyed that Bowknot was finally coming around, and giddy at the prospect of his old friend returning to him, replacing the often surly and obnoxious stranger he had become.

After Bowknot parked the car, the two of them got out and sate on the porch in the bright moonlight, talking late into the night. It was as if the wall between them had come tumbling down and they could now hear each other clearly. A healing of their once-strong bond—a bond that had been broken by distance, travail, and experience—was taking place, restoring them to a closeness that even most brothers didn't share.

Chapter 14

Jay-boy awakened the next morning with the bright sunlight pouring through his window. The sound of gospel music floated to his ears as his mother bustled about in the kitchen preparing breakfast, humming along with the radio. The Mighty Clouds of Joy, a staple of Sunday-morning programming, were proclaiming in passionate tones, "There will be peace in the valley when Jesus comes." His mother punctuated the refrain with "Yes, Jesus!"

Jay-boy, though he was now fully awake, continued to lie in bed. Only his eyes moved, watching the sunlight play with the bright-colored patterns on the wallpaper, highlighting some and casting others into shadow.

The mingled aromas of buttermilk biscuits and smoke-cured ham assailed his nostrils and his stomach growled, awakening his salivary glands. He sat up on the bed, swinging his feet to the floor. He wondered if Bowknot was awake, then he heard steps and realized that Bowknot was probably already up and dressed. Jay-boy stood up, stretching his arms toward the ceiling, and yawned deeply. He pulled on his pants and walked over to the door, pausing for a moment to look around once again at the sunlight playing on his wall. Then he turned quickly, opened his bedroom door, and stepped into the hall. He looked through the partially open door into Bowknot's room and saw him standing before the mirror, meticulously combing his hair. Jay-boy smiled to himself as he quietly observed his cousin standing there, primping. Bowknot seemed to be totally absorbed in what he was doing. He stood staring into the mirror, shifting his head ever so slightly, moving the comb with the precision of a seasoned barber, making sure he got every strand just right. Jay-boy eased closer until he was just abreast of the door; Bowknot was so engrossed that he was oblivious of his presence. Suddenly, Jay-boy reached out and rapped loudly on the half-open door with his knuckles, booming at the same time, "Good morning, Mr. Bow!" The sounds startled Bowknot, and he leaped like a deer jumped by a hunter, the comb flying from his hand, his eyes wide, and his mouth agape.

Bowknot collected himself immediately, flashing a sheepish grin at Jay-boy, who by then was grasping his stomach as laughter erupted from somewhere deep inside of him. Then Bowknot exploded, too, his laughter bouncing off the walls as his shoulders shook and he staggered weakly against the dresser for support. Jay-boy had fallen back against the door, doubled over with laughter.

Finally catching his breath, Bowknot exclaimed, "Man, what are you trying to do, give me a heart attack or something? I didn't know what in the world that was!"

Jay-boy stumbled into the room and slapped Bowknot on the back. "My man!" he said, "standing there styling and profiling like one of them big-time movie stars!" Again the two of them exploded with barrages of laughter. Jay-boy collapsed onto Bowknot's bed, still laughing. Bowknot leaned heavily against the dresser, his hand tightly grasping its edge for support.

Mrs. Johnson appeared in the doorway, her smile indicating that she was ready to join the merriment. "I came to see what all the laughing was about. What's so funny?" Then just watching them, she was overcome by the gaiety and laughter bounded from her with such abandon that she felt unsteady on her feet. She didn't know what in the world they were laughing about, and then, somehow, she just didn't care. Just the sight of them laughing together and the sense of warmth that now pervaded the room made the act of laughing more important than the reason ever could be. She felt exuberant with joy as the boys filled the room with their laughter.

Finally, after what seemed an eternity, peace settled over them and Jay-boy cleared his throat. "Well," he said slowly, glancing over at Bowknot, who lowered his head, still giggling softly. "I was watching my man combing his hair. He was just standing there preening and primping like one of them Hollywood stars! Jay-boy moved his hand over his head in imitation of his cousin. "Oh, he was just combing, trying to get every single strand in place." His mother cupped her hand to her mouth to suppress a stream of giggles as she watched and listened in amusement. "Well, I stood there and watched him for a while, then I knocked on the door real hard and said, 'Good morning, Mr. Bow.' Man, he jumped like somebody had shot him out of a cannon!"

Mrs. Johnson's hand came away from her mouth now as laughter bellowed from her lungs. Her laughter was contagious; Jay-boy and Bowknot broke up again, laughing so hard that tears came to their eyes and their stomachs hurt. Finally, they all collected themselves and Mrs. Johnson said, "You boys go on out there and feed up and come on back so you can eat."

Jay-boy rose from the bed, cutting his eyes at Bowknot as he walked out of the room. He winked, and said in a teasing voice, "My man, my main man!"

Jay-boy's morning bath had refreshed him and made him feel cool clear through. He felt invigorated, and a sense of warmth and peace settled over him like the morning mist had settled over the green landscape, leaving it with a new luster and vitality. As he and Bowknot made the rounds feeding the chickens, hogs, and mules, they talked animatedly. He was glad to see Bowknot back to his old self, and the good feelings that coursed through him made everything that had happened seem far away and insignificant now. It was as if Bowknot were a long-awaited butterfly that had emerged from a cocoon of sullen, morose resentment. The family's patience had paid off, and Jay-boy was ecstatic that the Bowknot he once knew, more brother than cousin, was back again.

Jay-boy paused a moment and straightened, looking out toward the highway. Bowknot paused, too, and followed Jay-boy's gaze. They saw Mr. Johnson coming along the dirt path, the old car bouncing over the uneven earth, lifting a large cloud of yellow dirt behind it.

"I thought I heard something," Jay-boy said abstractedly, still staring at the car. Then he turned his head toward the western horizon. He shrugged. "Looks like it's going to be another hot one and I don't see a cloud in the sky. So I reckon that means we'll just have to wait a little longer on that rain."

There was a leaden sadness in his voice, and a sickening feeling of utter helplessness washed over him as his eyes moved over the fields.

"Well, Bow," he said, shaking his head as if to shake the depressing reality of what he had just observed from his brain, "I guess we're all done here. Let's go in and get some breakfast."

Jay-boy sat down the large bucket that he had been holding and started walking toward the house; Bowknot fell in beside him. When they reached the back porch, the smells of ham and buttermilk biscuits overwhelmed them and left them with a most pressing desire to pull up to the table and get busy. After washing their hands in a tin of warm water that Mrs. Johnson had placed on a small table on the back porch, they entered and took their places at the table. Jay-boy heard his father come in the front door, then move around the living room. Seconds after, he heard the rustle of the morning paper, then he heard the television come on. He sighed deeply, watching his mother place a large bowl of scrambled eggs on the table and wondering how long his father was going to hold up the meal.

Suddenly, he heard what he was sure was a Negro voice on the television and the sound of it made him wheel in his seat. Jay-boy shot a quick glance over at Bowknot, who had snapped to attention. "Hey!" Jay-boy said, "who in the world is that on TV?" As soon as the words had cleared his lips, the two of them were rising from the table. His mother turned from the stove.

"Where are you-all going, heading out of here like you're going to see a fire?"

Jay-boy spoke, his words coming in a rush. "We're going to see who that is on TV." The boys crowded into the living room, their eyes bright with curiosity; they stood as though riveted before the television screen and stared at it breathlessly. What they saw struck them dumb.

"I am the greatest! I'm the king of the world! I shook up the world! I am pretty!"

"Hold it!" a reporter began, "you're not that pretty!" Before he could continue, the tall, magnificently handsome Negro with the superbly chiseled body spouted on. "I am the greatest! I am the king! Put me on a throne!"

The man was surrounded by white reporters, though it seemed as if he was determined not to really talk to any of them. He wanted to make statements, not answer questions, and make statements he did. As he reeled and shouted, "I am the king of the world!", the words seemed to shoot out of the television set like bullets, hitting everyone within earshot with devastating impact. Finally, after what seemed an interminably long time, the voice of an exasperated reporter came over the set as the picture of this strange and wonderful Negro slowly began to fade, saying "This is Cassius Clay, the new heavy-weight champion of the world."

Then another voice came on, talking about the weather and Jay-boy was finally able to tear his gaze from the screen. His lips were slightly parted as he turned to Bowknot, still dazed as if he was coming out of a trance. "Man, did you hear that!"

Bowknot shook his head in the affirmative, his eyes still wide and glassy; the spell the booming warrior had cast over him still had his head spinning and his mind reeling between dream and reality. Turning and looking at his father, who had been sitting in a chair with the newspaper in his lap, Jay-boy smiled a smile that lit up the whole room. His dad beamed.

"They got a big write-up on him in the paper right here." Mr.

Johnson lifted the paper and pointed to the front page. "When I got to the store this morning, old Moses Roberson came up to the car and told me to make sure I got the Sunday morning paper. You know old Moses used to prize-fight for years and he's always up on stuff like that." Jay-boy's dad paused and cleared his throat. "They say that this-here Cassius Clay is from Louisville, Kentucky. Man, he sure put a whipping on that-there Sonny Liston," he chuckled. "I'll let you-all read it as soon as I finish. I turned on the television because I figured they might have something on the news about that fight."

Jay-boy was glowing with pride. He had never heard a black man talk like that. The wondrous sense of exhilaration that moved over him made him giddy with delight. He looked around at his cousin and saw the same sense of wonder and pride in Bowknot's eyes. Jay-boy started to say something, but after groping feverishly for a moment for words to describe the way he felt, he gave up. He walked over and slapped Bowknot on the shoulder. "The man is bad!", he exploded, and the two of them burst into laughter. He saw his father's shoulders shaking with laughter, too. Then he became aware of his mother standing in the doorway. Having been the last to come into the room, she had caught only the end of the news story.

"Who is that man?" she asked, wondering what all the commotion was about.

"Mama, that is the new heavyweight champion of the world!" Jay-boy exclaimed, lifting his fist and dancing around the room. "That man is Mr. Cassius Clay, the king of the world!" Watching Jay-boy's antics, they all broke up with laughter.

"Well," his mother said, "I reckon you-all better come on in here and eat before your breakfast gets cold."

Chapter 15

"Precious Father, I stretch my hand to thee; no other help I know. If thou withdraw thyself from me, whither shall I go?" The old deacon stood, gaunt and lean, his worn suit hanging off his stooped shoulders. His raspy voice was trembling with the fervor of his supplications as his words echoed around the sanctuary. "My Father," he continued, his hands clasped tightly together in front of him, his grizzled gray head bowed in humble submission, "it is once more and again that one of your servants comes before your throne of grace. Father, I ask you to look on us with an eye of compassion this morning. Father, I ask you to strengthen us where we are weak and build us up where we're torn down."

"Yes, Jesus!" "Have mercy, Jesus!" "Please, Jesus!" The refrains floated up from the congregation.

"My Father, we know that you are a doctor in our sick-room and a lawyer in the courtroom."

"Yes, yes, Father!" "Have mercy, Lord." The responses came almost in rhythmic cadence.

"My Father, we ask you to look upon the sick ones among us, Father."

"Please, Jesus!"

"We ask you to look on the ones bound in jail, my Father."

"Sweet Jesus, look on them, Lord!"

"My Father, we ask you to send us some rain, my Father."

"Please, Jesus!" "We needs it bad, Lord!"

"My Father, we ask you to open up the fountain of heaven and pour us down some rain, Lord."

"Do it, Lord!" "Have mercy, Jesus!"

"My Father, folks' crops are just burning up in the fields, Lord."

"Burnin' up, Lord!"

"My Father, we needs your rain, my Father."

"Please, Jesus, we needs it right now, Lord!"

Jay-boy had been thinking about the brash young Negro who he had seen on television earlier that morning. He had unabashedly boasted of his athletic prowess in a way Jay-boy had never before heard a black man speak, and this had affected him deeply. Here was this young southern Negro on national television, not bending and bowing or smiling apologetically for his blackness, but proud of who he was and proclaiming to the world that he was indeed the king of the world! The words echoed up and down the canyons of Jay-boy's brain: "I am the king! I shook up the world! I am the king; put me on a throne! I'm a bad man! I'm pretty!" The things that Jay-boy was feeling were so new to him that he stopped trying to understand what was happening to him and just sat back and luxuriated in the fact that this wonderful thing was happening. This man wasn't much older than he was and yet the man's words had smitten him like blows and sent his mind reeling and made his heart dance like a leaf in a strong breeze.

Jay-boy stood and held a hymn book open and heard people around him standing also. He read the parts that they were supposed to read from the hymnal for the responsive reading, but the sound did not register in his brain. He was aware of Kathy standing next to him and Ruth standing next to her and Bowknot next, and then his mother and father. But still, somehow he was far away. Suddenly, the answer to all his questions exploded in his brain like a blinding flash of light, illuminating the dark recesses of his mind where the answers he needed had lain shrouded in mystery. Yes, now he knew why the young man he had seen on television had affected him so strongly! It wasn't just the fact that he had won the heavyweight boxing title. Perhaps it wasn't anything to do with boxing at all. Wasn't the man who Clay had defeated a Negro, heavyweight champion of the world? There had been other Negro boxing champions—Joe Louis, Sugar Ray Robinson, Jack Johnson—and they all had made Negroes feel proud. However, this Cassius Clay was different from them, much different. This unashamed son of Africa, this satin-cinnamon warrior, beamed with a kind of pride that Jay-boy had never seen a black man exude. The man seemed to be basking in the mystical glow of a kind of unassailable arrogance that made his dark eyes flash like live coals as his tongue lashed defiantly, "I am the king of the world!" That shocked Jay-boy into believing that he was without a doubt the kind of the world. However, this was only part of what mesmerized Jay-boy. The other—and perhaps more important—reason was that the man not only personified athletic greatness, but he celebrated his own blackness in a way that had stunned white folks and was absolutely captivating to Jay-boy. That was what really made his heart dance with pride and his spirit soar into the heavens like a rocket on wings of gladness. The man just made him feel like he, too, was somebody, and this strange new pride gave a new zest to his step. Now, when he looked in the mirror, his white teeth flashed in sweet self-satisfaction as he realized that yes! he, too, was a son of Africa and was, for the first time in his life, proud of it.

Later that same evening, Billy-Boy had come by to get Jay-boy to help put brake shoes on his car and Bowknot had come along. As the boys lay on their backs in the dusty grass beneath the old car, they were impressed with Bowknot's knowledge and skill in automotive mechanics. With Bowknot's help, they finished the job in half the time and they were certainly glad of it, too, as they wriggled out from the under hot car, brushing the dust and dry grass from their clothing.

"Well, I sure thank you fellows," Billy-Boy said, looking from one to the other with a glad smile on his face.

"Any time, any time, home," Jay-boy said, shaking the other

boy's hand in a playful manner.

"And my man here know his stuff, don't he!" Billy-Boy exclaimed, looking at Bowknot with admiration. "Man, you can really make you some money working on cars."

Bowknot smiled shyly and laughed softly. "Oh, it wasn't nothing," he said, shrugging his shoulders. "My old man works at the Ford plant and he's showed me a few things here and there."

"Well, like I said," Billy-Boy continued, "you seem to know your stuff. Hey!" he broke off sharply, "how would you guys like a cold one?"

"A cold what?" Jay-boy asked, feigning ignorance of what Billy-Boy meant.

"A cold beer, my man."

Bowknot's face broke into a wide grin; he stared at Jay-boy, waiting for his answer, hoping that it would be in the affirmative. Jay-boy shrugged and laughed. "I guess that's all right."

"All right," Billy-Boy said.

The three of them headed for the house. When they reached the porch, Jay-boy said, "Man, I'd just as soon have a seat right here. As hot as it is, I know it's got to be a little cooler out here."

"All right," Billy-Boy said. He opened the screen door and disappeared into the house. It was getting late in the evening and the sun had fallen below the horizon, leaving only its faint red after-glow on the canvas of the pale-blue sky. There still wasn't a cloud to be seen, and only a hint of a breeze stirred. Jay-boy was staring out over the dry, dusty landscape, his eyes moving abstractedly along the horizon and his mind drifting like a leaf on a slow-moving stream. Finally he awakened from his lethargy and glanced over at Bowknot sitting across from him. Bowknot's face was calm and expressionless and his eyes were wide and staring, as if he were in deep thought.

Billy-Boy stepped back out onto the porch carrying a tray laden with a six-pack of Black Label beer and a large bag of potato chips. "All right, fellas," he said, placing the tray on an empty chair, "let's eat, drink, and be merry!" He pulled up a chair, and the three of them dug in with the self-satisfying smiles of adolescents breaching the barriers of youth and trespassing into adulthood.

For a long while, they swilled beer and munched on potato chips in silence. Billy-Boy's mother was away at an evening church service, and he knew that she wouldn't be back for some time yet. He had stopped at the store and bought the beer when he was on his way to pick up Jay-boy and Bowknot. Old man Scott had never asked him for proof of his age and he had never offered any. He had been buying beer for about a year now at various places around the county and no one had bothered to ask him for proof of his age. He figured that the fact that he had grown a beard must make him look older, and chalked his good fortune up to that. A lot of people had told him that the beard made him look like a grown man and he liked that.

Jay-boy spoke, "Hey, Billy, did you see the paper this morning?"

"Yeah, I saw it, and I read about this guy, Cassius Clay, who knocked out Sonny Liston for the heavyweight title."

"Yeah, I read it too," this from Jay-boy again, "and man, they had Cassius Clay on TV this morning." Jay-boy paused a moment, feeling the effects of the alcohol seeping into his brain, making his head spin. "Man, that guy is something else!" he continued excitedly. "You should have heard him: 'I'm the king! Put me on a throne! I shook up the world! I'm a bad man! I'm pretty!' Man, he was really talking some stuff!" Feeling more uninhibited because of the alcohol he'd drunk, Jay-boy stood up suddenly and began strutting back and forth, imitating Cassius Clay, beaming with the great pride the man had inspired in him. "I am the king, put me on a throne! I'm pretty, I shook up the world!" he boomed. The three of them broke into laughter. Billy-Boy had bent double, holding his stomach. Bowknot shook so violently that he had to set his can of beer down beside his chair to keep from dropping it. Jay-boy went back to his chair and sat down heavily, weak from laughter.

Almost simultaneously, the three of them looked up to see a car moving along the path toward the house. Jay-boy straightened up and cleared his throat, peering at the car intently. "Who is that?" he asked no one in particular. The other two boys also stared at the unfamiliar beige Chrysler coming toward them.

"Aw, shoot!" Billy-Boy exclaimed. "That ain't nobody but old Pigfoot Parker."

Jay-boy felt a sobering sensation wash over him. This was the guy who had been liking Ruth. Jay-boy thought that he had better cool it with the beer and keep his wits about him. He was sure that nothing serious would happen here—Billy-Boy wouldn't have it—but he was going to keep his head clear to make sure. He knew that alcohol had a strange way of bringing out the worst in some people and made folks wake up feeling sorry the next day for something stupid they had done while under the influence of the liquor. He never bought the notion that alcohol, in and of itself, made people do the dumb things that they did sometimes: he was sure that the idea was already there; the alcohol just gave them nerve enough to do it and served as a handy excuse. The car pulled to a stop in the yard.

"Hey," Billy-Boy called out, "you-all come on up and have a seat."

Pigfoot climbed out of the car and a tall, thin boy got out on the other side. "This-here is my cousin, Rip," Pigfoot said, nodding in the direction of the boy with him. "He's down here visiting from D. C. How you-all doing?" Pigfoot included each of them in his question, sweeping his gaze from one to the other.

"Oh, man, everything is everything. We just trying to beat the heat, that's all," Billy-Boy responded for all of them.

"How you doing?" Pigfoot nodded at Jay-boy specifically.

"All right. How are you?" Jay-boy greeted him politely, watching Pigfoot's eyes as they traveled to Bowknot. Bowknot and Pigfoot exchanged a quiet, polite greeting.

"Oh!" Billy-Boy started, remembering his manners, "let me go in here and get you-all some chairs." He opened the door and stepped into the house.

There was a brief, uncomfortable silence in his absence, which Jay-boy broke. "So, what's been going on, Pigfoot?"

"Nothing much, man. Just working hard, trying to save up a little money to get my school clothes and keep that old car running." Pigfoot spoke softly and shifted his weight nervously from one leg to the other as he leaned against the house, staring out over the fields.

Jay-boy knew that Pigfoot didn't care much for Bowknot or, at least, that's what he had heard. Pigfoot probably wouldn't even have stopped at Billy-Boy's house if he had known that Jay-boy and Bowknot were there. Pigfoot had told Bobby Lee Adams that he didn't appreciate that fancy city-slicker trying to move in on his girl, and if things didn't change pretty damn quick, they were going to meet in fist city and somebody was going to end up getting hurt. That was before he had found out the kind of man he was venturing to trifle with. After he had heard about how Bowknot had dispatched with Big Tiny Oliver—no doubt from Bobby Lee—his baleful threats had melted like thin ice under a hot sun. And one thing in Pigfoot's favor, as far as Jay-boy knew, was that none of the threats had gotten back to Bowknot.

Billy-Boy returned, carrying two straight-backed chairs. "Here you go, fellas," he said, shoving one toward Pigfoot and the other toward Rip. The boys took the chairs; Pigfoot sat next to Jay-boy and Rip pulled his chair over next to Billy-Boy, conspicuously eyeing the tray, which still held three unopened beers and the bag of potato chips. Noting him, Billy-Boy smiled broadly and laughed. "Oh, I am forgetting my manners! You boys go ahead and drink up!" He didn't have to say it a second time; the two young men had already risen from their seats and were reaching for the beer.

Pigfoot popped the tab-top and took a long guzzle, then

belched loudly. Startled by the noise, the others swung around to find its source. Upon meeting Pigfoot's eyes and seeing the amused look on his face, they exploded into laughter. Recovering himself, Pigfoot patted his stomach and declared, "Man, that really hit the spot!" He lifted the can to his lips again. Jay-boy shook his head in mock disgust as he watched Pigfoot's bobbing adam's apple and heard the rhythmic gulps as the liquid spilled down his throat.

Man! Jay-boy thought, he drinks the stuff like it's water!

"Hey, Pig!" Billy-Boy gibed, "I got another six-pack in the refrigerator, but the way you're swilling that one, I'd have to have a fifty-gallon drum to keep you going!"

The other boys laughed heartily. Pigfoot lowered the can to speak, but Billy-Boy cut him off. "And besides, you got to drive, so you know you'd better take it easy, jack."

"Heavens to mergatroid! Holy mackerel!" Pigfoot teased, gesturing with his hand, waving them all aside, "can't a poor boy drink him some beer in peace?"

"Yeah," his cousin spoke up for the first time, his natural shyness melting away as the intoxicating warmth of the beer settled over him. "We don't mind letting a man drink his beer in peace, Cousin, but I just don't want to you to sit here and get drunk as a skunk and I can't get back home."

The other boys erupted in loud laughter and Pigfoot, feeling the weight of his cousin's remark, lowered his head and grinned sheepishly. "Hey, you-all," he said, trying to change the subject and direct their attention away from him. He drained his can and placed it beside his chair. "Did you-all hear about this bad brother that just won the heavyweight boxing title?"

"Oh, yeah!" Jay-boy replied excitedly. "That guy is something else, ain't he, though? They say he came out of Louisville, Kentucky."

Sitting up and leaning forward in his chair, Bowknot interjected, "The man sure can talk his talk!"

Jay-boy launched into his routine, parrotting Cassius Clay. "I am the king! Put me on a throne! I shook up the world! I'm a bad man!"

The others watched him with pride and amusement. "Yeah," Bowknot added, his hands pawing the air in front of him, jabbing at an invisible opponent, "the man is bad! I mean, sure-enough bad, and that's a fact!"

They all laughed with such abandon that they found themselves wiping their eyes as the heavy guffaws wracked their frames. When something like peace settled over them again, Billy-Boy glanced at the tray and saw that the remaining beer had disappeared. He swung his gaze around the group to locate it. When his eyes rested on Pigfoot, he was greeted with a wide grin, a wink, and a sly chuckle.

"Well, while you-all was laughing and carrying on, that poor little-ol' beer was just setting there getting hot." He motioned toward the beer with his hand. "So I just reached over and picked it up and put it out of its misery." He held the can upside down to show them that it was empty. They gaped at him in wonder and then all broke up laughing again.

"Pig, how in the hell did you grab that beer off the tray and drink it up that fast, man?" Billy-Boy asked, his eyes lit with astonishment and his shoulders still shaking with laughter. Pigfoot just wagged his head and grinned, flashing his white teeth. Billy-Boy rose and turned, stepping into the house.

"Pig," Rip admonished him, "I ain't playing, man. Don't you sit here and get drunk."

"Hey!" Pigfoot cut him off. "Don't worry, cousin, have no fear; your cousin Pigfoot can handle his beer! So don't you worry about the mule going blind, you just stay in the wagon and hold the line!" He laughed at his own witticism. Then he abruptly straightened and turned to Bowknot, staring at him as if he wished he could see the truth of the matter. "Hey, dude," he began. Bowknot turned his head slightly and met Pigfoot's stare. "Did you really kick old Tiny Oliver's ass like they said you did?"

Bowknot was silent. Jay-boy's eyes moved from one to the other of them, his stomach tightening with dread. He had been hoping that no one's tongue would become loose when the alcohol started flowing, but it was beginning to look as if his hope was futile. Finally, Bowknot answered coldly, his eyes hard and unblinking, "Now just what do you think?"

"Hey, fellas," Jay-boy interrupted, his eyes still moving back and forth between them, "let's let sleeping dogs lie, okay?" The two boys averted their eyes from each other and Jay-boy knew that they were content to drop the matter. He sighed heavily and his taut muscles relaxed.

Billy-Boy returned just at that moment with the second six-pack; he sat it on the tray beside the potato chips. "All right, fellas," he said, "help yourselves but don't hurt yourselves. Especially you, Pigfoot."

"Yeah, man, you looka-here," Rip spoke up, "one more beer for you and that's it."

"All right, all right," Pigfoot conceded in an aggravated-sounding voice. "Man, you're worse than an old woman!"

"I know you, Pig," Rip cut him off sharply. "If your ass get stopped out here for drunk driving, I'm gonna get my ass chewed out, too, and you know that!"

The other boys laughed, and Rip almost wished he hadn't said anything. His face flushed hot with embarrassment.

"All right, man," Pigfoot said grudgingly, "one more brew and that's all she wrote." He lifted a can of beer carefully from the tray, then reached out and got a large handful of potato chips. The other boys, save for Jay-boy, reached out for beers, also. Popping the tops, they raised the cans to their mouths and drank luxuriantly, savoring the smooth feel and the acrid bite of the brew.

After a couple of rounds of stuffing their mouths with potato chips and washing them down with beer, Billy-Boy spoke. "Hey, I've got a good joke, if you-all want to hear it." They all nodded expectantly. "Well," he began, smiling broadly, "there was this blind man with his dog, standing on the street corner." He paused a moment for effect. "The blind man was waiting for the light to change, but meantime, these two old ladies walked up to him and asked if they could help him get across the street. The man said, 'No, that's all right. I got my dog here; he can take care of me.'" Billy took a long swallow of his beer before continuing. "Well, the light changed and the two little old ladies went on across the street. Once they got to the other side, they turned to watch the blind man and his dog, who were still standing on the opposite side. They saw the dog lift up his leg and piss all over the blind man's pants leg, then real quick-like start to pull him across the street. When they got to the other side, the man reaches into his pocket and hands the dog a cookie. Man, these two ladies are just beside themselves now; they don't know what to make of this scene. So, one of the little old ladies strolls up to the blind man and taps him on the arm and says, 'Sir, you gonna give that dog a cookie after what he just done to you?' 'Yeah,' the blind man smiles. 'You see, I'm just giving him a cookie to find out where his head is, cause I'm going to kick his ass." They all laughed uproariously and told other stories late into the evening.

The beer seemed to have a mellowing effect as the night wore on and the atmosphere cooled somewhat. Dusk deepened into night and the stars came out bright and shimmering like finely cut diamonds as their voices floated on the cool night air. Billy-Boy's mother had come home from church and had seen the beer cans but had said nothing. She knew that he drank beer and, realizing that he was almost a man, she gave him that freedom.

Chapter 16

Jay-boy's shirt collar shivered under the throb of the electric bass that boomed from a jukebox somewhere in the rear of the place. He and Bowknot were in Beulah May's Cafe and the place was packed "wall to wall, tree-top tall," as the young men liked to say. A long, mahogany bar with a row of bar-stools ran along the front of the cafe; the back wall held a long row of tables with booths on either side. At the other end of the elongated room was the kitchen, which filled the place with the mouth-watering aromas of the reputed best danged cooking below the Mason-Dixon line. The air was filled with the babble of speech as young and old men and women of all sizes, shapes, and shades lined up along the bar and crowded in the booths. Jay-boy and Bowknot threaded their way through the crowd, nodding at familiar faces, their eyes roving around the room looking for a seat. Bowknot spotted a booth in the back, and they moved slowly through the clusters of bodies toward it. They slid into the booth on opposite sides of the table.

Jay-boy's gaze wandered around the room. He knew most of the people there and, as his eyes caught their glances, their faces brightened with recognition and they flashed broad smiles and waved or nodded. Now and then, friends and acquaintances of his parents would amble by and inquire about them, smiling and sending their regards. He nodded politely and thanked them. From time to time, various friends of his would strut past the table, favoring him with a multitude of colorful salutations. Turning to Bowknot, he asked, "Well, sir, what would you like to have?"

Bowknot's face was quiet and pensive, but his eyes had been moving around the room and his mind was busy, noting everyone and everything under his gaze. His mind analogued the bright cotton dresses that hugged the blooming swell of ripe, young breasts and clung with painted-on tenacity to curvaceous hips. His mind also filed with meticulous care the freeze-frame pictures of the large, dark eyes that gazed back at him with the seductive glint of romantic possibilities. Jay-boy's words had sounded in his brain like some distant bell or the vague rattling of an alarm clock rousing someone from a deep, restful sleep.

"Oh," Bowknot blinked as if trying to focus on his cousin, "what was that you said?"

Jay-boy chuckled softly. "My man, checking out the ladies?"

Bowknot grinned slyly. "Man," he quipped, "if some of these country girls ain't sure-enough nice, I'll have to throw up my hands and say mouse ain't mice!"

Jay-boy wagged his head in agreement as he crowed with laughter. "I'll have to say, I second that motion. But, as I was saying, what would you like to eat?"

Bowknot paused a moment, reading the large menu board on the wall behind the bar. "Oh, I think I'll just have a pop and two hot dogs."

"Okay," Jay-boy said, "is that all?" He added, "The treat's on me."

"Yeah, that's all I want. But are you sure, man? I've got some money; I can pay," Bowknot said, nodding to indicate his gratitude.

"I know. Just keep it—we can spend yours later," Jay-boy said as he slid out of the booth and stood. "I'll be right back." He turned and edged his way toward the bar.

Bowknot watched him melt into the bustling crowd, drumming his fingers on the tabletop in time with "Twist and Shout," which blared from the jukebox. Then he resumed his favorite pastime, girl watching. Again, his curious gaze flitted around the room, taking in one female after another in a single glance.

His active mind critiqued and filed vital statistics: breast size, hips, legs, facial tone, gestures. His mental file was so accurate that, hours later and in vivid detail, he could summon any specimen he had seen to the luminous screen of his consciousness to tease and tantalize him.

Suddenly, he felt a strange and disturbing sensation move over him and he stirred nervously in his seat. Feeling someone's eyes on him, he looked up, and his gaze locked with that of pretty lemony-colored girl with large brown eyes and a smile that made him glow.

"Hi," she said, smiling down at him.

"Hi, there," Bowknot responded, barely above a whisper.

"Is anyone sitting there?" the girl asked, motioning toward the seat Jay-boy had occupied.

"Oh, no," Bowknot stammered confusedly. "I mean, yes, my cousin is sitting there."

The girl laughed, looking pointedly at the empty seat and then back at him with a glint of amusement in her eyes. Bowknot felt the blood rush to his face and he flushed with embarrassment. Then he shook his rapidly, fighting for control of the tempestuous impulses that flickered wildly between delight and fear.

"I meant," he said, trying to appear calm, "he was sitting there. He went to get us some hot dogs and soda pop, but you can sit here if you'd like," he said, gesturing to the space beside him.

The beautiful girl exuded the elegance of a debutante and her graceful movements matched the self-assured poise of a fashion model. She lay her purse on the table and slid into the booth beside him.

"My name is Linda Howard," she said. "I gave your cousin my address and told him to give it to you."

Bowknot's mind flashed back over the recent past and, yes, he did remember that Jay-boy had given him a small piece of paper with a girl's name and address on it and had told him that the girl wanted to meet him. He had also said that she was a good-looking girl and worth getting to know, but Bowknot had never followed up on the offer. He sat, speechless, staring vacantly at her with a corny smile plastered on his face, his mind reeling with bafflement. Why had he not at least gone to meet her? Then he remembered. That was the same night that he had gotten into the horrible fight with Big Tiny Oliver and, in the aftermath of all that shit, he was so messed up that what Jay-boy had said had gone in one ear and out the other.

"So, mister," she broke in on his thoughts, "are you going to talk to me?" She was looking straight at him.

"Oh, sure," Bowknot stammered. "First, let me say that I'm very sorry for not getting in touch with you. My cousin told me about you and gave me your note but, dumb me, I misplaced the doggone thing. Then every time we went by The Shack, I was hoping that I might see you, but no such luck." He paused and smiled, feeling excited. "It's a real pleasure to meet you, Linda, and if you still want me to, I'd love to come by to see you."

She smiled again and he beamed, his senses alive and charged with the thought that she was actually sitting next to him. She was indeed a very pretty girl, he thought and, for a brief moment, he envisioned her in his arms. He quickly pushed the thought from his mind.

"Sure," she said, "I'd still like to see you."

"Just let me know when," he said, trying to restrain his excitement and appear calm and mature.

"Well," she said, looking for a moment at the milling crowd, "I'm free tonight."

"Are you sure?" he asked, trying not to sound too eager. "What time are we talking about then?"

"Around seven o'clock."

"Seven o'clock, then. I'll be right there."

"Then it's a date." She reached out and placed a hand on his forearm; a slight shudder ran through him.

"All right, then, it is a date," he said, still feigning calm and sophistication. This lady was something else. He would have to be on top of his game to deal with her. Her calm self-assuredness and feminine charm titillated and frightened him, beckoned and threatened him, leaving him feeling unsettled. When she looked at him, she stared straight into his eyes and held her face only a few inches from his. Whenever she gestured to make a point, she touched him unhesitantly, her soft fingers patting him on the arm or poking him in his ribs. He thought she must be two or three years older than him and maybe that accounted for her poise and maturity and the velvet ease with which she expressed herself.

After a while, Jay-boy returned, carrying four hotdogs and two bottles of soda pop on a tray. Placing the food on the table, he said, "Well, hello, Linda. I'm glad to see you two have finally met."

Bowknot took his hotdogs and soda from the tray and pushed them in front of Linda, who protested, "Oh, no thanks. You go ahead and eat." When Bowknot tried to insist, she said, "No, really, I've already eaten something. I'm not at all hungry. And anyway," she laughed coyly, "those hotdogs would be too heavy on these hips." The boys laughed, too.

"You see," she added, "I don't want to straighten out my curves. I've heard that there's nothing more dull and uninteresting than a straight road." As they were laughing together at her homespun wisdom, they were joined by another girl. Her smooth, copper skin and finely chiseled features made her mighty pleasing to look at, and she was vivacious and animated when she talked. She made it clear that she could—without much persuasion—be sweet on Jay-boy, but he did not take matters beyond polite conversation, for Kathy was his one and only girl. The young lady, knowing about Kathy, understood that his lack of pursuit was not intended as a rejection and perhaps really didn't expect him to reciprocate her flirtatious passes.

The four of them chatted easily together, talking about people they knew, school, the weather. The weather had finally changed; a soaking, healing rain had come at the beginning of the week, bringing life back to the land and people. Things were green and growing again and the people felt more vitality. It had rained for two days.

The heavy thunderstorms had marched across the land like a liberating army with booming cannons that seemed to crack the heavens. Spectacular displays of lightning had stabbed savagely at trees, farmhouses, and barns as the rain came down in sheets. The dying vegetation drank greedily and lifted once-drooping heads in triumphant splendor.

Jay-boy had not failed to notice the bright optimism that had come back into his father's face and the mirth that had returned to his laugh. Everyone seemed reinvigorated and energetic and ready to smile or laugh at the slightest provocation. Jay-boy and Bowknot had put in two days that week, Thursday and Friday, helping Mr. Green with his tobacco. It was their first chance of the summer to work for pay, and they had been overjoyed. The fourteen dollars apiece that they had earned was now burning in their pockets and they itched to spend it. Their little group sat and engaged in small talk until the shadows of the office furniture store across the street had grown long in the afternoon sunlight.

Chapter 17

Jay-boy and Bowknot sauntered up to the pool room and peered through the glass door to see who was inside. Jay-boy turned to his cousin and said, "You can go on in. I'm going over to the grocery store to see how much longer Mom is going to be."

Bowknot nodded and entered the building. Looking around at the twelve or so tables, he noted that everyone seemed to have a game in progress. They're pretty busy in here today, he thought, making a mental estimation that there were about twenty-five or thirty patrons. He edged his way over to the snack counter and a tall, husky man smiled politely. "Can I help you there, young man?"

"Yes, I'd like a Pepsi, please."

While the man was at the long cooler behind the counter, Bowknot turned his head slightly and looked over his shoulder, his eyes moving slowly through the crowd. The man returned, saying "Here you go." He set the bottle down in front of Bowknot, then punched fifteen cents on the cash register. Bowknot paid him and retreated to a wall from which he could watch a game that looked interesting. He leaned back and sipped his bottle of soda. A short, stocky, dark-skinned boy with a baseball cap turned backwards on his head was deftly handling the pool stick, strutting around the table cockily, bending and posturing unabashedly. He was obviously aware that he was being watched, not only by Bowknot, but by several other boys standing quietly along the opposite wall. He sunk the final ball with a flourish, and flashed a gloating smile. His opponent, a tall, lanky boy with yam-colored skin and large, expressive brown eyes, threw up his hands in mock exasperation. "Man, that's all of my money you gonna get today!"

"Oh, come on, now, Peter Rabbit," the stocky boy began plaintively, "I thought you wanted to shoot some pool."

"Yeah, I did," the other boy replied, "but I ain't gonna stay here and let you beat me out of all my money."

"Man, that's why they call you Peter Rabbit," the other boy scoffed. "You always ready to run. Man, don't you know that scared money don't win?"

"Hey, man," the tall boy cut him off before he could continue, "I'd rather be scared and have some money in my pocket than be brave and broke." He patted his pocket and grinned, then turned and started toward the snack bar.

"Chicken!" the stocky boy called scornfully after him. "You chicken-hearted sucker." Realizing that his taunts were having no effect on his former opponent, he frowned and scanned the faces of Bowknot and the other boys who had been watching, obviously hungry to get someone else's money. "Any of you-all game to play me?" His words sounded more like a threatening challenge than a cordial invitation, which rankled Bowknot to the core. In a heartbeat's time, he stepped away from the wall, speaking as he advanced.

"Yes, I'd like to play you."

The boy eyed him suspiciously for a moment, taken aback at the swiftness of his response. The other boys unconsciously edged forward, their eyes wide and curious. The terse sound of his citified speech alerted them to the fact that he was not from around there, and his boldness in challenging one of the best pool-players in Emporia riveted their attention.

"All right, Beebop," a tall, dark-skinned boy wearing glasses spoke up, "there's your man.

Beebop looked around at the on-looker who had spoken and smiled widely, then winked, as if to say, "This guy obviously don't know who I am and now I'm gonna make the sucker pay for opening his big mouth." "Well, now," Beebop said, turning his attention to Bowknot, "let's rack them up and get down to business, shall we?"

"How much do you want to play for?" Bowknot asked, meeting his eyes levelly.

"Fifty cents a game."

"Is that all?" Bowknot spoke scornfully, deliberately goading him.

Beebop's face flushed and he stopped racking the balls to stare at Bowknot. "I thought I'd do you a favor by playing just fifty cents a game. That way, you wouldn't get broke so fast and I'd have the privilege of playing you a little longer." The sneer in his voice was evident.

Bowknot laughed in spite of himself. Show-off or not, the boy certainly had flair. The other boys laughed, too, but quickly cut it off lest they antagonize Beebop. Flattered with himself, Beebop decided to press the matter. He picked up his stick and looked up at Bowknot, who stood about six or eight inches taller than he. "Well," he drawled, "what about a dollar a game?"

The onlookers drew in a collective surprised breath. Bowknot simply smiled and said calmly, "How about two dollars a game?"

Beebop stared at him a moment as though to gauge his sanity, then broke into a low chuckle, his eyes glinting with confidence. Then he said sarcastically, "Well, my man, it's your money and if you just bound and determined to lose it, I might as well be the recipient of your charity. So, let's go on and raise it to three dollars a game."

Bowknot cleared his throat and reached down for a pool stick. He inspected it carefully for a moment, then looked straight at Beebop and laughed. "Look here, man, why don't we just can this penny-ante shit and raise the stakes to five dollars a game and get the show on the road?"

Beebop's mouth dropped open, rendering him temporarily

speechless. The other boys stood barely breathing, straining not to miss Beebop's answer. It took Beebop a full minute to recover from the shock of such audacity, but he finally mustered a sardonic smile. "Five dollars it is, then."

"Man," one of the boys burst out, "that's a lot of dough!"

Two more boys had come over; one of the original group turned to them and said, "Man, they're shooting for five bucks a game!"

"What?!" came the disbelieving response.

"Yeah, five bills a game!" the first boy reiterated, gesturing toward Bowknot and Beebop.

The game was on. Bowknot and Beebop placed their money on the edge of the pool table and Beebop positioned himself to take the first shot. All eyes were riveted on his every movement. The deftness with which he handled the stick, his steady hand, the interesting angles he employed to sink the balls, the ease with which he moved all showed he was definitely no stranger to billiards. But Bowknot knew that Beebop's undoing could be the fact that he was playing to the audience. In his attempts to amuse and impress the by-standers, Bowknot knew that he would take risks and that the risks he would take would doubtlessly increase as the size of the audience increased. He had seen the phenomenon countless times back in Detroit. Fairly good pool- players lost their shirts because they allowed themselves to become intoxicated by spectator praise and to overrate their own ability. Yes, this guy was pretty good, Bowknot thought, observing him bouncing around arrogantly, brimming with the unfounded confidence that a drunk man has in his ability to drive an automobile safely. But Bowknot knew that he was better. He would not brag or boast about it, he would just calmly show this loudmouth pretender who was best.

When Bowknot's turn came, he lifted his pool stick and quietly went to work. Beebop glared at him for a moment, then sneered disdainfully. "Man, you're gonna have to do a hell of a lot better than that-there to beat Beebop."

The other boys laughed, and Bowknot's stomach muscles tightened; he struggled to remain calm and to concentrate on his game. Back in Detroit, he had met an old ex-prize-fighter sitting on a park bench, sucking at a bottle of cheap wine. Relishing the fact that he once again had an audience, that someone was interested in what he had to say, the old man had shared some hard-won words of wisdom with Bowknot and three friends. "You know, boys," he had said, glancing around the circle of faces, "nine times out of ten, it ain't a question of not being prepared to fight that makes a guy lose." He paused and scratched his grizzled, gray beard. "The reason why most people lose is because they lose their concentration. Then they forget everything they've ever learned about the proper way to box, so they resort to street fighting—and a street-fighter ain't got a snowball's chance in hell of beating a real boxer." The old codger straightened his furrowed brow, his eyes narrowing with the effort of reasoning. "You see, fellows, when a man gets mad, he gets emotional, and when you get all emotional, you lose your ability to reason, to think clearly." He gestured with a finger pointing at his head, smiling faintly as he took another long gulp of his cheap wine. He chuckled, then sighed heavily."This helps my heart." Noticing that the boys' attention was still riveted on him, he hurried on so as not to lose ground. "As I was saying, the difference between a real professional fighter and a pretender is the ability to concentrate, and when you can concentrate, you can execute your strategy. Now, I knows what I'm talkin' about," he added, "because it helped me win thirty-nine bouts and that ain't half-bad for a poor boy from North Carolina."

Bowknot and his friends had been intrigued with the old man, and they were awed at the stories he told of his boxing days. Bowknot's admiration for him grew immeasurably when he learned from his father that the old guy had indeed been an outstanding fighter in his day. Bowknot had even gone to the public library and found old clippings about him and proudly showed them to his friends, who, like Bowknot, had at first thought the old devil was just making up stories to get attention. They had only hung around that first time because it was enjoyable to listen to him; he told the stories with such vividness and passion that it had seemed as though they were living every detail themselves. But, after that, whenever the boys found themselves with not much to do, they would seek out the old man. Hearing his stories had the result of arousing Bowknot's interest in the sport of boxing. He joined the boys' club and begged his father to buy him some boxing gloves. He had had a pretty good boxing instructor at the boys' club, but the instructor couldn't hold a candle to the old wino, who spent many afternoons giving Bowknot lessons in the park. The old man had told him he had what it took to be a champion and all he had to do was to want it bad enough to quit running around with his gang and dedicate himself to the sport. Bowknot had never taken this advice to heart—hell, he was having too much fun hanging out with the fellows—and when the old man challenged him one day to piss or get off the pot, he stopped going around him. He knew that the old warrior knew that he did not want it bad enough. About a year later, Bowknot read in the paper that his old friend had been found in an unheated apartment in the dead of winter, frozen to death. His heart had sunk and the sense of loss that had swept over him had filled him with regret as scalding tears flowed down his face.

Suddenly, his mind snapped back to the present and his eyes moved around the table. The word had raced like wildfire through the pool room that he and Beebop were playing for five dollars a game, and a large crowd had gathered. Even the tall, husky man who had waited on him at the shack bar had come over and was watching the game. Bowknot's eyes went back to Beebop. He watched him gesturing elaborately with the stick, grunting loudly now and then, whistling and shifting his gaze back and forth between the pool table and the on-lookers, winking and smiling confidently as if he had matters under control.

Bowknot just watched in silence. He had intentionally missed shots that he could make with ease, just to make Beebop think that he had himself a real sucker. Now they were down to the last ball and it was Beebop's shot. "All right, city man, get ready to get in your pocket and pay me!" He smiled broadly, then laughed. "Corner pocket," he declared. He leaned over, aimed, straightened for a moment, then aimed again. He shot—and missed. A murmur went up from the crowd. Trying not to appear shaken, Beebop stepped back, tapped his stick on the floor, and said nonchalantly, "Well, city boy, let's see what you can do with it."

Bowknot calmly leaned over the table and gestured with his stick. "Side pocket," he said, then sank the ball. A heavy, tension-releasing sigh went through the crowd of on-lookers, then exclamations of grudging admiration. "Wow! That was a hell of a shot!" "That man is for real!" The tall husky man boomed heartily, "You better watch out, Beebop! That man might have your number!"

Beebop waved him off and said, "Oh, he was just lucky. It was about time; he was due for some luck, anyway." He jammed his hand into his pocket and pulled out another five-dollar bill. Laying it on the table, he said tersely, "Rack 'em up."

Bowknot racked the balls and they started the next game. Again, he employed the same strategy, missing easy shots and shying totally away from those that looked difficult. Now, it was Beebop's turn. He want to work, his face now serious, his eyes narrowed, and his aim deadly accurate. One by one, the balls sank, and it seemed like an interminably long time before he finally missed. He straightened up and smiled with great self-satisfaction, as echoes of praise fell over him like soft raindrops sifting down through the leaves of a tree. Bowknot sighed heavily, glanced around for a moment, then went to work. He continued to play poorly, though not so poorly as to make it obvious. He missed, swore softly under his breath, and straightened slowly.

Beebop beamed confidently. "Don't worry, my man. The only thing you got to lose is your money." Then he moved in and pointed, "Corner pocket." He sank the ball, then another and another, then missed.

Bowknot leaned forward calmly, saying softly, "Side pocket." He sank the ball. He sank another, then straightened and looked around at the crowd a moment. Then he said, "Corner pocket," leaned forward, aimed, and sank the ball.

"Damn," Beebop gasped disgustedly as he watched Bowknot pick up the money.

"Are you still game?" Bowknot asked in an almost timid voice.

"Hell, yeah!" Beebop retorted.

A voice called out from the crowd. "Hey, Beebop!" Beebop looked around into the eyes of a short, barrel-chested, copper-colored boy, holding a bottle of soda in his hand. "Just do like old nappy chin—keep on betting, you bound to win!" The crowd exploded with a volley of rocking laughter, as Beebop rolled his eyes in disgust. "Rack 'em up," he said irritatedly.

Bowknot obliged him and the game was under way. Bowknot watched Beebop's face as he moved around the table, calling out the shots and sinking the balls with the precision one might use to cut precious stones. His face was placid as a stone; all the emotion had drained out of it and Bowknot knew that Beebop had his head in the game now, possibly for the first time. He had lost ten dollars and stood to lose five more; this realization made him shed the persona of the swaggering showboat and get down to playing some heads-up pool. Yes, he was good, real good, but Bowknot still knew that he was better. It was time to push aside all pretenses and play the game.

When Beebop finally missed, the crowd heaved a collective sigh of admiration for his skill. Bowknot said nothing, but leaned over the table and quietly called out his shots. The balls disappeared one after the other until the last one fell. Beebop's lips parted. He started to speak, but thought better of it. Instead, he just stared for a long moment at Bowknot. The crowd, too, was silent, more stunned than amused. Beebop's face told the story. He realized that he had been the sucker all along: his opponent was a superb billiards player and could no doubt beat him all night.

Bowknot looked at him and slowly picked up the money. "Are you still game?"

Though Bowknot's tone was not threatening in the least, his words smote Beebop like a blow. Through clenched teeth, he hissed, "Yeah, man, I'm still game. You see, man, money don't make me—I make money!" He reached down and started to rack the balls. Suddenly, a voice called out from behind him, "Beebop, you'd better quit while you're ahead. Cause if you get broke, you might as well go on home to your folks." A subdued snicker coursed through the crowd. Beebop acted as though he had not heard a thing; he reached into his pocket and pulled out another five. Laying it on the edge of the table, he said grimly, "Let's go."

Bowknot glanced at him and saw in his eyes a glint of challenge tinged with admiration, an admiration that one who is skilled in a thing has for another who is just as skilled. The look was an affirmation and appreciation of Bowknot's ability, a look of respect that could only be born of having been defeated. Bowknot nodded his agreement that he was ready to begin.

Both men put on a superb exhibition of billiards that left the on-lookers gaping in awe and wonderment; however, Bowknot came out the winner.

Beebop smiled in almost open admiration now. He was clearly impressed with Bowknot's ability, but still unwilling to concede that Bowknot was the better player. "Man," he sighed, "it would be worth risking five more dollars to play you just one more time. I still think I can take you." The spectators gasped in disbelief. "Rack 'em up and let's do it one more time, city man." His whole tone had changed from one of scorn and contempt to one of respect and near reverence.

Again, they dazzled their audience with phenomenal shots. Their concentration, their strategies, the adroitness with which they made difficult shots look easy, stunned and delighted the crowd. They played with the kind of grace and finesse that couldn't help but exact a tribute of mutual respect for each other. Their spell-binding exhibition rendered the crowd mute and transfixed with admiration and awe at what they were seeing.

Beebop was superb, but Bowknot was brilliant and, just as he had done four times before, came out the winner. As Bowknot sank the last ball, he straightened and found himself staring into Beebop's smiling eyes. He felt himself smiling back. Beebop laughed softly and moved around the table toward Bowknot, thrusting out his hand. Bowknot extended his hand and grasped that of the other man. "Man," Beebop chuckled, "you are one hell of a pool-player!"

Bowknot flushed and smiled shyly. "You ain't so bad yourself."

"Well," Beebop shrugged, "I think I've had enough for one day, but I still want to try you again."

"I'll be around."

"Where you from anyway, man?"

"Oh, I'm from Detroit. I'm out here for the summer, so I'll be around for a while." Their conversation was now so cordial that Bowknot began to feel uncomfortable that he had won twenty-five dollars from Beebop. Beneath his facade of arrogance, he was actually a pretty nice guy, and a good sport, too. Bowknot strangely wished that Beebop had beaten him at least once.

Suddenly, Bowknot became aware of the large crowd that had gathered to watch. He and Beebop had become the center of attention and most of the other pool tables had been abandoned. He looked around and smiled into the eyes beaming back at him in silent admiration. Then someone said, "Man, you just beat the second-best pool-player in this town!" "Yeah," another voice sang out, "damn if you ain't something else with a pool stick!" Bowknot flushed, embarrassed and uncomfortable under the weight of the admiring stares. "Man," someone in the crowd called out, "I'd sure like to see him and ol' Fat Daddy get together. I bet that would be something to see!" "Yeah," another voice said, "Fat Daddy thinks he's so hot. I bet this man can put him in his place." "Yeah," another voice piped up, "I wonder where he is right now. Any other time, he'd be up in here show-ing off and taking folks' money, talking stuff."

Bowknot kept glancing around the circle of faces, shifting his weight from one foot to the other nervously. He liked praise, but somehow this time, it made him uncomfortable. This boy who he had just relieved of twenty-five dollars—which was probably all he had—wasn;t the arrogant bastard that Bowknot had thought he was. He was a nice fellow and a damn good pool-player, certainly a worthy and formidable opponent. These facts gnawed at him and made him flush with something akin to shame. Somehow he felt that the on-lookers gloated in Beebop's defeat, that they had not really understood or appreci-ated his skill or talent. He had heard about this "Fat Daddy" and, if he was better than Beebop, Bowknot wasn't sure that he wanted any part of him. As he was thinking these thoughts, his eyes still roving over the crowd, much to his relief he spotted Jay-boy. When their eyes met, Jay-boy smiled warmly and winked. Bowknot jerked his head toward the door, indicating that Jay-boy should meet him outside, then turned and moved off.

"Take care, boss, " Beebop called after him, "I'll be seeing you again."

"All right," Bowknot tossed over his shoulder, "nice game."

He threaded his way through the crowd to the door. He hadn't realized how crowded the room had gotten since he had arrived. As he passed, people were whispering and pointing toward him excitedly. "Man, that guy can sure handle a pool stick. He beat old Beebop five times—for five dollars a game, too!" "Say what!" "Yes, he did! He took Beebop back to pool school!" The first voice laughed. "Man," another voice said heartily, that-there guy is a mess, I suggest!" A spattering of laughter rippled through the crowd. When Bowknot emerged from the pool room, he drew in a long, deep breath of fresh air. He filled his lungs and exhaled slowly, savoring the feeling. He was reinvigorated suddenly and now, outside and away from the gawking stares, a strange wave of exhilaration swept over him, animating the smile he flashed at people passing by him on the street.

Jay-boy came up beside him, touching him lightly on the arm. He turned in response to the touch and was met by Jay-boy's smiling face, beaming with admiration and pride. "Man, I didn't know you could shoot pool like that! Old Beebop is one of the best pool-players in this whole county! Man, you really took him to school in there; where did you learn to play like that?"

"Oh," Bowknot shrugged, reveling in his cousin's admiration, "a friend's daddy was a pool shark. He told me that his old man had supported their family with nothing but his pool stick for about a year once when he was out of a job. He claims that they lived high on the hog, too! Anyway, they had a pool table in their basement and my friend, Roscoe, had been shooting pool since he was about seven years old. His old man had taught him all the tricks, and I learned from him.

Jay-boy chuckled in appreciation of the story, then sobered and said, "We'd better get going. Mom and Dad are waiting for us." They started down the street.

"Man," Bowknot picked up his story, "you would have had to see this guy play one time, then you would believe and know that I'm for real! Man, Roscoe's dad was like a demon with a pool stick. He could bank shots and play angles that you couldn't dream of!" He paused for a moment, overwhelmed by his vivid recollections, then exclaimed again, "You would just have to see this guy to believe him! And old Roscoe was just as good. He would just smile when the fellas got to praising him too much, and say that his dad taught him everything he knew. Man, guys would beg Roscoe to teach them how to play, but he wouldn't, jack, not unless he really liked them. I was real tight with him, so he taught me. Old Roscoe would grin and say, 'Man, I'm gonna show you how to keep some money in your pocket.' We spend many a day in his basement shooting pool and it took me about four years before I got to the point where I could beat him every now and then. I remember the first time I beat Roscoe, too. Man, I was so happy! Old Roscoe looked shocked, then he walked over to me and said, 'Man, that was pure skill you beat me with, not luck. You're damn good now; you shouldn't have to go hungry a day in your life, not as long as you can find a sucker ready to play you.' I beat him a few times after that, too, and one day he looked at me and said, 'Shucks, man, I done taught you too well. You're almost as good as me! But hey, you remember now, I taught you everything that you know—I didn't teach you everything that I know!'"

Jay-boy and Bowknot were laughing heartily as they turned the corner of the drug store and saw the car parked in the shade of a large, old oak whose limbs and leaves stretched out over a corner of the parking lot. "Yeah," Bowknot continued, "that Roscoe Bryant is something else. I reckon he's the most talented guy I've ever seen. Man, that guy can dance better than anybody—he's always the first to learn the new dances and then he would show me. Oh, the boy can cut a rug, and all the girls just fall all over themselves to dance with him. He can sing, too. I mean, he can croon like Sam Cooke! He is good in everything he does. I think he's a genius myself, because I've never before seen anybody good in everything they do. He's a good boxer and he's smart as a whip in his school work. I used to tell him all the time, he's gonna be famous one of these days. He would just laugh and say, 'Well, my man, I hope so, I really hope so."

"Bow," Jay-boy said in a serious tone, "they said that you-all were playing back there for five dollars a game."

"Yeah, that's right," Bowknot said calmly.

"Man, what if you had lost? That guy could have cleaned you out."

"Yeah, I know," Bowknot chuckled. "But I knew that I was better than him."

"You couldn't have known that for sure and, besides, you didn't know that he was one of the best pool-players in town."

"That's true," Bowknot said matter-of-factly, "but I stood back and watched him play for almost an hour and I felt that I was better. I was content just to watch until he started showing off on some guy he had almost cleaned out because the guy wanted to quit. He challenged everybody, and I thought I was good enough to take him down a peg or two."

"Man," Jay-boy said with relief, "I'm just glad you weren't wrong."

Chapter 18

The two boys strolled toward the car, skirting the edge of the parking lot and sauntering along in front of the many rows of parked cars. As they came near, they saw a short, round woman with gray-streaked hair and a suitcase of a purse leaning into the car window, talking animatedly to Jay-boy's mother. Noticing their approach, she turned and smiled up at them. "How you young men doing?" "Fine," Jay-boy replied, nodding politely. Bowknot did the same, then moved around to the other side of the car. As he was opening the back door, Jay-boy noticed that she was still staring at him; he slid into the seat, his face flushed with embarrassment. His mother's friend cackled, "I declare! He is the spitting image of his daddy!"

His mother laughed softly and agreed, "Yeah, I reckon he is, ain't he?"

Jay-boy glanced over at his father, who was standing on the opposite side of the car talking to a tall, very dark-skinned man with a receding hairline and a huge pot-belly. Mr. George Jackson, one of his dad's oldest and closest friends, wore wire-framed bifocals and smiled a lot, sporting a mouth full of tobacco-stained teeth. Mr. Jackson owned a large farm about fifteen miles down the road from them. He had been quite prosperous over the years; his was one of the largest Negro-owned farms in the whole county. He was always one of the first to get a new tractor or a new type of farm implement, which made some of the white farmers label him as uppity, but all of the black farmers admired and respected him, including Jay-boy's dad. Their collective lofty opinion of him was born out of the fact that they admired his stature as a man as well as his ability as a farmer. He was always willing to loan his equipment and to help people in whatever way he could—and he would flatly refuse to accept payment for his help in money or in kind. He would just shrug his shoulders and say, "If I let you pay me for it, I don't feel like I've helped or really done you any favor." He turned now and spat a brown stream of liquid into the grass, wiped his mouth, and smiled wryly.

"You know," his brow clouded thoughtfully, "if it hadn't been for the rain, we all would have been in some kind of a hurt."

"Yeah," Jimbo said, pausing to take a long draw from his cigarette and releasing the smoke slowly. "Man, I was more than a little bit worried, too. I had gone into debt to get me some more land, I had bought two new plows, and you know I had just got them new mules." He inhaled deeply on his cigarette, then let the smoke escape in a long, luxurious exhalation, as if he thoroughly enjoyed the sensation. "Man, it looked like I was going belly-button deep in the hole this year. The crops looked like they was gone," he raised his voice to emphasize his point, "burning up in the field."

"Yeah," Mr. Jackson said, looking pensive. "Man, all I could do was walk the floor and pray. Sometimes my wife would get after me, you know, because I sat up so late at night. She'd say, 'George, why don't you come to bed? You gonna worry yourself to death and there ain't a thing you can do about this-here weather.' I know she was right, but man, even when I'd lay down, I still couldn't sleep. I would just toss and turn all night long and keep her awake."

Jimbo smiled, nodding his affirmation. "Yeah, George, I know exactly what you mean. I was the same way. Man, I couldn't eat nothing much, I couldn't sleep, my mind was just so troubled I didn't know what to do. I would try my best not to let my wife know how worried I really was. So, man, I'd ease out of the bed at night while she was asleep and just pace the floor till almost daylight, a-many a night. He leaned down and knocked the ashes from his cigarette against the car's front tire. Then when morning would come, I'd get up, feed up, and then go out and walk over the fields, looking at my crops dying right before my eyes." He took a final drag from the dwindling cigarette, then exhaled with a sigh. "Man, I tell you, I felt like something was drawing the life right out of me, too."

"You ain't kiddin' a bit!" Jackson broke in fervently. "I know just how you felt, cause I felt the same way. Look like your stomach just tie itself up in knots and you just feel sick and weak."

"Yeah," Jimbo agreed, "that's just the way I felt. But they say the good Lord never puts more on us than we can stand."

Jackson flashed his brown-stained teeth in an animated smile and unconsciously massaged his bald pate as he warmed to the subject. "Yeah, they say that He may not come when you want Him, but He's always right on time. He sure 'nuff was on time this time!" He clapped his hands and laughed triumphantly. "Man, that rain saved us!"

"Yeah," Jimbo answered, "it sure did, so I reckon somebody's prayers got through. That rain just seemed to make everything come back to life. Who in the world would have thought two weeks ago that the crops would be looking like they do now?"

"Nobody!" Jackson boomed, slapping his thigh. "But the Man Upstairs got everything under control and I guess it takes something like this every now and then to remind us of that. We can only do but so much, but He can do it all!" "Yeah," Jimbo chimed in, "and I certainly thank Him for it, too!" He glanced around and noticed that everyone was sitting quietly, waiting for him. "Well, I reckon they're ready to go now, so I reckon I'll be seeing you, George." He reached out and clapped the older man's hand and smiled warmly into his eyes.

George Jackson smiled back. "You-all take care, now, Jimbo." Releasing Jimbo's hand, he stepped forward and leaned into the car window. "You-all take care, now, and have a good evening, you hear?" He straightened and said, "I'll be seeing you, now."

He patted Jimbo on the shoulder affectionately and ambled off, threading his way through the parked cars.

Jimbo slid under the steering wheel of his car and started the engine. He eased the car backwards a few feet, then drove forward down the aisle created by cars parked on either side of him until he reached the edge of the lot, then turned out onto the street.

As they moved east along Maple Street, Jay-boy noticed that the sun had sunk precariously low and was hanging just above the tops of the buildings along Main Street. As his father turned south on Main Street, he could see the crimson reflection of the sun's dying rays bouncing off the windows in the stores and shops along the street. There were still quite a few people milling about, carrying boxes and bags of every description, bustling in and out of stores in a frenzy of activity, trying to take advantage of the last few moments of shopping before the stores closed for the day. Pulling up to a traffic light near the edge of town, Jimbo patted his shirt pocket and a look of mild panic swept across his face. "Doggone it, I forgot to get me a carton of cigarettes and I don't have a one!"

"I thought you picked some up in the grocery store," his wife said, glancing at him.

"Yeah, I said I was gonna get some, but then I got to talking with Sam Dixon, standing there running my mouth and forgot all about it. Well, at least I thought about it before we got way out of town. I'll just stop down at Boxdale's and pick me up some."

The traffic light changed and the car lurched forward, moving smoothly in the flow of traffic. A few moments later, Jimbo turned off of the main street and pulled into the parking lot of a red-brick building. Bowknot lifted his eyes to the blue-and-white sign above the the door that read, "Boxdale's Grocery." The building sat at the corner of Main and Baker streets. There was an abandoned gas station directly across the street and a large warehouse stood diagonally across the intersection from the store. Boxdale's was flanked on its immediate left by another large warehouse and, across Baker Street on the right side of the store was a large, metal-colored building whose sign proclaimed it to be "Jones' Hardware." Bowknot's eyes took in the scene and his brain processed every detail, filing the information in his memory. His mind came alive with possibilities. He noticed that everything around the store was closed and that there were a number of trucks of all sizes and descriptions parked in the lots of both warehouses, sitting in straight lines along the fronts of the huge, ashen-colored buildings.

"Here, son." Jimbo looked over his shoulder and handed a ten-dollar bill to Jay-boy. "Go in there and get me a carton of Lucky Strikes, please." Jay-boy took the money, opened the door, and stepped out of the car. Bowknot wheeled in his seat and murmured, "I'm going in, too. I want some gum." He hurried to catch up with his cousin, who was now almost at the door.

Jay-boy glanced behind him when he heard Bowknot's footsteps, then stopped to wait for him. He opened the heavy, metal door and they entered the store.

Hearing the door open, Boxdale looked up from what appeared to be a ledger of some kind. Drumming his pen on the counter, he asked, "Can I help you boys?" He watched them through bifocals set low on his nose and straightened as they approached.

Jay-boy's eyes had been busy scanning the shelves near the counter, looking for the cigarettes. Suddenly, he snapped to attention when Boxdale's voice sang out again. "I said, can I help you-all." This time, his words sounded cold, almost angry. Jay-boy's eyes flickered to Boxdale's face, which was rapidly turning red, and followed Boxdale's eyes to Bowknot, who was returning the man's hard stare. "I'm gettin' ready to close the store," Boxdale hissed through clamped teeth, never taking his eyes from Bowknot's face. "So whatever you want, put it on the counter." His eyes narrowed and his voice trembled with emotion.

Jay-boy felt the hair at the base of his skull begin to quiver and the blood began to pound in his temples. Quickly, he moved closer to the counter and, clearing his throat, which had become surprisingly dry, he stammered, "Yes, sir. I would like to have a carton of Lucky Strike cigarettes, please."

At first, the old, stoop-shouldered man stood stone-still, as if he hadn't heard a word Jay-boy had said; his gaze remained locked on Bowknot, his face beet red and full of agitation. Then slowly he turned and moved back toward the counter. Jay-boy shot a sidelong glance at his cousin, who was still staring fixedly at Boxdale, his face screwed up in a disgusted scowl. The tension was almost tangible; it had filled the place and was now weighing heavily on Jay-boy.

"That will be three dollars and fifteen cents," Boxdale spoke unexpectedly, pecking at the cash register as he rang up the sale. Jay-boy thrust the ten-dollar bill at him hurriedly. He wanted to get out of that place, and damn quick. He didn't want to get into an altercation with the old bastard who could, if he chose to, make serious trouble for them. Tom Boxdale was a pillar of the white community, and his grocery store had become an institution in the town. He had been some kind of a hero in the war and was a big wheel in the local V. F. W. He had inherited the store from his father, David Boxdale, who had died right after the war. Boxdale had taken over the business and expanded the store. The talk was that, at first, he had been pretty nice and would even let colored folks have credit, but that had changed pretty quickly. Rumor had it that he and old Charley Thomas had gotten into an argument about the amount of Thomas's bill. Thomas maintained that Boxdale was wrong about the amount Thomas owed and Boxdale, of course, said Thomas was wrong, the result being that Thomas refused to pay more than he thought he owed, vowing that he would never let anyone cheat him. Right after that, Boxdale had put up a sign in the store that read "NO MORE CREDIT." Mrs. Ruth said the sign only applied to the colored folks, because he still gave the white folks credit; she claimed she was in the store one day when he had done so. Then old man Taylor said the same thing. The word got around and, for a while, a lot of colored people had stopped shopping there—though they eventually drifted back. Still, a lot of folks had said that he really didn't care for colored folks. He had a way of watching and peeping at every move you made, like you were going to steal something. And he would never take your money directly from your hand, he would just motion for you to lay it on the counter. And he would invariably throw your change down on the counter; no matter how many times you reached for it, he would never give it back in your hand.

As these thoughts flashed through Jay-boy's mind, a tight ball of smoldering rage began to form in the pit of his stomach, rising into his chest and then his throat, where it lodged and made him feel as if he were choking. Slowly picking up his change from the hardwood surface, he lifted his eyes, glaring at Boxdale with contempt, not attempting to hide his disgust.

Boxdale was looking past him at his cousin. "Do you want something?" he asked, his voice edged with irritation.

"Yeah, this," Bowknot replied, in an ice-cold tone. Bowknot slammed two packs of gum onto the counter, which made a sharp, slapping sound that startled Boxdale. He flinched, averting his gaze to the gum to avoid looking at Bowknot. Bowknot threw exact change on the counter, turned, and headed for the door without another word. Jay-boy followed him.

When they emerged from the store, Jay-boy confronted his cousin. "Man, what in the hell was you trying to prove in there?"

Bowknot's eyes fell and he looked perplexed. "What do you mean?"

"This is what I mean!" Jay-boy screwed up his face and stuck it in Bowknot's face. "That is what I mean!"

Bowknot opened his mouth to speak, but Jay-boy cut him off. "Man, you ain't in Detroit no more! This is Emporia, Virginia, the south, Klan-land U. S. A.! You're getting ready to get in more trouble than you can handle and I'm gonna tell you right now, you'd better cut that shit short, son! We have to put with enough shit from these white folks around here now without you causing more trouble and, besides, I still got to live here after you're gone!" Jay-boy calmed down when he stopped his tirade to regain his breath. He sighed heavily, then frowned. "You ain't been in the city all your life. You know how it is around here."

Bowknot nodded, then reached out and patted Jay-boy on the arm, saying apologetically, "Yeah, man, I know. I'm sorry about that, but that son of a bitch just pissed me off to the damn core! He acted like we were bothering him or something. Hell, I started not to get a damn thing." Bowknot's voice was now quivering with passion. "Son of a bitch take your money and treat you like shit."

Jay-boy placed an arm around his shoulder and said comfortingly, "Let it go, man. I guess you being away from around here and all, you kinda forget about that kind of shit. It's hard to take it any time, but especially when you ain't used to seeing it all around you."

Moving off toward the car, Jay-boy glanced again at his cousin, but Bowknot was looking straight ahead. Jay-boy felt hot shame streak over him for chiding his cousin. For what, for frowning back at a son of a bitch who had frowned at him? For being indignant in the face of indignation? For being hostile toward hostility? He climbed into the car and struggled valiantly to control an impulse to scream and release the tension that compressed his chest like an over-inflated tire.

As Jimbo drove back out toward the main street, Bowknot's eyes surveyed the scene again, with a queer interest growing somewhere deep in his brain. It was now about quarter after six, and the man had been getting ready to close the store when they'd entered around six o'clock. He noted reflectively that the other businesses on the street were already closed. He smiled to himself, as if only he were privy to some private joke.

Chapter 19

It was about eight-fifteen that evening when Jay-boy turned the car into Linda's driveway. Bowknot smiled animatedly, still bobbing his head to Sam Cooke's "Let the Good Times Roll," blaring from the car radio. Glancing over at his cousin, Jay-boy asked for the third time, "You sure you-all don't want to go with us to the shack?"

Bowknot looked at him, still bobbing his head to the music and smiling broadly. "Well," he said, "let me go in and see what she wants to do."

"All right," Jay-boy replied, turning off the engine.

Bowknot climbed out and sauntered toward the door. He stopped and pulled a small piece of paper from his pants pocket and checked it to make sure he had the right house. "Yes," he sighed, "1123 Halifax Street; this is it." He continued toward the house. It was a small, single-family, white frame house with a cement porch running length-wise across the front. The lawn was small and neatly manicured. In fact, all the houses on the street, as far as he could see both ways, looked similar to hers. A wave of nostalgia washed over him; the street—frame houses, nice lawns, neatly trimmed hedges—reminded him of Detroit, of home. He shook off the feeling and stepped up onto the porch. He started to knock, but spotted the doorbell and rang it, instead. After a few moments, the door opened and a tall, slender, middle-aged man appeared, holding a cigar in one hand. Bowknot smiled into the man's dark eyes and asked politely, "Is Linda home?"

The man smiled back and spoke congenially, "Yes, she is.

Come on in and have a seat while I get her. I'm Linda's dad, Horace Howard." He extended his hand to Bowknot.

"My name is Kevin Woods, but everybody calls me Bowknot," Bowknot said, shaking the man's hand.

Mr. Howard chuckled softly and gestured to a large, overstuffed chair. Bowknot nodded and moved over to the chair and eased himself into it.

"Let me go up and tell her you're here." Mr. Howard paused, glancing around at Bowknot. "Oh, can I get you something cold to drink, young man?"

"No, no thanks," Bowknot said quickly. "That's all right; I'm fine."

"Okay," Mr. Howard said. He disappeared up the stairs.

Bowknot's eyes moved around the room and he deduced right away that the family must be pretty well off. The large, carpeted room was decked out with what looked like fairly expensive furniture. There was a huge, exquisitely plush couch along one wall, flanked on either end by two stout mahogany end tables sporting large ceramic lamps with satin shades. Then, there was a large, floor-model television in one corner, adorned with a large glass bowl filled with artificial fruit. There was also a long mahogany coffee table in front of the couch, graced by two high-stepping golden ceramic horses pulling a brass cart laden with artificial fruit. The sight made Bowknot chuckle softly to himself. Then he noted the two other overstuffed chairs across from him and the expensive-looking record player sitting on a shiny wooden table between them. He smiled with self-satisfaction and drummed his fingers softly on the arm of the chair. "I sure hope we can become real good friends," he smiled to himself, "yes-sirree buddy!"

Presently, Mr. Howard reappeared. "Linda said she'll be right down," he said, smiling at Bowknot.

"Okay," Bowknot nodded, still smiling but trying not to appear too obsequious.

Mr. Howard walked over and clicked on the television, then

took a seat on the couch. He leaned forward and flicked the ashes from his cigar in an ashtray on the edge of the end table, then settled back on the couch. He puffed gently on the cigar, exhaling blue smoke. Clearing his throat, he glanced over at Bowknot. "Linda tells me that you're from Detroit."

"Yes, sir," Bowknot replied, "I'm out her staying with my Uncle Jimbo and them for the summer."

The man's eyes brightened and a broad smile moved over his face. "Shucks, I know your people," he chuckled. "I've been knowing Jimbo for years. Me and him was in the service together. I know his wife, too. How are they doing?"

Bowknot smiled delightedly, his tensed muscles relaxing as he settled down into the comfortable chair. "Oh, they're doing all right."

"Wait a minute—what did you say your name was again?"

"Bowknot Woods."

"I know your daddy, too!" The man laughed and was beaming with satisfaction as if he had just figured out some cryptic code. "Didn't your daddy used to work for old man Colfax and live back there on the Robinson place?"

"Yes, sir."

"Yeah, man! I know your daddy. What's he doing now?"

"He's working at the Ford plant in Detroit."

"Well, all right!" Mr. Howard exclaimed, slapping his thigh with one hand and raising the cigar to his lips with the other. "I remember he was trying to get on down there with us one time at Georgia Pacific." He paused momentarily, his eyes reflective and his brow furrowed. "Yeah, he came down there a number of times, but I guess they wasn't doing no hiring back then. I remember him telling me that if he couldn't find him something better, he was going to leave here."

Suddenly Bowknot's nostrils were assaulted by a fragrance so divine that it made his head spin. He quickly recovered himself and looked up into Linda's large, brown eyes; she was smiling down teasingly at him. She placed a hand on his shoulder.

"I'm sorry I took so long."

"Oh, that's all right," Bowknot said hurriedly. "I was just sitting here getting acquainted with your dad and come to find out that he already knows my folks."

Mr. Howard laughed. "Baby, that's George Woods' boy. You know, he used to work for old man Barrett. He used to come here and help me work on my old car. He used to drive an old Desoto with a tire behind it."

Linda's eyes flashed with recollection. "Yes, I remember him. But I don't remember you," she said, bemusedly looking back at Bowknot.

"Well, I was just a little tike then and momma was a real homebody and she would keep me home with her a lot back then. You know, it got pretty lonesome back out there on that old place."

"Well," Linda said, leaning over, touching Bowknot on the shoulder, "you want to come on with me back into the den?"

Bowknot rose automatically, and Mr. Howard said, "Nice talking to you, young man."

"Same here," Bowknot responded. He turned and followed his date back down a hallway and into another, smaller but equally well-furnished room. She led him to a plush sofa, where he sat down. She walked over to the table against the far wall where another record-player sat.

Realizing how long he had kept his cousin waiting, Bowknot leaned forward to catch Linda's attention. When she looked his way, he said, "Linda, my cousin is waiting outside in the car for me to come and tell him if we're going to The Shack with him and his girlfriend."

He could immediately tell that she did not care to go, and it made him feel sorry that he had even asked. "Well, she said, "if you want to go, we can, but I'd just as soon stay here. We can play our own music and have our own party."

Bowknot smiled, his eyes bright with glee, then rose from the couch. "Well, let me go on out there and tell him to go ahead

on, then." He strode out to the car and told Jay-boy their decision; he was back within a few moments. When he reentered the
room, Linda was sitting on the couch listening to Joe Tex as he
crooned, "You Had Better Hold on to What You Got." Looking
up, she caught his gaze and rose from her seat. As she moved
toward him, his muscles tensed and his stomach felt the sensation of a thousand butterflies fluttering their wings inside him.
He stopped. He didn't know why exactly, but he felt as if something had nailed his feet to the floor. Still, she came toward him,
her eyes wide and staring deep into his, a flicker of a smile
playing at the corners of her sensuous mouth. Suddenly, he felt
her arms gliding upward around his neck, pulling him gently to
her. His arms seemed to automatically enfold her and she
melted into them. Her perfume made his nostrils tingle with
sweet delight and when she nestled her face against his, waves
of titillation washed over him like warm rain.

"I'm glad you came," she said softly. "I hope this won't be
the last time."

Bowknot's head spun like a top, and his mind reeled with
ecstasy. Thoughts cascaded through his brain with the liquidity
of a waterfall, fluid, interlaced, and indistinguishable. His
mouth moved as if to speak, but the connection had been interrupted somewhere in his brain. They danced in silence, letting
Joe Tex's voice fill the room. Then they danced through Wilson
Picket's "I Found a Love" and Solomon Burke's "The Price I
Paid for Loving You." Then Sam Cooke's "Let the Good Times
Roll" hit the turntable and she released him, stepped back,
smiled deep into his eyes, and took his hand. "Come on and let
the good times roll," she said.

He laughed and then launched into his fancy footwork. She
watched him for a moment and then mimicked his steps as if
she had always known them. Noticing her uncanny ability to
pick up new dance steps so quickly, he laughed, his eyes lit with
admiration. "Hey, you're something else, lady! I ain't never seen
nobody pick up new steps that quick."

She smiled, her face flushed, and she laughed softly. They danced their way through several more up-tempo records and finally the stack was finished. She sighed, pushing her cascading hair back from her face. "Getting kind of hot in here. I think a cold glass of soda pop might help the situation, don't you?" Bowknot smiled and nodded in agreement. She put a new stack of records on the machine, then turned and disappeared from the room. Bowknot walked over and sat down at one end of the couch. He crossed his legs and scratched his ankle a moment, then reclined, letting his full weight sink into the soft pillows.

In a short while, Linda returned with two tall glasses of soda pop. She handed one glass to Bowknot, then sat down next to him and lifted the glass to her lips. Bowknot shot a quick glance at her, then lifted his glass, taking a long, luxurious drink. The cold liquid seemed to refresh him and settle his screaming nerves in some strange way. He lowered his glass and cast another furtive glance her way. Yes, just as he thought, she was staring. So, he stared back, suddenly emboldened and strangely calm in her presence.

She reached over and placed her hand on his. "I'm glad you came to see me," she said softly.

"I'm glad, too, mighty glad," he smiled.

"So, are you enjoying yourself?"

He looked at her, and their eyes held. When he spoke, his voice was soft but loud enough for her to hear. "Yes, I am. You know, you are the most beautiful lady I think that I have ever seen." He paused for a moment, trying to keep his tone firm and steady. "And I'd rather be here with you than anywhere in the whole world."

Stroking his palm, she leaned slightly forward and said, in a sincere voice, "That's about the nicest thing I've ever heard. I'm really flattered. Here," she said, handing him her glass, "will you put this over on the table for me?" Bowknot took the glass and placed it on the table along with his own.

The record player was about to drop another record and

Bowknot was waiting to see what it would be. There was a dull, metallic clicking of the hi-fi needle arm moving, a soft "splat" of a record falling down onto the turntable, then several seconds later, Joe Simon declared, "I can say that you are my adorable one." Bowknot glanced around slyly at Linda and smiled. She caught his glance, furtive though it was, and smiled back, then chuckled to herself.

"So," she said, straightening and turning her full attention to him, "tell me about yourself."

Bowknot cleared his throat and started to drum his fingers softly on the arm of the couch and tap his foot to the music. He paused a long while, staring abstractedly at her, then finally spoke, sudden-like, as if he had just remembered what she had asked. "Well, there's nothing much to tell about me. I used live here, as you know. We moved to Detroit when I was thirteen. Jay-boy is my first cousin, but we grew up more like brothers, I guess because he's an only child and I'm an only child." He paused a moment and looked at her quizzically. "Uh, exactly what about me would you like to know?"

Linda smiled warmly. "I would like to know where you learned to dance like that."

"Oh, that's nothing," he shrugged, trying with all his might to appear modest. "You should see some of my buddies back in Detroit; they make me look sick! Now, those guys can really shake 'em down!" He smiled reflectively and chuckled deep in his throat.

"Can the girls dance like that?"

"Can they!" he laughed, "they can out-dance most of the guys. You see," he paused a moment, reached over for his glass of soda, and took a long drink, "there is this record company in Detroit called Motown and they got a lot of young groups." He cleared his throat and shifted his position on the couch to face her more directly, aware that he had her undivided attention. "A lot of these young groups perform around Detroit: The Temptations, Smokey Robinson and the Miracles, the Supremes, the

Marvelettes, the Contours, the Four Tops, and so on. So you see, everybody that can sing and dance—or everybody who thinks they can sing and dance—wants to be a star, so that's what most of the young people spend a lot of time on. The ones who are good get better and the ones who are not so good, like myself," he smiled, "I guess get respectable. Some folks say that I can sing a little bit, but Smokey Robinson and Marvin Gaye ain't got nothin' to worry about from me."

"Oh, I bet you can sing," she poked him in the ribs. "Sing me a song, please."

Bowknot was silent, suddenly sorry that he had opened his trap in the first place.

"Please, please, please," she begged, staring deep into his eyes and leaning closer until her face was only inches from his. His stomach muscles flexed taut, his heart started to hammer against his chest, and he could feel the blood rush to his head. He tried to tear his gaze from hers, but something in those big, dark eyes captivated him. Or was it something in the sweet plea of her mellifluous voice? He couldn't be sure, but he was charmed like a field mouse hypnotized by a moccasin, and he was now like clay in her hands. Suddenly, from somewhere—he didn't know where—he heard the opening strains of Otis Redding's song, "That's How Strong My Love Is." He chimed in, singing from the depth of his soul and twisting every drop of feeling out of every word. He watched two large, dark eyes inches from his own mist over, and a voice echoed sweetly in his brain, "Sing to me, baby!" Then he felt her moist, warm lips full on his. She drew back for a moment, and looked deep into his eyes.

"You really feel that way about me?" She watched his eyes glisten with tears as he mumbled "yes," just above a choked whisper. She could see his feelings etched vividly in his face, and she knew that he was hers. She rose, walked over to the record player, and put on another stack of records, making sure "That's How Strong My Love Is" was first. She walked back over to the couch, leaned down, took Bowknot's hand, and led him to the middle of the room, gathering him in her arms. As they glided around and around, she raised her head and whispered softly in his ear, "Sing to me, baby." Bowknot obeyed without hesitation, singing again from the very depths of his being and holding her as if he would never let her go. Yes, he was smitten, just like that, and there wasn't a doggone thing he could do about it. This woman, this angel, this ethereal being had captivated him, mind, body, and soul. For the first time in his life, he was feeling emotions that he could not explain. His mind reeled with sheer delight, his heart soared, taking to the sky on wings of gladness as his blood sang like wine through his veins, making him giddy and light-headed.

When he finally came to himself, she was stroking his cheek softly with her fingers and staring deep into his eyes. He cleared his throat and tried to speak, but the words froze. She smiled, and as if reading his mind, she drew his face down and kissed him long and luxuriantly, squeezing him tight against her. Finally, she released him an led him back to the couch. He sat down and she sat on his lap, slipping her arms around his neck. Bowknot felt his arms go around her, one around her back and the other around her waist. She was soft, sensual, passionate, and the most beautiful woman he had ever laid eyes on. She patted his cheek playfully, and asked, "Wouldn't you like to know something about me?"

"Yes," Bowknot whispered softly, his eyes lit with unspeakable happiness.

"Well," she began, shifting her weight a little in his lap, "I graduated high school two years ago and decided that I would work a while before I went off to college. My folks were dead set against it at first, but they finally came around. So, I got a job at the garment factory out on route fifty-eight. I worked my regular shift and all the overtime I could in the beginning so that I could save up enough money to buy a car. After about seven months, I had almost enough and, when my folks found out what I was trying to do, they chipped in and gave me the rest. I bought a Ford Fairlane." She smiled with self-satisfaction and giggled a little. "I already knew how to drive; Mom taught me when I was fifteen. I am the kind of person who just likes to have my own. You know, "Mama may have, Papa may have, but God bless the child that's got his own."

Bowknot nodded and smiled admiringly at her. "This is really some kind of woman," he thought. This was a real woman. Deep inside of him he became aware of an unsettling sense of doubt about whether he was enough man for this woman.

She continued. "I have two brothers. One lives in Washington, D. C. He is married and has three children. My other brother is in the service, stationed at Fort Dix, New Jersey. He has two more years. I'm planning on going to college this fall."

Bowknot's heart sank at the mere thought of her going anywhere that meant separation. He was sure that he would just dry up and wither away like a broken-stemmed flower without her.

She noticed the startled look in his eyes and the streak of panic that crossed his face when she mentioned going away to college. "Well, now," she said, lifting his chin with her fingers, "why the sad face?"

"I just met you," Bowknot said, "and now it looks like I'm going to lose you."

There was a leaden sadness in his voice and the words stung her. She nestled closer to him, then planted a long, passionate kiss on his lips. Drawing back slowly, she said, "I'll be in touch with you. I'll write you every day and you'd better write me back." She laughed, patting his face.

Bowknot's eyes brightened and he smiled.

"And when are you going back to Detroit?"

"My folks will be back for me around the first or second week of September."

"Well," she broke in, "enough about going away. Let's enjoy the time right now. Besides, we have a whole lot of time before either of us has to go anywhere."

Bowknot raised his hand and stroked her long hair, pushing it gently back from her face. Her large eyes sparkled and she smiled and purred softly under her breath. He pulled her to him and kissed her with all the passion in him, his tongue probing deliciously, exploring the inside of her mouth. He felt her squeezing him tighter, her firm breasts pressing against his chest and her arms tightening around his neck as she began to moan softly, her breath coming in deep gasps. She kindled a flame in him that quickly burst into an all-consuming fire that made his body ache with desire. He could his manhood throb with such intensity that it racked his frame and made him tremble with passion. His hand automatically went to her breast and his fingers seemed to have a mind of their own as they cupped and caressed and made her moan louder and sigh more deeply. After a while, he let his hand move down over her stomach and onto her thigh. He caressed the top of her thigh, feeling her squirm and press against him as his manhood strained against her buttocks. Keeping his tongue wedged in her mouth, kissing her passionately, he moved his hand up her skirt to her inner thigh, and let his hand rove until his fingers rested on her silk panties. Beneath the sheer silk of her panties, he could feel a triangle of thick hair. He stroked the zone with his fingers and she opened her legs wide and began to grind her hips rhythmically against his straining manhood. Suddenly, Bowknot let out a deep, guttural moan as his insides seemed to explode; he gripped her desperately in his arms, trembling. Then spent and utterly embarrassed, he slowly released her.

She drew back slowly, then leaned in again and kissed him. "That's all right, baby."

Bowknot was silent.

"I want you to come by tomorrow morning about nine-thirty. Everybody will be gone to church."

Chapter 20

The next morning, Bowknot awoke and bounded out of bed, his mind spinning so fast he could hardly think. Pulling on his clothes, he forced himself, through sheer determination of will, to calm down. He had to figure out some way to get his uncle to let him have the car. After pondering a range of excuses, he finally came up with one that his uncle might go for. Yes, it sounded plausible enough. He would ask for the car so that he could go down and help Linda's dad put on some brakes and, besides, the man had promised to pay him.

By the time breakfast was over, he had worked up enough nerve to ask. He lingered in the kitchen, hoping that his aunt would step out. It looked like she wasn't going to, so he came out with it. His uncle hesitated for a long moment, and his aunt spoke up. "I don't know about this-here working on Sunday. He ought to be going to church. He's got plenty of time to do that sort of stuff all next week."

His uncles brow furrowed as he reached up and ran his hand through his thinning hair. "Maybe Horace ain't got time to do it next week, with the way they work and all. He said he's gonna pay you, huh?"

"Five dollars." Bowknot spoke softly and hoped desperately that his uncle wouldn't persist with questions.

"Well," Jimbo said finally, with a deep sigh, "let the boy go on and make himself a little change. I reckon the good Lord will understand."

Bowknot's stomach was still tied in knots as the family climbed out of the car in the churchyard. "All right, now," his aunt said sternly, you be back here by two o'clock, you hear?"

"Yes, ma'am," Bowknot answered. He nosed the car between the rows of parked cars and out onto the hard-surface road. He drove at a moderate speed while he was still in sight of the church, but when he reached the woods, he gave it the gas. He watched the speedometer needle move past forty, fifty, sixty, and finally jump over to ninety as he careened through the countryside, radio blaring. Finally, he reached the city limits and slowed his speed. After a few moments, he passed Boxdale's grocery. He sneered as a picture of the man's frowning face flashed across his mind. Minutes later, he was pulling up in front of Linda's house. He stepped from the car and sauntered toward the porch, trying to still his screaming nerves. He mounted the steps and rang the doorbell; Linda appeared in a few seconds. She was lovely, and the mere sight of her made his mind reel and his senses alive with wonder and awe.

"Come in," she said, smiling at him. He entered and she closed the door and turned to face him. She had on a sheer, cotton bathrobe, tied in front with a rope-belt. She was as fresh as a rose bathed in early-morning dew and her perfume permeated the air about her, making his nostrils tingle as he drank in the fragrance. She reached up and locked her arms around his neck, pulling his face down to hers so that she could plant a long, hungry kiss on his mouth. She kissed him for what seemed to him like forever. When she finally released him, he found himself panting and throbbing with desire. She smiled, staring deep into his eyes. Then, taking his hand, she said calmly, "Come on, let's go make love."

She led him down a hallway, past the den, and upstairs. "Here we are," she said softly, preceding him into her bedroom. She closed the door behind them, locked it, then turned back to face him. She moved slowly toward him. "I want you to undress me," she told him. Bowknot moved to obey. He reached down and untied her belt, her robe falling open to reveal her firm, round breasts with nipples jutting forward. His eyes slid down the front of her to the triangle of thick, black hair between her thighs. When he lifted his eyes, she caught his gaze and smiled. "Like what you see?"

Bowknot smiled and said nothing. She wriggled her shoulders and came out of her bathrobe to stand completely naked before him in the dim light of the room. She pulled him to her and kissed him, her tongue now probing hungrily inside his mouth as her fingers quickly unbuttoned his shirt and unbelted his trousers; Bowknot helped her relieve him of them. Then they were in bed. "Take your time," she whispered, "there's no need to rush anything."

She took him on a sexual odyssey that exploded all of his preconceptions about lovemaking. She lifted him to the apex of bliss, far beyond his wildest fantasies, then sent him tumbling back to reality in blissful agony, satiated and spent. She had given herself to him totally, and he would never be the same. Yes, he was now hers, mind, body, and soul, to shape and mold like clay.

Chapter 21

"What you-all gonna do, just stand around here and gawk all day or help us hand some of this tobacco?" said a stout woman, glancing from Jay-boy to Dallas Green. Green laughed and Jay-boy smiled wryly. Then he said humorously, "I do believe I was hired to pull tobacco and not to hand it." A ripple of laughter went around the crowd.

The stout woman and a fairly attractive girl of about eighteen stood on one side of the long trailer laden with tobacco leaves. On the other side stood a tall, thin girl who looked to be about twenty, with large eyes and long braids. At the opposite end stood a pretty, coffee-colored girl with dimples and thick, cascading hair swept back over her shoulders. They were picking up the leaves of tobacco, pressing three of them together and handing them to Tom Wright, who stood just within arm's reach on one side of the trailer, and to Sister Bullock, who stood on the other side. Sister Bullock held a long, narrow stick on a wooden horse, where they would tie the tobacco onto the stick with heavy twine. Dallas Green and Jay-boy were standing at the back of the trailer watching the others work.

"So, you-all ain't gonna help us, huh?" the stout woman repeated. There was a sassy bite to her tone.

"Well," Green said, then paused for a moment.

"Well, hell!" the woman cut in. Laughter erupted, and even Green couldn't resist crowing at her indignation.

"Now, you-all just wait till we get ahead of you-all and see if I come out to that field and pull one leaf of tobacco."

Jay-boy and Green looked at each other and laughed. Suddenly, the little doll of a girl standing next to the stout woman let out a terrified scream. She started to tremble, her face etched with horror as she pointed at something on her upper arm. It was a large, green worm, crawling slowly up her shoulder. Green quickly stepped around the trailer and brushed the worm away. Seeing what she had been screaming about, they all laughed. The girl finally smiled, too, and admitted, "I'm just terrified of those things."

Tom Wright cleared his throat and said loudly, "That ain't the worm you should be scared of." Again, they all broke into prolonged laughter.

Presently, Bowknot came up from the barn, where he had gone to get a drink of water. He looked around as if to say, "What's all the laughter about?", but he said nothing. The tall girl with the long braids looked over at him and smiled. Bowknot returned her smile.

"Hey, city man!" Tom Wright called. "That girl's been peeping at you all day. I told her if she got something to say to you, she ought to come on out and say it."

"Oh, Tom Wright!" she said in exasperation, swinging at him with a handful of tobacco leaves. "You make me sick!"

Wright ducked, and laughed uproariously. The rest of them laughed, too, and the girl's face flushed with embarrassment.

"I think you a little too late, baby," Green said, smiling and glancing from Bowknot to the girl. "That man is up-tight with the Spence girl."

"Oh, yeah!" Wright jumped in, "I know; I been seeing them at The Shack a lot together. Man, oh, man!" he laughed, "them two are just like two peas in a pod." He chuckled a moment, then added, "She got that boy's nose open so wide, you can drive a tractor up in there without touching either side." They all laughed uproariously. Bowknot's face was flushed with embarrassment, but laughter overtook him, too. He secretly wondered if the burly old cuss knew just how right he really was. Every chance he got, Bowknot was at Linda's house. They had been virtually inseparable for the past four weeks. He was in love, and she was the first thought in his mind when he rose and the last thought in his mind when he went to sleep. Thoughts of her flowed through his mind like water all day long. He replayed things that they had talked about, over and over in his mind. He could hear her voice resonating in his brain, he could see her face on the screen of his consciousness.

As the weeks drifted by, a gnawing dread began to lurk beneath his happiness. Bowknot knew that, soon, Linda would be going away to school and he would be going back to Detroit. He tried to push those thoughts to the back of his mind, but they would, with relentless persistence, shoulder their way into his consciousness and leave him with a sickening feeling that made him wince with pain.

One Wednesday night as he was leaving her house, she told him that she would be going to Richmond with her aunt early that Friday morning to do some shopping for school. Bowknot's face fell. She patted his cheek lovingly and kissed him. "It'll only be for the weekend."

His heart sank into the pit of his stomach and his eyes glazed over. She drew back and looked at him for a long time. "You really love me, don't you, Bowknot?"

"Yes," he said softly, "you know I do."

"I love you, too, and believe me, I really miss you when we're not together. Sometimes, I just ache inside, baby." He quickly embraced her.

"That's the way I feel, too," he said, his voice quivering with emotion.

"I don't know what I'm going to do when you leave and I have to go away to school," she said in a bewildered tone.

"I know what you mean. I don't know if I can make it on just a letter, baby. I already talked to my folks about letting me stay out here to finish school and all they keep saying is they'll think about it. I mentioned it time and time again to Uncle Jimbo, but he says it's up to my folks. Well, maybe things will work out.

Anyway, I can come to see you on holidays."

They stared into each other's eyes for a long time, and whispered "I love you" to each other.

"Well, Bowknot," Jay-boy said, starting the ignition, "you want to go with us to The Shack tonight?"

"I guess so.""Cheer up, man!" Jay-boy poked at him, "you look like you just lost your best friend."

Bowknot plastered on what could pass as a smile, then looked out of the window. Jay-boy headed the car along the dirt path out to the hard-surface road. Turning onto the road, he quipped, "Old Tom Wright was telling the truth about you and that girl, wasn't he?"

Bowknot was silent. Jay-boy continued, "Man, she's just going away for the weekend." He glanced over at Bowknot, not sure that his cousin was listening. He said nothing else. After all, he knew how it felt to be in love, and he knew how he felt when Kathy was away, even for a few days. He silently chided himself for not being more understanding; he, of all people, should know how Bowknot felt. "Bow," he said apologetically, "I'm sorry for ribbing you, man. I know how you feel."

Bowknot smiled and shrugged his shoulders. "Oh, that's all right."

"No," Jay-boy protested, "I'm really sorry. If Kathy was gone out of town, I'd feel the same way." He cleared his throat and was silent for a moment. Then he said, "Love is a hell of a thing, ain't it?"

"You ain't kidding a bit!" Bowknot laughed, knowing the truth in his cousin's words.

A few minutes later, they were sitting in front of Kathy's house. Jay-boy opened the door. "Come on in, Bow."

"No, that's all right. I'll just wait out here."

"All right," Jay-boy said, then he turned and disappeared up the stairs and into the house. A few moments later, Jay-boy returned with Kathy at his side. She was all smiles and nodded when Bowknot spoke to her. He had climbed out of the front seat and gotten in back so that she and Jay-boy could have the front seat. Bowknot looked at Kathy and knew that Jay-boy felt about her the same way he felt about Linda.

They drove in silence to The Shack and, though it was still early in the evening, there were quite a few people there. The jukebox was blaring as usual, and the place had begun to rock. Jay-boy parked the car and they all climbed out and headed for the door, Kathy and Jay-boy in front, Bowknot bringing up the rear. His eyes combed the grounds, taking in everything as they made their way to the entrance. Suddenly, he caught sight of Ruth in the crowd that always seemed to mill for hours just outside the door. Ruth saw Kathy, and started toward them— Pigfoot Parker beside her, smiling with smug self-satisfaction. He spoke to Jay-boy and Kathy and, with less congeniality, to Bowknot. Ruth just nodded to him and immediately engaged Kathy in enthusiastic chatter; Pigfoot struck up a conversation with Jay-boy. Bowknot touched Jay-boy's shoulder and said, "I'm going on in."

"Okay," Jay-boy said, "we'll be on in in a few minutes."

As Bowknot stepped inside the place, Rufus Thomas was asking, "Can Your Monkey Do the Dog?" Bowknot found a spot where he could lean against the wall and watch the dancers answer Thomas's question with gyrating profundity.

Suddenly, he felt a hand on his arm. He looked around into the sparkling eyes of a copper-colored girl, hair in an upsweep, flashing pretty, white teeth. "So, you're going to be a wallflower tonight, huh?"

Bowknot smiled warmly, noticing that the girl was quite attractive.

"Well," he said, clearing his throat, "I just got here. Would you like to dance?"

"Yes," she answered. He led her onto the dance floor. They danced through several fast records; she was quite a dancer. He had seen her there before and kept glancing around to see who she was with. They danced through two slow records, then someone played "That's How Strong My Love Is." He gathered her into his arms.

"Are you with anybody?" he asked.

"Yes. He's outside, but he don't mind if I dance with other people."

When Bowknot finally released her, he turned to see two cold eyes staring at him appraisingly. He met the boy's gaze for a moment, then turned and chuckled to himself, mimicking the girl, "He don't mind if I dance with other people." Bowknot knew better.

He resumed his post against the wall and watched abstractedly, his mind light years away, until Jay-boy came and tapped him on the shoulder. "Snap out of it, cousin, it's party time. Look over there, there goes two girls who just walked in alone and the short, cute one been giving you the eye for the past five minutes. Go on over there and ask the girl to dance."

Bowknot met the girl's gaze, smiled broadly, and started moving toward her. "Would you like to dance?"

He took the hand she held out to him, and they stepped into the beat of "Green Onions." They danced their way "The Way You Do the Things You Do" and "I Found a Love," with Bowknot wishing the whole time that she were Linda. The record ended and he thanked her for dancing with him.

"Any time!" she responded, with a flirtatious smile.

Bowknot's eyes moved around the room looking for his cousin; he spotted Jay-boy coming toward him. "Hey, Bow!" Jay-boy greeted him, a serious look on his face. "Come on outside with me for a minute where we can hear. I got something I want to ask you."

Bowknot followed him through the door and into the fresh evening air. Jay-boy headed toward the car, with Bowknot trailing behind him. When they reached the car, Jay-boy turned to face his cousin. "Bow, would you do me a big favor?"

"What is it?"

"Fat Daddy's car broke down and he ain't got no way to get

back to town. He's got to be at work by seven o'clock—can you run him up to the hospital for me?"

"No problem. Is he ready to go now?"

"Yeah. I'll send him on out here. Hey, thanks, man. Thanks a million."

"Like I said, man, no problem."

Bowknot got into the car and waited. Rolling down the window, he hooked his elbow over the side, resting his other hand on the steering wheel. His eyes moved over the landscape, taking in the scene as if he was seeing it all for the first time. The large, weather-beaten house exuded a kind of earthy animation that beckoned one's soul with an irresistible allure to come and let one's hair down.

The hard-packed earth around the structure had an ever-so-gradual outward slope leaving the building itself on an incline. This made rainwater run away from the building and, due to the firmness of the earth, there were no mud puddles around The Shack even after a heavy rain. The water would drain out toward the road into ditches dug along the highway. The incline made The Shack look almost majestic, and gave it a kind of gaudy splendor. The thick-set poles that ringed the yard in front of the place—ostensibly to keep people from driving right up to the door—could have been a courtyard packed with royalty. So many counts and countesses, dukes and duchesses and earls, princes and princesses, and all manner of genteel society festooned in their elegant finery pranced about the courtyard. Suddenly, Bowknot was jolted from his reverie by a hand touching his arm. He looked up, startled.

"Oh," she laughed, "I didn't mean to startle you." Her soft, brown eyes smiled down at him.

Bowknot cleared his throat, pausing a moment to recover. "I didn't hear you come up."

"I know," she chuckled, "you were a million miles away from this place."

Bowknot smiled, not so much at what she had said but with

the self-satisfaction of remembering who she was. Her name was Josephine; he had danced with her on several occasions. She looked about his age, but was definitely where the comparison ended. She was an eyeful of woman, with a thin waist, substantial bosom, and shapely hips. Her uncommonly smooth copper skin, pouty lips, and large, dark eyes gave her an air of sensual sophistication that belied her rural background. She had a certain urbanity, a mercurial quality that gave weight and force to her presence.

"So, what's new, Miss Lady?"

"You got the business; I'm just the customer," she laughed.

Bowknot laughed, too, but he was strangely off balance, fighting inwardly to stay calm and self-possessed. Summoning all his force of will, he stilled himself and said, "Well, now, customer, what can this-here proprietor do for you this evening?"

She smiled coquettishly, then said, "Well, let me think on that a moment." Then, in a more serious voice, she asked, "Where's your lady friend tonight?"

"Oh," Bowknot said, "she's gone out of town for the weekend."

"And left you here all by your lonesome?

"Where's the guy I usually see you with?" Bowknot countered.

"Oh," she said, waving her hand as if to wave away some bad memory, "we had a slight disagreement. I disagreed with him being around so much."

They both laughed. Bowknot was feeling more at ease now.

"So," she continued, "I told him to make like the wind and blow."

As they both exploded in uproarious laughter, she leaned forward, pressing against his arm.

"Hey," Bowknot said, recovering from laughter, "I'm getting ready to take a friend of my cousin's downtown. Would you like to ride with me?"

She was thoughtful for a moment, then smiled broadly. "Are

you sure you're going to behave?"

Bowknot smiled, "Cross my heart, hope to die, stick a sharp stick in my eye."

"Well," she said haltingly, "I'd better tell you, I can't promise that I'll behave." She laughed, then said, "Really, I would love to ride with you, but I've got to stay here and wait for my girlfriend. I promised to meet her here at seven o'clock, and if I'm not here, the child might panic. Anyway, thanks for the invitation; I hope I can get a raincheck on that."

"Sure," Bowknot agreed.

"Are you coming back here?" she asked.

"Yeah."

"That's good. Maybe we can have a chance to get better acquainted then."

"I'd like that," Bowknot said, smiling into her eyes. Just then, a voice boomed near them, shattering their moment of intimacy.

"Hello, Josephine. How you doing?"

They both looked around at the thin, wiry, coffee-colored man wearing a derby hat with wisps of grizzled, gray hair peering out from under it. "Do you remember me, baby, like I remember you?" He clapped a bony hand on her shoulder. "I'll be danged if you ain't as pretty as a picture in a book could look."

Josephine laughed at his good-natured ribbing. "Oh, go on, Bumsey!" she said, making a lame effort to push him away.

"How you-all doing?"

"All right," they both said politely.

Bumsey paused a moment, glancing over the yard. "Looks like we gonna have ourselves a crowd here tonight."

"Yeah, they gonna be wall to wall and treetop tall in there tonight."

They laughed, then Bumsey's gaze shifted back to Josephine. He shook his head wistfully. "Girl, looks like you look better every time I see you. If I had a woman like you, I'd work three jobs! Better yet, I'd work twenty-four hours a day and then some overtime for you." They all laughed at this. He continued, "I ain't lying, baby. If God made anything prettier than you, He kept it in heaven. Nations go to war over women like you. Hey, I'd give ten years of my life for one night with you, you know that?

Josephine laughed, then her lips curled into a teasing pout. "If I did spend a night with you, Bumsey, you couldn't handle me. I'd give you a heart attack, and I wouldn't want that on my conscience."

"Hey," Bumsey broke in, "kill me, baby! You can kill me dead." He paused a moment, taking a draw from the dying cigarette he had been holding, exhaling the smoke. Eyes twinkling, he went on. "I sure can't think of a better way to die. And, look here, when I die, don't bury me at all. Just put my body in alcohol. Fold my arms across my chest, and tell all the women, Bumsey's gone to rest!" He cackled with glee at his witticism and they, too, broke up with laughter.

"Hey, baby!" Bumsey was on a roll. "I might be a little old, but Bumsey ain't dead yet. Just because there's a little snow on the roof don't mean it ain't no fire in the furnace."

"But, Bumsey," Josephine said, egging him on, "what would I tell people if me and you spent the night together and I woke up and found you dead? How could I explain a dead man in my bed?"

Bumsey laughed, his eyes sparkling with delight. "Just tell them that 'it' brought me here, now 'it' done took and carried me away!" He crowed with laughter, slapping his thigh, his bony frame shaking. "Girl," he said, slapping Josephine on the shoulder, "you're a mess, I suggest. Hey, but just like 'Moms' Mabley said, 'I don't want nothing old but some money.' The only thing an old woman can do for me is show me which way a young woman went. Hell," he paused for a moment, taking a last draw from his stub of a cigarette, "I'm old; what would I want with an old woman? I want me something young and full of life that can keep me warm on a cold, rainy night. Somebody that can make my liver quiver and my toenails curl!"

"Oh, hush your fuss, Bumsey!" Josephine stammered through a stream of giggles. "You talk more stuff than a dime-store lawyer."

"Greetings, greetings, greetings!" a voice broke in. They all looked around and saw Fat Daddy in front of the car.

"Hey, there!" Bumsey called out, "how about lending me twenty dollars there, Big Money?"

Fat Daddy smiled sheepishly, never taking his eyes from Josephine's face. "Man, if I had it, you know that you could get it."

"Could I get it?" Josephine asked teasingly.

"Oh, baby," Fat Daddy gasped, his face flushing with delight, "I'll turn my pants upside down for you."

"Wait a minute!" Bumsey interjected. "Don't you do that, Fat Daddy, don't you do it! Man, if you took off your pants, somebody might shoot you, boy, thinking you're a buffalo or something." They all laughed.

"But that's all right, Bumsey," Fat Daddy retorted, "at least I ain't two days older than water and I don't have to stuff rags in my drawers to try to impress the ladies." Again they all exploded in laughter.

"Well, now, Fat Daddy, you can say what you want to, but don't get mad with me because nothing don't want to grow in the shade."

Fat Daddy didn't respond, apparently missing Bumsey's point. "Well, let me get on downtown," he said, moving to the passenger side of the car. "I'll see you-all later," he said to Josephine and Bumsey.

"I'll see you later," Josephine said, patting Bowknot on the arm.

"All right," he answered.

Bumsey winked at him and said, "I wish I was twenty years younger. I'd give you a run for your money, young man." Then he slapped Bowknot on the arm and laughed, moving off with Josephine toward The Shack.

Bowknot started the engine, eased the car into gear, threading his way through the parked cars and out onto the road. He accelerated, feeling the stream of air whip across his arm, where it still protruded from the window.

"Well," Fat Daddy said, after a few moments of silence. "I hear that you are a pretty good pool-player."

"Oh, I'm all right, I guess. I heard that you're the man."

"I don't know about all that," Fat Daddy grinned, feigning modesty. "I would like to get together and play you some time. I think you could give me a real good game—Beebop said that you could probably beat me. He said you're the best he ever seen."

Bowknot laughed. "Well, I don't know about all that, now. The night that I played him, I was damn lucky."

"Yeah," Fat Daddy quipped, "but Beebop said that you were putting some hellified angles on them balls! He said that you beat him five games straight." Fat Daddy paused a moment, leaned over, and spat out of the window. "Now, some of that might have been luck, but I bet you most of it was skill. And besides, old Beebop ain't no slouch with a pool stick. Yeah, he said that you were good, all right."

Bowknot was silent for a long time, then he said, "Like I said, I guess I'm all right; nothing to brag about, though."

"Well," Fat Daddy said, scratching his temple, "I'd still like to play you sometime."

"We'll get together," Bowknot said, glancing over at him with a kind of indifference that indicated that the whole matter was really no big deal.

"I sure wish that I didn't have to go to work this evening," Fat Daddy mumbled with a note of regret in his voice, "but I promised my supervisor that I would come in and work over-time tonight. Hell, I need the money anyway, so ain't no need to complain."

They fell silent. After a few moments, Bowknot reached down and turned on the radio. He found a station playing jazz and leaned back in his seat, drumming his fingers softly on the steering wheel in time with Duke Ellington's "Satin Doll." Fat Daddy smiled and started wagging his head and tapping his fingers on the windowsill, softly patting his foot, all in time with the music. A short while later, they were pulling into the city limits; Bowknot looked over at Boxdale's grocery store and frowned, then like a flash of lightning, the frown turned to a wicked smile. He shot a quick glance at Fat Daddy to see if he had noticed and was glad to see that his passenger was staring straight ahead. Fat Daddy was still bopping to the music, staring fixedly ahead, his face calm and placid. Finally, they pulled up in front of the hospital.

"Well, here we be," Bowknot said.

"Yeah," Fat Daddy replied, coming out of his music-induced trance, "I guess it's time to punch that clock and meet that man."

"Yeah, I know what you mean," Bowknot said, looking after him as Fat Daddy climbed out of the car.

Closing the door, Fat Daddy turned around and said, "I sure thank you, man."

"Oh, that's all right, anytime."

"Well, I still appreciate this favor. And you tell Jay-boy I said I really appreciate this. Tell him I owe him one, too, you hear?"

Bowknot smiled warmly," I'll tell him."

Fat Daddy straightened and began walking away from the car. Abruptly, he stopped and turned back. "Hey," he called out, leaning down to see inside the car, "don't you forget, now! I still want to get together with you to shoot some pool, okay?"

"It will have to be one night this week, then, cause my folks will be coming for me over the weekend."

Fat Daddy's brow furrowed and his eyes narrowed as he stared at the ground as though in serious thought. "Hey," he said, looking up suddenly, "what about this coming Thursday night? I should have my ride fixed by then, and I can come out there and pick you up. We can stop somewhere on our way back and have a few beers and then come on down and shoot some pool."

Bowknot thought for a moment, then said, "All right, it's a deal, then." They shook hands.

Fat Daddy turned and headed for the hospital. "Thanks again, you hear?" he threw back over his shoulder.

"No problem. Catch you later," Bowknot called to his back.

Chapter 22

He started the engine and slipped the car into gear. As he nosed the car out into the street, he felt something tightening in his stomach. Looking down at the dashboard clock, he saw that it was a little after six o'clock, and wondered if he would have enough time. All his senses suddenly heightened like those of an animal on the prowl. With every fiber of his being alive and alert, he drove with meticulous care to a back street about five blocks away from Boxdale's grocery store, parked the car behind a furniture warehouse, and got out. Before closing the door, he reached beneath the front seat and pulled out a stocking, which he stuffed in his pants pocket. It belonged to Linda; she had left it in the car after one of their love-making sessions and he hadn't bothered to give it back, knowing that he would have another use for it in time. He closed the car door, locked it, and started off walking at a brisk pace, though not so fast as to attract attention to himself. He weaved his way through a series of back alleys, frequently peering back over his shoulder to make sure that he was not being watched or followed. Finally, he came up behind the store on Baker Street. Glancing about, he moved cautiously around the side of the store toward the front. When he reached the corner of the building, he stopped a moment to gauge the traffic flow. Traffic was pretty heavy now; most of the stores were closing or had already closed, and folks were leaving town. Bowknot leaned against the building for a moment, casually glancing around, noting that the parking lot was empty and knowing that it must be right around closing time for Boxdale's. He began to walk nonchalantly toward the door, glancing around the area one last time, making note of the trucks parked in front of the warehouses that could provide cover for him if he needed a quick place to hide.

He ran his hand down into his right-front pants pocket and curled his fingers around the handle of his blade, which he had already opened. It was razor sharp. He reached out and casually turned the doorknob, eased the door open, and stepped inside. The old codger hadn't heard him, and he smiled as his heart started to hammer against his chest. He could feel the blood pounding in his temples as his roving eyes took in the scene. There were no customers. He quickly drew the stocking from his pocket and snatched it down firmly over his head, adjusting the slits for his eyes. Boxdale was standing behind the counter with his head down, poring over his ledger. With cat-like agility, Bowknot sprang stealthily forward. Boxdale looked up, and his pale blue eyes went wide with horror as Bowknot pressed the cold steel of the blade against his throat.

"Wha . . . wha . . . what do you want?" the old man stammered in terror, his voice breaking and tears beginning to fill his eyes.

"I want you to reach down, real slow, and get a large paper bag from under that counter and put all the paper money from the cash register and the safe into the bag. Now, be damn quick about it!" Bowknot hissed.

The stocking had flattened his features, making them grotesquely distorted and making him all the more frightening. With trembling hands, the old man obeyed.

"Now, if you make one sound, old devil, the groundhog is going to be your mailman. You got that?" he snapped, pressing the knife roughly against the man's throat, causing a thin trickle of blood to stream down into the collar of his shirt. After a short while, the man had the bag almost filled with money and Bowknot smiled inwardly.

"Now, give me the key to the back door of this place and make it snappy," he said, shoving the old man roughly against the counter. The man pulled out the key, and Bowknot snatched it from him. "Now, lay down on the floor."

The old man made as if to lie down; then suddenly, from somewhere beneath the counter, a gun appeared in his fist. He turned, swinging the gun around toward Bowknot, who slashed down savagely with his knife, hitting mostly collarbone. A fountain of bright red blood spurted from the man's neck as Bowknot dropped the knife and grabbed frantically for the gun. The old man was surprisingly strong and put up quite a struggle, even though he was bleeding profusely; Bowknot fought for the gun in fierce desperation. Suddenly, the gun fired. A bullet struck the old man in the throat, and he slumped to the floor.

Panic streaked across Bowknot's face as he looked around wildly for a moment, trying to gather his wits. Quickly, he grabbed up the money and the gun, then looked around desperately for his knife. Fear gripped his guts like a steel vise as he heard the front door opening; he turned and leaped toward the back of the store. He made his way to the back door and with trembling fingers managed to get the key into the double deadbolt lock, open the door, and slip out. He closed the door softly and crept off down Baker Street, turning blindly into the first alley.

Big Tiny Oliver lumbered into the store, his bones still aching from a long day's work lifting logs. He had just gotten paid; he was on his way home when he remembered that he didn't have any more cigarettes. So he had stopped in Boxdale's to get some. He hadn't heard the gunshot as he had stepped inside the door, probably because of the huge tractor-trailer turning at the intersection in front of the store. His eyes swept the store, but he did not see Boxdale. Thinking that Boxdale was probably in the back somewhere, Oliver strode forward.

"Mr. Boxdale! Mr. Boxdale!" he called. There was no answer. As he came nearer the counter, he saw something that stopped him in his tracks. There was a huge puddle of blood on the floor at the end of the counter; Boxdale was lying in it, face up, with his mouth partially open and his eyes wide and glazed over. His white shirt was almost totally crimson, soaked with his blood. Then Tiny's eyes lit on something. He moved forward, bent down, and picked it up—it was a knife. A wicked-looking thing it was, with a curved blade like a hawk's bill. Tiny's mind reeled, his brow wrinkled and his eyes narrowed as he looked closer. Now, where had he seen something like this before? Somewhere deep in the caverns of his brain was a vague hint of recollection, but he just couldn't seem to pull it to the fore of his consciousness for the life of him.

Big Tiny was suddenly jolted out of his cogitation by the sharp, nasal tones of an icy voice hissing through clenched teeth.

"Don't you move a muscle, boy, or this-here twelve-gauge just might go off."

Big Tiny stood stone still, and his heart sank into the pit of his stomach. Beads of sweat began to pop out on his forehead, his eyes misted over with terror, and a profound sense of doom washed over him like a cold rain as his mind grasped the severity of his predicament. Here he was, alone in the store holding a blood-stained knife, with Boxdale lying dead on the floor. For a brief moment, he had a wild impulse to turn and spring upon the man behind him. No, he was too close, or maybe not close enough to grab in a single lunge; the man had the gun on him and, no doubt, his finger was itching to pull the trigger at the slightest provocation. So Tiny thought better of it and struggled to control his conflicting impulses, trying to harness his tempestuous emotions with the strength of reason. He remained still, his face drained of emotion and his eyes dull and expressionless. Then he heard another voice call out. It was an airy voice, high pitched, with a twang.

"Earl, I flagged a taxicab down at the light, and I told him to get the police right away," the man said excitedly, struggling to catch his breath. "I stood right there and watched him call, too, and they'll be here directly."

"All right, Dave, good work," the other man, Earl, said.

"We'll just stay right here and keep this-here boy company until they get here." Then to Tiny, his voice still cold and seething with disgust, he commanded, "Turn around, boy!"

Big Tiny started to turn to face the two men. "Careful, boy, and drop that knife real easy-like, now, because I don't need much of a reason to blow you to hell."

Big Tiny dropped the knife and turned ever so slowly to face them. His face glistened with hot perspiration and his lip dropped as he stared dumbly at them. Dave was a thin man, whose stature matched his small voice. Earl, the one holding the shotgun, was big and burly, with reddened cheeks, a thin mustache, and an unruly thatch of thick, brown hair.

"It's that-there boy they call Big Tiny Oliver!" Dave exclaimed. "He's always in some kind of trouble or another."

Earl glared at Big Tiny; his faded blue eyes were as cold as death, and there was an unmistakable glint of revenge in them. He glanced down at Boxdale's prone figure for a moment, then back at Big Tiny. His eyes narrowed, and a sneer curled his lips.

"I ought to blow five miles of daylight through you right now and just save the taxpayers the expense of putting you on trial."

He shot a glance at his friend to gauge his feelings about the idea, but kept an eye on Big Tiny, inwardly hoping for the slightest reason to shoot. The little man looked stricken, his face flushing as he fidgeted about, shifting his weight nervously from one foot to the other.

"We can say that, when we came, he was still holding the knife," the burly man continued, "and he made a break for us and I had to kill him."

Without waiting for Dave's response, he raised the shotgun, leveling it at Tiny's chest.

Terror streaked across Tiny's face, and tears streamed down his cheeks as he blubbered pitifully, raising his hands as if to ward off the shot. "Please, mister, please! I didn't do it!"

"Sure, you didn't," Earl hissed with mounting disgust.

"I didn't, sir, I swear I didn't!" Tiny's voice had now risen toward hysteria, and his pleas became more and more muddled and incoherent. A few moments later, still pleading through his tears, he made out three or maybe four blue uniforms moving quickly toward him.

Chapter 23

Bowknot was approaching a men's store. Seeing a thin, stoop-shouldered, white-haired man ambling toward the door with a ring of keys in his hand, he quickened his steps. He reached the door just seconds ahead of the man he had been watching through the large plate-glass window. Pulling open the door, he asked, "You-all closed yet?"

The man smiled drily. "Just on my way to lock the door. What is it that you want?" he asked, his eyes moving speculatively over Bowknot's clothes.

"Oh, I just wanted to pick me up a shirt for church tomorrow."

The man paused a moment, staring at him. Bowknot stared back at him ingenuously, his hand instinctively tugging at the front of his coat, hiding the bloodstains on his shirt. Though he knew that the man could not possibly see them, the mere staring made him damn uncomfortable just the same.

"All right," the man snapped, turning on his heel, "follow me."

The man led Bowknot back to a section of the store where there were racks and racks of men's shirts of every color and style. Bowknot's eyes flitted over the rack for a moment, then he walked over and picked up a light-blue shirt almost exactly like the one he was wearing.

"Sir, I'll take this one here."

The man looked up at him, his expression puzzled and somewhat amused. Then he shook his head slowly and turned down an aisle that led to the check-out counter. He rang up the sale without a word, and handed Bowknot his change.

"Thanks," Bowknot said. "Thank you very much, sir."

"No problem," the man replied, "no problem at all."

As he watched Bowknot leave the store, he shook his head and chuckled under his breath. "Why in the devil did he go through all of that to get a shirt just like the one he was wearing?" the man mumbled to himself. He shook his head again, still smiling at the thought, picked up his keys, and went over to lock the door.

When Bowknot stepped out of the woods into the purple twilight, his eyes moved slowly over the large corn field. Then he looked back toward the hard-surface road that he had taken to this dirt path, which wound through the woods back to the corn field that, itself, was ringed by woods. He saw no one. He stood still and listened for a long time; the only sound he could hear was the rhythmic throb of tree frogs and cicadas lifting their shrill chorus in the cool night air. He walked over to the car, pausing to brush the small bits of twigs and forest debris from his clothes with meticulous care. After a few moments, he straightened and smiled wickedly. Satisfied that he had hidden the money, gun, and shirt in a safe place, he opened the car door and slid in.

Starting the engine, he decided to back the car out to the road—that way, the tire tracks would be less conspicuous than if he turned around at the edge of the corn field. He slipped the car into gear, then positioned himself so that he had a good view through the rear windshield and began to ease the car backward along the dirt path. A few moments later, he had reached the road; he paused and looked both ways, up and down the road. He could see no one coming either way in the deepening twilight, so he continued to back onto the road, shifted the gear, and headed toward The Shack.

Cruising down the road, he felt the incredible numbness that had enveloped him back in the store finally giving way. His mind seemed to slip into gear, and he was again able to think, to reflect, to plan. Until now, he had been like a frightened animal, operating mostly on instinct rather than reason, and now that fact gnawed at him, chewing at his guts like a determined rat. Had he done everything he could to ensure his escape? The questions began to needle at his mind as their consequences weighed on his shoulders with relentless gravity. What if Boxdale wasn't dead? Had the person entering the store caught a glimpse of him running to the back? Had anyone seen him on the street, clutching the large bag to his chest to hide the blood stains on his shirt? Why hadn't he taken his coat into the store to begin with? Had the old man at the clothing store seen something, suspected something? Bowknot had noticed the man staring at his clothes curiously several times while he was perusing the racks: had he seen blood somewhere on him?

Bowknot reached down and turned on the radio in a vain attempt to calm his screaming nerves, but it was to no avail. Finally, he recognized the opening strains of "Baby, Baby, Where Did Our Love Go?" and his mood brightened. The music evoked thoughts of Linda and gave him the mental fortitude that he needed to push off the heavy sense of dread and break the tenacious hold of fear that had begun to twist his guts into knots. He began to relax somewhat, and the thoughts of Linda made his heart quicken. Now that he had the money, he could definitely come back out here to see her. Hell, he could take a plane if he wanted to. He smiled to himself at that, but immediately reconsidered. He didn't want anyone to become suspicious, so he'd just take the train. That way, he could say that he was using money he had saved from working during the summer. Well, at any rate, he had money now, and lots of it, too. He had counted almost fifteen thousand dollars and there was more. It was more money than he had ever seen in his life, and when he thought of all the possibilities this could mean for him, his heart danced with excitement.

But he had killed a man. The thought smashed into his consciousness, smiting him like a blow and jarring him to the very core of his being. Yes, he had killed a man, and the naked realization of it was so fantastically horrid that his stomach began to heave and lurch, making him so sick that his limbs went weak and he had to pull over and stop the car. He flung open the door and leaned out, face contorted with anguish, mouth agape, expecting to gag, but nothing came up. He poked his finger deep into his throat trying to induce vomiting, but still nothing came as he coughed and spat his lungs into the dirt. He leaned back against the seat and sighed wearily. Suddenly, panic flushed over him. What if someone came along and saw him sitting here and started to ask questions. He had to get his ass in gear and get the hell out of here. He glanced into the rear-view mirror; there was no one coming. Hurriedly closing the door, he put the car into gear and pulled off; he hadn't bothered to shut off the engine earlier.

The engine droned and the rubber tires whined along the gravel road. Bowknot hadn't noticed that the radio station that he had been listening to had gone off the air, leaving a soft, hissing sound coming from the dashboard speakers. His mind was still reeling from the fact that he had killed someone, and it made it all but impossible to concentrate on anything else.

Suddenly, he slammed his foot down hard on the brake and the car went sliding across the intersection. Bowknot glanced around him, his eyes wide and flashing with horror. There were no cars coming. He shuddered, his stomach tying itself in knots. When he looked down at the steering wheel, he saw that his hands were trembling. He quickly backed up and straightened the car, then turned onto the road that led to The Shack. He eased off, still glancing nervously now and again into the rear-view mirror, but there was no one in sight. He just had to get hold of himself. He just had to, or he would be found out, for sure!

As the car droned along the winding road, his mind groped feverishly for some position to anchor his reason and balance his emotions. With a herculean effort, he finally calmed his screaming nerves and quieted his boiling emotions enough to harness his intellect. Yes, he had killed a man, but, he rationalized, it was really in self-defense. He had had no intention of hurting Boxdale if he had just done what he was told; he just would have taken the money and left. But, no, that fool had to grab that damn gun. So, really he caused his own death. He was trying to kill me, wasn't he? Boxdale would not have hesitated to shoot him, and if he hadn't fought like hell, he would have been the one lying there and Bowknot was sure that that damn Boxdale would have had a smile on his face, too, after putting a bullet into his skull. So, he hadn't really killed Boxdale in cold blood; he had killed to keep from being killed. Yeah, that was it. So, why was he feeling this way, sick to his stomach and all? Hell, he had just been defending himself. Well, he figured, maybe it was just the thought of killing someone. He had stabbed guys before, cut them up pretty bad—like Tiny Oliver—but this was the first time he had actually killed someone. Well, had he really even killed Boxdale? They had been struggling over the gun and it had gone off. After all, it could have been him. Finally, a strange calm flooded his being and, for the first time since the whole ordeal, he was feeling self-possessed and in control. He smiled to himself, gratified that he had thought it all out and thrown off the sickening fear that had gnawed at his guts and the icy dread that had weighed so heavily on his shoulders.

When Bowknot pulled up at The Shack, the dusk had deepened into night. The air had cooled significantly and it had started to rain, not a heavy rain but a misty spray. He noticed that the place was packed, because the yard beyond the poles ringing the grounds just in front of the place was full of cars and he had difficulty finding a parking space. Finally, he nudged into a space between an old truck and a sporty, new Chevy. He climbed out of the car and threaded his way between cars toward the entrance. He noticed that there were only a few people still milling around outside now. Walking up to the door, he saw a middle-aged man come out. He tapped him on the arm and the man turned to face him.

"Say, buddy, could I get you to do me a big favor? I'll pay you."

The man's eyebrows went up and he smiled broadly. "What can I do for you?"

Bowknot motioned for the man to follow him; they walked a few paces away from the place and Bowknot turned to him. Leaning forward, he whispered to the man, "Say, I'll give you three dollars if you'll go in there and get me a pint of bourbon."

The man was silent for a moment, then he said, "Shucks, man, you got yourself a deal. I got just one request."

Bowknot stiffened, leveling his gaze at the thick-set, balding man.

"I want me a little taste of it."

Bowknot grinned and stuck out his hand; the man took it. "Deal!" Bowknot laughed. "Look, I'll be waiting for you around there by the side door."

"All right," the man said.

Bowknot handed him the money and the man turned and made his way back into The Shack. Bowknot went around to the side of the building and leaned nonchalantly against the rough boards, waiting. After a while, the man emerged from the side door, flashing the bottle and grinning at Bowknot.

"Come on," Bowknot said, "follow me." Bowknot led him out to the car and the two of them climbed in.

The man handed him the bottle. "What's your name, sport? I like to know a man's name if I'm going to drink with him."

"They call me Bowknot. What's yours?"

"They call me Pap."

"Well, Pap," Bowknot smiled, "nice meeting you."

"Same here," the man said.

Bowknot broke the seal and lifted the bottle to his lips. He flinched as the hot liquid gurgled down his throat. Then he felt it warm in his belly. He wiped his mouth and handed the bottle to Pap. The man took it and drank greedily, gulping it down like water. For a moment, Bowknot was alarmed and started to speak but, before he could, Pap lowered the bottle and handed it back, grinning delightedly.

"I sure thank you, young man, and I sure 'preciate that drink, too."

Bowknot took another big drink, trying to do it with the non-chalance of a seasoned drinker like his new friend. However, the liquor still seared his throat like fire and scalded his belly. He closed the bottle and they climbed out of the car. Again, he thanked the man and they shook hands and parted company.

By the time Bowknot had made his way back to the front door, his head was starting to spin and he could feel the alcohol warm in his belly, moving up and out into his limbs. Stepping into the place, his eyes peered through a haze of thick cigarette smoke at wall-to-wall gyrating bodies. Rufus Thomas was asking "Can Your Monkey Do the Dog?" and the building was rocking under their rhythmic sway. He eased inside and found a perch against the wall and let his eyes canvass the room. He chuckled to himself as he recalled what Bumsey had said earlier that evening about people being wall to wall, tree-top tall. They sure enough were, that was a fact. The place was packed. He thought he spotted Josephine, but he wasn't sure. In the dull glare of the overhead lights, he moved toward her, eyes fixed as he pressed his way to the area on the dance floor where he thought he had seen her. Now the girl had her back turned. What the hell, it looked like her and, even if it wasn't, he would find out. When he was near enough for her to hear him above the loud music, he called out and she looked up. It was indeed Josephine; she smiled deep into his eyes. He was beaming as she moved toward him.

"So, you made it back, huh?"

"Yeah," he responded. Before they could say more, the opening strains of Joe Simon's "Adorable One" filled the room and a hand shot out, swiftly grabbing Josephine's arm and almost spinning her around.

"I just got to have this dance with you, baby. I been watching you all night," said a big, broad boy with large arms and rough hands, steadily drawing her to him. Josephine stiffened and her face flushed with indignation as her eyes flashed from the boy's face to Bowknot's. Then she stared pleadingly at Bowknot and his muscles tightened as he hissed through clenched teeth, "Let the lady alone, man."

The boy glared at him contemptuously and sneered, "Whose daddy are you, mister?"

"I said, leave the lady alone. She doesn't want to be bothered." Bowknot moved closer, raising his voice. The crowd around them moved back, sensing what was coming.

The boy looked down at Josephine, whose arm he was still holding, and snapped, "Can't you speak for yourself, baby?"

"I don't want to dance with you," she blurted, her eyes bright with reproach.

"Oh," the boy said loudly, "I got it now. So, you just prefer dancing with sissies, huh?" He glared at Bowknot and smiled derisively, stepping back, his legs apart.

Bowknot's fist came like a blur, smashing the boy in the mouth, making blood spurt forth. Before the boy could recover, Bowknot had landed another in his temple and the boy's legs went rubbery as he reeled backward. Quickly, Bowknot moved in, ramming his fist deep into the boy's stomach and feeling him slump to the floor. However, he didn't see the hard fist coming at his jaw, and Josephine's shrieked warning was too late. The hard knuckles of a thick-set, coffee-colored boy with a wicked scar under his left eye and a mean, petulant mouth caught Bowknot squarely on the jaw from his blind side and he went down with a thud.

Jay-boy appeared, his eyes moving from Bowknot, who was lying groaning on the floor, to the boy who had hit him. Jay-boy's eyes glittered with speechless hatred as he said coldly through clenched teeth, "I'm gonna give you more of a chance than you gave him." He stepped quickly in front of the boy, landing a hard right to the jaw. The boy staggered backward and came back swinging wildly at Jay-boy's head and missing. Jay-boy came back with a devastating uppercut to the chin, and the boy went down. Jay-boy bent over him, reaching down and snatching him up by his shirt collar. "I'm just getting started," he sneered disgustedly in the boy's face. Then he smashed his fist into the boy's ribs, making the boy stagger drunkenly before another blow smashed him in the temple and he went down hard.

As Jay-boy moved toward him again, he heard Kathy calling out, on the verge of tears, "That's enough, Jay, please! He's had enough!"

Seconds later, Dallas Green broke through the crowd. "All right, son, leave him alone now. They told me who started it, so I ain't blaming you and your cousin, but that's enough, now. I want you-all to go on home and cool off. You know I don't like this sort of stuff around here, no matter who started it."

Chapter 24

It was late the next morning when Bowknot dragged himself to the kitchen table and sat heavily down in a chair. His head throbbed with such force that it made his eyes blurry and he could only focus with great difficulty.

Jay-boy glanced up at him and laughed. "Man, you must have really taken a shot last night, huh? I didn't know that that chump hit you that hard."

Bowknot chuckled softly to himself, knowing that the joke was on his cousin. He hadn't been hit that hard. Most of his misery, especially the pounding in his skull, he knew was from the bourbon. Except for the slight swelling on his cheekbone, there would have been no sign that he had been hit. "Yeah," Bowknot said finally, playing along with him, "I guess he really stole one on me that time. I never knew what hit me." He paused a moment, rubbing his brow. "One moment I was kicking this guy's ass for bothering Josephine, and the next minute you was helping me up off the floor out to the car."

Jay-boy laid down the newspaper the newspaper that he had been perusing and looked up at Bowknot. "Well, Mom left your breakfast in the stove to keep it warm. We've already eaten, and she and dad left about an hour ago for church. I was just getting up and Mom said she didn't wake us because she didn't want us sitting up in church falling asleep. So, like I said, your food is in the stove."

"I'm not hungry right now; I'll eat in a little while. Finish telling me about how I wound up on the floor last night. It's one thing when a man knows that he's had an ass whipping, but it's another when he wakes up wondering who in the hell hit him."

Jay-boy laughed drily, then continued. "Well, just as I pushed my way through the crowd to see what was going on, I saw Tommy Jordan hit you in the jaw. I didn't ask no questions, just went for his ass. Then out of the corner of my eye, I saw his brother, Jimmy, laying on the floor beside you and I figured you and him must have been fighting and Tommy jumped into it. I knew that you never saw the lick coming because, man, you fell like a tree. That shit made my blood boil. So I evened up the odds and gave him a hell of a better chance than he gave you."

"Could he fight?" Bowknot asked, glancing up at his cousin.

"He tried," Jay-boy laughed, "but I left his ass laying on the floor beside his brother." They both laughed, Bowknot wincing from the pain shooting through his head.

"Hey," Jay-boy said, motioning to the paper laying on the table in front of him. "It says here that Tiny Oliver was arrested for robbery and murder."

Bowknot wheeled in his chair, his eyes wide with surprise. "What!" he exclaimed, nearly breathless.

Jay-boy paused and stared hard at him, and Bowknot felt the blood rush to his temples. Glancing back down at the paper, he continued. "Yeah, it says right here that two prison guards on their way home from work caught him with the knife in his hand."

Bowknot listened as Jay-boy began to read. "'The two men held Oliver at bay with a twelve-gauge shotgun until police arrived. Boxdale had been shot and stabbed in the neck, however, the coroner says that the gunshot wound to the head was no doubt the immediate cause of death.'"

Bowknot listened in amazement as his cousin read the article. His emotions flickered from surprise to fear to relief, and back to fear. That was his knife. He just knew he had left his knife. He'd dropped it when he'd grabbed for the gun. He could have kicked himself for not remembering to pick up his knife, but there hadn't been time, someone had been at the door. "Damn!"

he said to himself, no longer listening as his cousin read, catching only snatches of words between his swirling thoughts.

So, Tiny Oliver had been the hapless customer. If Bowknot had taken a split second longer to find the knife, he no doubt would have been caught or at least seen running from the building. He could feel a ball of tension building in his stomach, moving into his chest, then his throat, choking him. He started to cough so violently, reeling in his chair, that Jay-boy stopped reading and looked up at him in alarm.

"Man, are you all right?"

"Yeah, yeah," he said, staring hard at the tabletop, afraid that something in his eyes might betray him.

"Let me get you some water." Jay-boy rose and got him a glass of cold water from the refrigerator. Bowknot took the glass and thanked him, then drank slowly. The cold water moving down his throat had a settling effect on him.

Jay-boy finished the article in silence, then looked up at him thoughtfully for a moment. Bowknot met his gaze reluctantly and said softly, "That's too bad."

"Yeah," Jay-boy said. "If they find him guilty, he'll no doubt get life or maybe the chair."

Snatching his gaze from his cousin's open stare, Bowknot began to blink rapidly and fidget in his seat. Jay-boy said almost abstractedly, "Well, I reckon old Tiny done finally bit off more than he can chew. Robbing and killing a white man here in Emporia, wow! I sure hope he can send his soul to Jesus, cause his ass is grass!"

Bowknot was silent. He just shrugged his shoulders and sighed heavily.

Finally, Jay-boy rose and stretched lazily. "I reckon I'll go back and lay down awhile until the baseball game comes on. After he had left the kitchen, Bowknot snatched up the paper and read, fear clinging to him like a wet garment. The article said that the approximate time of the incident had been between six-thirty and seven o'clock p.m. The police had arrived at seven-ten. The coroner said that death had been instantaneous, the result of a gunshot wound to the head. Tiny had no doubt walked in, seen Boxdale, picked up the knife, and been accused of murder because he was found holding it when the prison guards arrived. The newspaper article stated that Tiny had insisted that he was innocent and also that police had been unable to find the gun or the money. Tiny was being held without bail. Bowknot shuddered and forced himself to push aside the pangs of sympathy stabbing at him. "After all," he sighed derisively, "he probably had it coming, anyway." It wasn't hard not to feel sorry for a man like Tiny Oliver, the brute and bully that Tiny was, and now the reputation that he had cherished so much would be the very thing that would seal his sorry fate.

Bowknot finally pushed the paper away and rose, a dull ache still throbbing somewhere in his brain and walked on out to the front porch in the morning air. He needed time to really think, to plot and plan which way he was going to ride this thing out.

Chapter 25

"What is it, Jay?" Kathy asked, with a pitiful plea in her voice. "What's wrong? You haven't been yourself for days now! There's no need to try to brush me off with that innocent smile. I know that something's wrong and, whatever it is, it's got you in a fix."

Jay-boy stopped the swing and stared at her for a long time. His eyes were sad and his face was etched with anxiety as he spoke, his voice charged with emotion. "Baby, I think that Bow-knot had something to do with that robbery last Saturday evening."

"What!" she exclaimed, her mouth hanging open in shock.

"Listen," Jay-boy continued, "you remember when I asked him to take Fat Daddy home—no, I mean, to work?"

"Yeah," Kathy nodded, her eyes riveted on him.

"Fat Daddy said that he had to be at work at seven o'clock and it was five-thirty, quarter till six when they left The Shack. Now it takes about twenty or thirty minutes at the most to drive from The Shack up to the hospital."

"So?" she prompted him, still staring quizzically.

"So that means that he was in town during the time of the robbery."

"Jay-boy," she sighed exasperatedly, "so were thousands of other people. What does that mean? Just because he was in town doesn't mean he had something to do with the robbery."

Jay-boy paused a long while before he spoke again. "Listen, baby," he said, leaning closer to her. "I kept checking outside for the car last Saturday and the last time I looked, it was almost nine o'clock and he wasn't back yet. He sighed, straightening, then leaned back against the seat. "When I realized that he was back, it was during the fight. Sunday, when I got around to asking him why he was so late coming back, he said that he had stopped in the poolroom for a while. Matter of fact, he said that he had gone straight to the poolroom after he had dropped Fat Daddy off. No!" he said, catching himself. "He said that he had stopped and got some gas and then gone to the poolroom. He said that he had got to the poolroom around six-thirty or quarter till seven. I ran into Peter Rabbit at the feed mill yesterday and he told me that it was around eight when Bowknot came into the poolroom, and that if I didn't believe him, I could ask Big Buck."

"So, he didn't get to the poolroom at the time he told you that he did! He said that he had stopped to get some gas." Her eyes were lit with a still-skeptical curiosity, but her reaction was merely a catalyst now, prodding Jay-boy toward conclusions he dreaded with all his heart to reach.

"Baby," he paused a moment, staring hard at her. Their gaze locked, and she almost flinched at the deep sadness in his eyes. "I love Bowknot like a brother. I guess, in many ways, we are brothers. I couldn't care for him any more or feel for him any deeper if we were blood brothers, and I think it's both ways. So, I'm not trying to blame nothing on him; I'm the one who's been defending him. But if he had something to do with this-here robbery and murder, I can't let an innocent man take the blame, even Tiny Oliver."

"Jay," she said slowly, never taking her eyes from him, "what makes you so sure that he had something to do with the robbery?"

"I don't know. I just got this damn uneasy feeling and there's just too many things that don't add up, that's all. He lied about what time he got to the poolroom. I mean, I could understand if it were a matter of a few minutes, but a whole hour? Besides, he told me that he stayed there till almost nine, but Peter Rabbit said he left around eight-thirty." Jay-boy sighed heavily, looking away from Kathy, out across the field. "Then it's the way he's been acting, jumpy and all quiet and gets irritable when I ask him about where he was and why it took him so long to get back to The Shack. Seems like he's slipping back to the way he was when he first came out here. But, there is something else I could try that might tell me what I want to know."

"What's that?" Kathy asked.

"The paper said that Tiny was caught holding the knife in his hand, right?"

"Yeah," she nodded.

"Now, what if Tiny was holding that knife because he had just picked it up and was staring at it out of curiosity and just got caught in the wrong place at the wrong time?" He paused and glanced out across the field again, then turned back to her.

"Go on, Mr. Sherlock Holmes."

"You remember back here early this summer when Bowknot and Tiny got to fighting and Bowknot cut Tiny up?"

"Yeah."

"Well, when I pulled Bowknot off Tiny that night, I took Bowknot's knife. I literally had to pry it out of his hand and didn't give it back to him until the next day. Let me tell you, that knife was the wickedest-looking thing I had ever seen. It had a long, sharp blade that curved at the end like a hawk's bill, and it had some kind of a brand on the handle that looked like a diamond with a cross inside of it. Now, first thing tomorrow morning, I'm gonna make up some excuse to stay home and, after Bowknot leaves for work, I'm going straight downtown and ask the sheriff if I can see that knife."

Kathy gasped in horror. "You don't really think that that's Bowknot's knife, do you?"

Jay-boy nodded in the affirmative, his eyes misting over.

Chapter 26

The next morning, Jay-boy woke with a sickening feeling in his stomach that made him nauseous and weak as he lay thinking about what he knew he had to do. He didn't have to fake anything. When he ambled into the kitchen, his mother took one look at him and grimaced. "You look sick enough to go to the doctor, boy."

Bowknot and Jimbo swung their heads around to look at him. "What is it, son?" Jimbo asked.

"I don't know; it's my stomach, I reckon."

"Go on back in there and lay down," his mother said sympathetically. "You can't go out here talking about pulling no tobacco today."

"Yeah," Jimbo added, "I'll stop home for lunch and, if you don't feel no better, I reckon I'll take you in to see the doctor."

Jay-boy stumbled back to his room and fell sprawling across his bed, his frame aching with dread. After a while, he heard Dallas Green's old truck roll into the yard, coming to pick up Bowknot, and then heard his mother explaining that he was sick and wouldn't be working today. He heard Bowknot get in and Green drive off. A few minutes later, he heard his father leaving with Mr. Jackson's tractor, which he had borrowed to haul peanuts. Finally, Jay-boy could hear his mother cleaning up the kitchen, bustling and humming to herself.

He forced himself upright on the bed, then sat for a moment, staring around the room, hating what something deep inside of him was telling him he would inevitably find at the sheriff's office. He forced himself up, and made his way into the kitchen, sitting down heavily in a chair at the table.

His mother whirled. "You're supposed to be in bed," she chided, turning a pair of reproving eyes on him.

"Mom," he said, "sit down a minute."

She hesitated.

"Please, Mom, I've got to talk to you."

Noticing the sadness in his eyes and the pitiful plea in his voice, she obliged. "What is it, Jay?" she asked, slipping into a chair across from him.

He told her the whole story. His mother sat dumbfounded, stricken and unable to speak. Her face was flushed and contorted with anguish and self-recrimination.

"Lord have mercy, Jesus," she said finally, shaking her head from side to side in helpless resignation. "We've done everything we could for that boy," she sighed. "Let's go see what your daddy says."

"If I could just see the knife," Jay-boy said, "then I could be sure."

As he had recounted his story to his dad, Jay-Boy watched his father's face grow gray with worry and his broad shoulders seemed to droop as anguish settled on him like a heavy load. Like his mother when she heard his story, it was a long time before his dad spoke, and when he did, there was a leaden sadness in his voice.

"Son, I have had a feeling that something was going on. For the past week or so that boy ain't even been able to look at me straight. Yeah, I thought something was wrong, but I didn't know it was this serious. I've done everything I know to do to help that boy," he sighed and leaned heavily against the rear tire of the tractor and stared hard out across the field. He was silent for a long moment, then he said finally, almost as if he was talking to himself as much as to his wife and his son, "If he had something to do with that robbery, he's going to have to answer to the law for himself. It is time that he realize that there is a consequence for his actions and there comes a time when every

211

tub's got to stand on its own bottom." The words came in a choked whisper, in a tone of painful resignation.

In a little while, they were heading toward town.

Sheriff Allen Porter was a huge, fleshy, red-faced man with wisps of stringy gray hair peaking from beneath his policeman's hat, which he seemed to wear all the time.

"What can I do for you folks?" he asked curtly, looking up from a pile of papers on his desk as they stepped into his office. Before they could answer, a tall, pale woman with thinning blonde hair broke in tersely. "They come in here insisting on talking to you and you only. I asked them if there was anything that I could do."

"That's all right, Mary," the sheriff said, waving his hand. "I'll see them. Come on in, and close the door," he said, his tone now slightly more cordial. "Have a seat." He motioned to three chairs along the wall in front of his desk.

They sat down and Mr. Johnson cleared her throat and began. "Sheriff Porter, sir, my son here has got something that he would like to ask you."

The sheriff's blue eyes moved from him to Jay-boy. "What is it, boy?"

Jay-boy met his gaze, then quickly looked away. "Sheriff Porter, sir, I would like to know if you'd let me see that-there knife you-all took from Tiny Oliver."

"What?" the sheriff said, leaning forward in his chair.

"Sir," Jay-boy continued hurriedly, "I believe that if I could see that-there knife, I could clear up some things."

"Like what?" the sheriff blurted. His fleshy face was turning beet red and agitation crept into his voice.

"If I can just see that knife, sir, I can tell you whether or not you've got the right man in jail."

"Boy," the sheriff said, his brow wrinkling and his eyes narrowing with irritation, "just what in the hell do you mean coming in here telling me my job?"

Jay-boy bristled with indignation, but fought to remain calm.

"Sheriff, sir, he ain't trying to tell you how to do you job, sir. He just wants to see the knife so he can tell you-all who it really belongs to, sir," his mother said, leaning forward slightly.

Jay-boy was fuming, and was careful to keep his eyes averted and his face expressionless. He was angry with his mother for being so obsequious, angry with his father for saying nothing, and angry with this brute sitting before him who obviously had the mind of an ox and the sensitivity of a jackass.

The sheriff sighed heavily and picked up the phone on his desk. He dialed a number and asked for Paul, and asked Paul to bring in the knife that had been taken in as evidence from Tiny Oliver. Then he slammed down the phone and glared at them as if they were pests. The silence that filled the room was almost deafening. Jay-boy was glad when a tall, heavy-shouldered man with a thick, red mustache and wearing a policeman's uniform stepped into the room carrying something in a small metal box. He placed it on the sheriff's desk, then straightened and glanced around at them curiously.

"Well, Paul," the sheriff said somberly, "this-here boy thinks that he can tell us something that we don't already know about this-here knife." The sheriff opened the box, retrieved the knife, and handed it to the man standing in front of his desk. "Pass that to him, will you, Paul?"

Jay-boy's muscles tensed, his heart hammered, and his temples throbbed as the icy fingers of dread twisted his guts into tiny knots. The man handed him the knife and, before he even took it, he saw the markings on the handle. Jay-boy took the knife and examined it closely for a moment. He sighed heavily as his eyes clouded over. He said sorrowfully, his voice coming in a choked whisper, "This knife belongs to my cousin from Detroit. He's the man you want."

The sheriff's eyes went wide with shock, and the other man's mouth dropped open in surprise.

Jay-boy recounted to them what he had told his folks earlier. He then asked them to let him try to persuade Bowknot to give

213

himself up. He pleaded with them to wait and arrest Bowknot at home after he got off work, but the sheriff would not hear of it. His eyes were hard and angry.

"The only thing that I'll agree to is letting you talk him into coming along peacefully and that's more than he gave Mr. Boxdale."

So, less than an hour later, Jay-boy and his folks rolled up to Dallas Green's place. Everyone was surprised to see Jay-boy after hearing about how sick he had been earlier that morning. All the workers were standing around a trailer loaded with tobacco as the car drove up, but the moment Bowknot caught sight of the two police cars rolling up behind Jay-boy, he knew something was up and made a dash for the woods. Leaping out of the car, Jay-boy took off after him. Bowknot was running like a man possessed, bounding through the tobacco field heading for the woods. He would have made it had he not tripped and fallen, catching his foot on an above-ground root of a small sapling at the edge of the woods. He hit the ground with a hard thud, rolled over, and was getting to his feet again when Jay-boy sprang upon him.

Bowknot glared at him, his eyes wild with fear. Then he lunged at Jay-boy, his fist crushing into Jay-boy's jaw and then into his ribs like stones. Jay-boy fought back, catching his cousin on the chin with a hard right that sent him reeling backward. Jay-boy immediately followed up with a left to the stomach and Bowknot's knees started to buckle. He had barely touched the ground before he was up again, swinging his fist, smashing Jay-boy in the nose. Jay-boy's vision blurred for a moment as blood spurted.

Bowknot was fast as lightning and quite good with his fists— a lot better than Jay-boy had thought. Nevertheless, Jay-boy moved in again, swinging, catching Bowknot squarely on the jaw with a slashing right and following it up with a sharp left to the chin. Bowknot went down hard and didn't try to get back up. He had had enough.

"So, you found out, huh?" he gasped hatefully, his chest heaving from the exertion.

"Yes," Jay-boy said sharply, his breath now coming in gasps, "I found out." He heard what he thought was the jingle of keys and turned to see four red-faced policemen coming up behind him. His eyes moved to find the source of the jingling he had heard. The sound had not been made by keys, but by a pair of handcuffs dangling from the belt of the officer who stood nearest to him. He lifted his eyes further, watching the policemen trotting up, their chests heaving and their faces glistening with perspiration. Suddenly, one of the officers shouted, "He's got a gun!"

Startled, Jay-boy's gaze flew back to Bowknot, who was still lying on the ground. What he saw made his blood run cold with terror as he wheeled and dove backwards into the dirt. Even before his limbs could obey his brain, he saw the gun spitting flame in Bowknot's hand. Through eyes misty with shock and horror, he saw two officers already down, lying in the dirt not more than fifteen feet away. Another was clutching at his chest and clawing the air as he staggered drunkenly backward. The fourth officer had his gun out and blazing. Jay-boy's eyes frantically sought Bowknot, who was tumbling wildly about in the dirt. Coming part-way to a standing position, he was jolted backward and clutched his shoulder. He had dropped his gun, but with lightning quickness, he retrieved it. He spun in the dirt, rising to his knees, miraculously dodging a hail of hot lead. His gun spouted flame, and the fourth officer was slammed backward, but not before firing a last shot that found its mark in Bowknot's stomach. The bullet's impact knocked Bowknot to a sitting position and he leaned forward, clawing for the gun he had again dropped when the bullet had struck him in the stomach. He wasted no time drawing a bead, but his extended arm wavered for a moment, his strength ebbing as blood covered the front of his baggy shirt. It was the split second that the fleshy-faced man, now weak himself and bleeding profusely, needed. His hand came up, shaky and unsteady, with his service revolver.

Bowknot, his shirt-front now drenched with blood, his arm trembling with determination of will, and eyes hard and defiant, matched his draw. The guns seemed to buck simultaneously, belching fire and smoke. Both men were knocked backward, flat against the earth.

Jay-boy leaped up and ran over to his cousin, falling down beside him. Through the tears that flooded down his cheeks like water, he begged pitifully, "Why, Bowknot, why? Why didn't you just give up without all this?"

With a great effort, Bowknot shifted his head so that he could meet his cousin's eyes. He sighed heavily, then his eyes brightened and a wicked smile moved over his face. "Jay-boy, my man," he began. He was halted by violent coughing as hot blood moved up into his throat, choking him. He cleared his throat and tried again to speak. Jay-boy moved closer, leaning down over him to hear. "I didn't mean to kill Boxdale. It was an accident. We were struggling over the gun and that's how I dropped my knife. I didn't have time to get it because someone was coming."

He coughed again, convulsively, paroxysms racking his frame. He continued, "But I did mean to kill these sons-of-bitches here because that's what they were going to do to me." He paused a moment, his smile broadening. "You see, it's better this way, a hell of a lot better than frying." He coughed again and cleared his throat with excruciating effort. "This way, at least I got a chance to put up a fight."

Bowknot's last words were barely audible to Jay-boy as his own loud, hacking, wailing sobs filled his ears.

Order Form

To order copies of *Blood or Justice*, tear out this page, or photo-copy it, and send it with a check or money order to: In Step Publishing, P.O. Box 10235, Columbus, OH 43201.

Name_____ Phone (_____)_____

Street_____

City_____ State_____ Zip_____

SHIP TO (IF DIFFERENT FROM ABOVE):

Name_____ Phone (_____)_____

Street _____

City_____ State_____ Zip_____

_____ copies of *Blood or Justice* at $15.00 = $_____

Shipping: add $1.50 first copy, .75 each add'l copy $_____

Ohio residents only—add sales tax of .86 per copy $_____

Total $_____